PRAISE FOR MAGGIE

Who's Sorry Now?
The Second Lady Adelaide Mystery

"Rupert's back! And Lady Adelaide still wants to kill him—only he's already dead. If you like a clever mystery, a handsome ghost, and the far-from-bereaved widow who can't find the elusive killer without Rupert's help, *Who's Sorry Now?* is just your cup of English murder."

—Charles Todd, author of the Inspector Ian Rutledge mysteries and the Bess Crawford mysteries

"Readers will enjoy the lively exchanges between Addie, a thoroughly appealing narrator, and her two admirers, exasperating Rupert and smitten Devenand. Fans of witty, romance-infused paranormal historicals will have fun."

—*Publishers Weekly*

Nobody's Sweetheart Now
The First Lady Adelaide Mystery

"A lively debut filled with local color, red herrings, both sprightly and spritely characters, a smidgen of social commentary, and a climactic surprise."

—*Kirkus Reviews*

"Set in England in 1924, this promising series launch...is... frothy fun."

—*Publishers Weekly*

"*Nobody's Sweetheart Now* is a clever, charming mystery that perfectly captures 1920s society. Bored debutantes and rich bankers mingle in Lady Addie's world, which is sure to appeal to fans of Ashley Weaver or Rhys Bowen. Likable characters, a well-paced plot, and an intriguing detective make *Nobody's Sweetheart Now* an excellent first entry in this delightful mystery series."

—*Shelf Awareness*

Also by Maggie Robinson

The Lady Adelaide Mysteries
Nobody's Sweetheart Now
Who's Sorry Now?

Cotswold Confidential Series
Schooling the Viscount
Seducing Mr. Sykes
Redeeming Lord Ryder

Ladies Unlaced Series
In the Arms of the Heiress
In the Heart of the Highlander
The Reluctant Governess
The Unsuitable Secretary

London List Series
Lord Gray's List
Captain Durant's Countess
Lady Anne's Lover

Courtesan Court Series
Mistress by Mistake
Mistress by Midnight
Mistress by Marriage
Master of Sin
Lords of Passion (anthology)
Improper Gentlemen (anthology)

Novellas
Just One Taste
All through the Night
Once Upon a Christmas

JUST
MAKE
BELIEVE

JUST MAKE BELIEVE

A LADY
ADELAIDE
~MYSTERY~

MAGGIE ROBINSON

Published by Poisoned Pen Press, an imprint of Sourcebooks
P.O. Box 4410, Naperville, Illinois 60567-4410
(630) 961-3900
sourcebooks.com

Library of Congress Cataloging-in-Publication Data is on file with the publisher.

Printed and bound in the United States of America.
SB 10 9 8 7 6 5 4 3 2 1

MAKE BELIEVE

There are times when you feel sad and blue
Something's wrong, you don't know what to do
When you feel that way, stop and think awhile
Just make believe and smile
Make believe you are glad when you're sorry
Sunshine will follow the rain
When things go wrong, it won't be long
Soon they'll be right again
Tho' your love dreams have gone, make believe, don't let on
Smile tho' your heart may be broken
For when bad luck departs, you will find good luck starts
Don't grieve, just make believe
When your dearest friends have turned away
And blue skies above have turned to gray
Don't worry for it may not all be true
Here's my advice to you
Make believe you are glad when you're sorry
Sunshine will follow the rain
When things go wrong, it won't be long
Soon they'll be right again
Tho' your love dreams have gone, make believe, don't let on
Smile tho' your heart may be broken
For when bad luck departs, you will find good luck starts
Don't grieve, just make believe.

Music and lyrics: Jack Shilkret/Benny Davis, 1921

CAST OF CHARACTERS

FERNALD HALL, BROUGHTON MAGNA

Lady Adelaide Compton (Addie)

Major Rupert Compton, ghost

Sir Hugh Fernald, baronet

Lady Pamela Fernald, his wife

Lady Evelyn Fernald, his mother

John Fernald, his son

Mrs. Iris Temple, his aunt by marriage

Miss Marguerite (Margie) Jordan

Miss Amanda (Mandy) Jordan

Owen Bradbury

Captain Dennis Clifford

Simon Davies

Patrick Cassidy

Lord Lucas Waring

Philippa Dean, Lucas's new girlfriend

Beckett, Addie's maid

Jim Musgrave, Sir Hugh's valet

Trim, Sir Hugh's butler

Mrs. Lewis, the housekeeper/cook

Juliet Barlow, John's governess and Pamela's cousin
Murray, Pamela's maid
Mary, a maid
Colin Stewart, tutor
Barry Dunn, head gardener
Bert Dunn, his cousin
Charlie Dunn, Bert's brother
Robby and Liam, grooms
Bill Parks, landlord at the Pig and Shilling, Broughton Magna

DOWER HOUSE, BROUGHTON PARK, BROUGHTON MAGNA

Lady Cecilia Merrill, Addie's sister
Ian Merrill, Marquess of Broughton, their cousin
Carstairs, butler

COMPTON CHASE, COMPTON-UNDER-WOOD

Forbes, butler
Mrs. Drum, housekeeper
Mrs. Oxley, cook

SCOTLAND YARD

Detective Inspector Devenand Hunter
Sergeant Bob Wells

Dear Addie,

Hugh and I hope you can join us for a week at Fernald Hall Saturday next. We'll have a small, congenial group—a few old army chums of Hugh's and a pair of pretty twins who remind me of our debutante days. Such girlish glory. How time marches on.

Lucas agreed to be torn from his farming duties for most of the week, and I count on you to keep him out of trouble and away from disobliging sheep and reluctant root vegetables. It will be heaven to have dear friends here again. We've missed you!

Bring your riding togs. We'll have three new additions to our stables, brought all the way from Ireland. I can't wait for you to see the improvements I plan for the grounds here and will welcome your suggestions. I do hope you can come despite the late notice.

Yours affectionately,
Pamela

Chapter One

Fernald Hall, Broughton Magna, Gloucestershire
A Saturday afternoon in June 1925

The brick stableyard was clattering with laughing guests and lofty horses, the equines' blindingly shiny tack redolent of harness oil, brass polish, and saddle soap. The humans were equally well turned-out, and Lady Adelaide Compton was glad she'd had a new riding habit made. The jade tweed brought out the green of her hazel eyes. Even if she disgraced herself riding, she'd look damn good doing it.

She waited for her mount to be brought out to her from its box with just a touch of nervous excitement. It had been quite some time since she'd sat on a horse. Major Rupert Charles Cressleigh Compton, her late and sincerely unlamented husband, had converted their stables at Compton Chase into a garage to hold his car collection.

To be frank, she now preferred an automobile's horsepower to the real thing. Much to her late—and sincerely lamented—father's disappointment, despite years of Pony Club, she'd never been a natural horsewoman. It was doubtful she'd turn into Boudicca one month shy of turning thirty-two.

She swallowed as a horse was led to her. It was very…tall. Glossy as the rest of Hugh's mounts, perhaps even glossier. A lovely color, rather like an Irish setter, which made sense, since he was an Irish horse. But still…

Addie had reservations. Her reluctance must have shown, for the Irish horse stud owner Patrick Cassidy, as glossy and burnished as the horse itself, touched her shoulder. Ordinarily, she would have stiffened at the familiarity; she'd only met the man at lunch. But this week she was trying to be the woman everyone expected her to be.

A merry widow. Sophisticated. Rich and titled. Not a care in the world. Closets full of first-class fashion, half of which she'd apparently brought with her for the week-long house party, since her maid, Beckett, wanted her to make a good impression. Even if she changed ten times a day, she'd never repeat herself.

With her usual cheeky candor, Beckett had informed Addie that she needed some fun. A flirtation was just the ticket, one that might even turn into a fling, as was de rigueur at so many country-house parties.

Naughty nocturnal navigations.

What her maid left unsaid: something to take away the sting of Addie's unsuccessful attempt to seduce Detective Inspector Devenand Hunter of Scotland Yard. She had thrown herself at the man two months ago and he'd resolutely refused to catch her.

Patrick Cassidy looked more than capable of fielding flying females.

"I picked him out specially for you, Lady Adelaide," Mr. Cassidy said. "He's a touch over seventeen hands. Isn't he grand? And as gentle as any lovely young woman such as yourself could wish."

In other words, this particular horse was almost as big as horses grew. Addie swallowed again.

The man's Irish accent was charming. He accompanied his horses to the Fernalds for the sale from Belfast a few days ago. According to Pamela, his horses were world-famous, and he was as much sought after as a dinner companion as a horse breeder.

He certainly was attractive, if overly optimistic about her riding skills. Addie smiled up at him. "I'm afraid I'm a bit rusty. I haven't ridden in ages."

"Well, then Timothy Hay is just your cup of tea. And it's not as though we're going foxhunting. Lady Fernald's promised us a nice quiet ride on the estate. Wants to show us what that gardener chap is doing."

That gardener chap was Simon Davies, well-known in society for refreshing the existing landscape, a modern-day Capability Brown. A gentleman with very green fingers, he truly was a gentleman, a baron's cousin. Whether he took any remuneration or performed his magic as a hobby, Addie was uncertain. But one met him at the best houses, and he had been friends with her hostess's parents and had known Pamela from childhood.

"How delightful," Addie murmured. Truthfully, she'd much rather walk, but that would be a waste of her expensive habit and blister her feet in her shiny new boots besides. And she told herself it was past time to take some risks. She'd been in a dreadful state since Rupert died, except for helping to solve six murders. One wouldn't want to make a habit of that. It was…ghoulish for a proper marquess's daughter and required poor, unsuspecting people to be packed off early from earthly life.

Not to mention dangerous. She'd come much too near to knives and guns and poisons for comfort over the past year, and Rupert's ominous return as a ghost made him as annoying in death as he had been when he was alive.

Being haunted by her dead husband made Addie cross and completely quiet about it. She didn't want to be clapped in an asylum or strapped to a psychiatrist's couch for the foreseeable future. Hooked up to electric wires or plunged into ice baths. Stuffed with large doses of drugs so she didn't know who you were or who she was. There were all sorts of devilish ways to "cure" diseases of the mind. She still had her sanity, thank you very much, even if Rupert materialized to her dismay.

Though on several occasions he had proved useful and turned up to "protect" her, acting as an unfortunate harbinger of death. But surely he was occupied somewhere else at the moment, far, far away in whichever direction he deserved to be.

The day was a stunner, with bright blue, cloudless skies, much too perfect to think of Rupert or any other ghost. Addie drove over early this morning with Beckett and her overpacked suitcases, top down all the way. The journey was familiar—she wasn't all that far from Broughton Park, where she grew up. But she hadn't set foot over the threshold of her old home since she helped her mother and sister move to the Dower House five years ago, after her father, the Marquess of Broughton, had died.

As a little girl, she'd dreamed of being married in the family chapel, and had been. That June day was a stunner too. She wore her mother's trailing Brussels lace veil and carried masses of white peonies from the gardens, just as she imagined when she played dress-up with discarded curtains and dandelions. Her future groom was always a rather vague figure. The reality of Rupert in 1919 far exceeded her childhood expectations; his many medals blazing against his uniform promised a bright and shiny future.

But peacetime brought little peace to either of them. So much for romance.

According to Beckett, a fresh romance was just what Addie

needed. There were at least three eligible men present to consider, and one could not dismiss Simon Davies, even if he was closer to her widowed mother's age. It was too bad the dowager marchioness wasn't here—she could use a romance herself.

"Allow me to help you mount," Mr. Cassidy said, the pressure of his firm hands about her waist. Before she was entirely ready, she was atop Timothy Hay with very little effort on her part. It was rather heady being up so high, if somewhat horrifying.

"There. What a sight. You're made for each other." As he stroked the creature's nose, Mr. Cassidy whispered something in what Addie presumed to be Gaelic. She hoped it translated to "please don't break this foolish woman's neck." That would spoil the week ahead, wouldn't it?

The riding party comprised of the Ladies Fernald—her hostess, Pamela, and her mother-in-law, Evelyn; the very young Jordan twins, who at lunch appeared to be simpering idiots in Addie's jaundiced opinion; Captain Dennis Clifford, in whose honor the week had been organized prior to his deployment to India; his friend Owen Bradbury; and Mr. Cassidy. Addie's old flame, Lord Lucas Waring, was due to join them at dinner tonight—he had a farm auction in Cheltenham to attend—so the ladies outnumbered the gentlemen.

Mr. Davies was to meet them later at the new water feature at the bottom of the parterres, a fountain that shot up to the heavens. Addie hoped he wouldn't be dreary and attempt to explain the mechanics of its plumbing functions; never mind how it got there, as long as the water sparkled in the sunlight and cooled the air. The modern world was a marvel she could appreciate without knowing all the details.

But first, they would ramble across the countryside. The local hunt passed over Fernald Hall land, and as she remembered it, all was groomed to the nth degree. She'd visited Hugh since childhood, and the property was almost as familiar to her as Broughton Park had been.

Hugh, of course, couldn't ride anymore. But that didn't lessen his stewardship over the land, and his attention to detail was peerless. Between them, Hugh and Pamela had created an idyllic country showcase that was the envy of their neighbors.

Timothy Hay was uninterested, sidestepping and tossing his head in impatience as Pamela touted the delights of a future gingerbread folly. Addie held the reins in a death grip as they rode by Corinthian columns intended to support a wisteria walk to the heated swimming pool that Hugh used for physiotherapy. To the west was the expanded orchard, its new fruit trees balled in burlap and waiting to be planted.

All the projects were ambitious, and Addie squelched a smidgen of jealousy. Jack Robertson, her own gardener—and Beckett's swain—was managing to bring Compton Chase up to snuff after the austere war years, but not to this level.

A wide swath of grass opened before them, and with a whoop, Pamela took off, belying her promise of a nice quiet ride. There might as well have been baying hounds and a frightened fox. She was immediately followed by the giggling Jordan sisters. Not to be outdone, the men challenged each other with some good-natured shouts and were soon in hot pursuit.

Addie couldn't help but admire them as they raced off, crouched low on their mounts, giving new meaning to the term "good seat." She'd never much noticed a man's bottom before, but three of them were hard to ignore.

Only Evelyn Fernald hung back to wait for her.

"All right, dear?" Addie and Lucas had come here by pony trap since they were little to play with Hugh, and Evelyn was as good as a second mother.

"Oh, yes. Don't linger on my account. I know how much you love the thrill of the chase."

"I'd only be chasing Pamela," she said dryly. "I don't want to leave you behind."

"Oh, please do!" Addie said, feeling guilty. Evelyn was an accomplished horsewoman, every bit as keen as her daughter-in-law. Riding was a release to them both from their somewhat constrained lives. "It's been yonks since I've ridden. We're just finding our way, Timothy Hay and I." She patted his sleek neck, and he whickered in approval.

"He is a magnificent beast, isn't he? Well, if you're sure—"

"I am," Addie nodded stoically, feeling no such thing.

Evelyn took off with a little wave, and Addie willed herself to relax. The horse had enough confidence for both of them, and it wasn't long before she was cantering after the others, though with their considerable head start, they were not yet in sight.

She jolted over mowed emerald fields, warm sun on her face, the scent of sweet grass tickling her nose. This was…rather fun. Perhaps she should think about getting one or two horses for Compton Chase—riding was marvelous exercise and would allow her to eat more of Cook's cream puffs. She might ask Mr. Cassidy—

Suddenly Addie inhaled sharply four times and then sneezed in a most explosive—and unladylike—fashion. And found herself flying through the air, as Timothy Hay startled at the sound and reared up like the statue of Boudicca's horses on Victoria Embankment.

Her initial misgivings were proving true. Well, she'd had a good life and would make an attractive corpse in her new riding habit if she remembered how to fall as gracefully as she had learned to faint. Maybe with luck she'd only break a leg or two. Timothy Hay's four legs were working perfectly well as he galloped off on the greensward, leaving her tumbling through space. Addie allowed herself a brief prayer, and then landed on something surprisingly soft.

"Oof."

"Rath-er. Have you put on weight?"

Rupert! Addie was sitting on his pinstriped lap, all in one piece, comfortably held. Her glasses had flown off in her somersault, but she didn't need them to see the smug expression on her dead husband's face.

She punched his shoulder. "What are you doing here?"

"Saving your life once again. Honestly, you could show more regard for my perfect timing. I wasn't due to arrive until tomorrow."

Addie's wildly beating heart thudded to a stop. "T-t-tomorrow?"

"As I said. Do pay attention. I so hate to repeat myself. You mortals have remarkably short attention spans."

When Rupert turned up, it meant only one thing, and it was not good.

She punched him again. "No!"

He shrugged. "I cannot help my presence here, no matter how much you abuse my hospitality. Sit still or you'll step on your spectacles. Isn't this just like old times?" He beamed, the sunlight glinting on his dark hair.

"I never sat in your lap in my life!"

"More's the pity. Perhaps if we'd communed with nature thusly things might have ended differently. And no, don't hit me again—I know absolutely everything was my fault. I was a cad. A rotter. A rogue."

"A weasel," Addie muttered.

"Yes, that too, I'm sure. And any other Mustelidae you might mention. Stoats, badgers, etcetera. Nasty little brutes.

Pointy teeth and very bad breath, I'm told. Are you all right? No bruises or bones broken? Good. Stay put while I search for your specs."

Addie slid onto the grass as Rupert stood and brushed himself off. He still cut a fine figure, wearing the very same bespoke Savile Row suit she'd buried him in, although his complexion was unusually pale.

Unusual for a live person, at any rate.

Who else was about to join him in the afterlife? Unfortunately, she supposed she would find out tomorrow.

And that meant murder…and a murderer.

She heard the thunder of hooves behind them.

"Here they are," Rupert said, cleaning her glasses with his pristine handkerchief. "Good as new."

"Scram," Addie hissed.

"You could say thank you. It's only that Cassidy person, and he can't see me unless I want him to. Why should I leave?" sniffed Rupert.

"I can't concentrate with you here. He'll think I'm mad." Rupert was known to be deliberately distracting. He loved to interrupt her conversations, and her "short attention span" couldn't cope.

"Spoilsport. I'd watch out for him if I were you. Never trust a redheaded man. They're never the heroes." In a blink he was gone.

What rot. If she didn't know better, Addie would think Rupert was jealous, which he had absolutely no right to be. Rupert had broken his wedding vows left, right, and center before he plowed into that stone wall and killed himself.

And Claudette Labelle, his French mistress.

Thank the Fellow Upstairs the woman wasn't haunting Addie too. That really would have been insufferable.

Mr. Cassidy reined in his horse, leaped to the ground, and pulled her up. "Lady Adelaide! Thank God! When old Tim came after us riderless, we all thought the worst. The rest of the party is right behind me, but I flew. You are all right, aren't you?"

"Only my dignity is bruised. I did tell you I haven't ridden in a while. I think I may have developed an allergy."

"To horses?" Mr. Cassidy asked, aghast. A fate worse than death for him, Addie supposed.

She felt that tickle in her nose again. "Possibly. I'm afraid I frightened Timothy Hay with my gasps and sneezes. It's not his fault."

"Rubbish. I'll have to retrain him. A hunter is useless if he can't ignore the unusual sounds around him. You've done me a great favor. I would hate to sell an animal that could harm my clients. Timothy Hay is intended for their son, John, you know. If anything happened to Sir Hugh's heir, I couldn't live with myself."

Addie was fond of young John herself. He'd arrived nine months to the day of his parents' wedding, a blessing since his father was wounded soon after in the war. She wasn't really experienced in dealing with children—one couldn't count her sister, Cee, who was twenty-five, even if she sometimes acted like a spoiled five-year-old—but John had always shown both his parents' easy charm.

She spotted the others coming toward them, clouds of dust in their wake. It had been dry for early summer, and the farmers in the county were grumbling. Addie gave a violent sneeze. "I'm sorry I'm such a nuisance."

Pamela dismounted at once and rushed toward her, enveloping her in a hug. "Oh! We were so worried! Thank heavens you're not injured."

That would have cast a dreadful pall upon the house party. Addie didn't have the heart to tell her that, according to Rupert, much worse was coming.

Chapter Two

For an Elizabethan house, Fernald Hall displayed every modern amenity except for straight walls and even floors. Most of the guest bedrooms had an attached bath, and Addie was making full use of hers, soaking in the deep tub. She would worry about Rupert and everything else tomorrow.

The hot water, laced with her hostess' lavender oil, felt divine, and she scrubbed with a cake of violet-studded soap that Pamela also made with flowers gathered from the estate gardens. Would she smell purple after? Addie had been through a tour of the old-fashioned stillroom before lunch, impressed by the neatly labeled bottles and fragrant hanging herbs. Pamela was quite the apothecary.

After Addie's ignominious fall from the horse, Pamela kindly gave her a jar of homemade cream, claiming its efficacy as a painkiller. Its astringent smell alone would kill anyone, in pain or not. Addie would rather live with the minor discomfort than reek, so it sat unopened on the glass shelf table next to her Chanel No 5, a far more palatable scent.

She washed and rinsed her hair, then rose from the steaming tub and wrapped herself up in a crisp white linen bath sheet.

A shaft of golden sunlight poured through the open bathroom window, and she sat in it, basking like a cat on the seat cushion, rubbing her hair dry and combing through the tangles.

"Damn. You've gone and done it, haven't you? I didn't notice earlier, what with having to cushion the blow and all and save your bottom. You cut off all your glorious hair. What a shame."

Addie yipped and dropped the comb to the tiled floor. Rupert perched on the edge of the recently vacated tub, trailing a finger in the scented water. The cheek of him! Couldn't he respect her privacy? She wasn't his wife anymore.

She rose, pulled the chain on the plug, and stood over him. Her tone was frigid. "I hoped you were done with me today. And every other day." She'd prayed it was so on Sundays and all the days of the week ending with 'y.'

"Believe me, so did I. What a bore. How many good deeds must I perform? I must confess, it's a cracking disappointment to be back in Old Blighty after our last adventure. But what can one do in this tenuous position but go along with a smile? Make the best of it, eh? It's not as if one belongs to a union and can go on strike. One cannot argue with this Boss. I wonder who's about to get the chop," Rupert said, sounding altogether too cheerful.

Addie sighed and sat back down. He was always as vague as a charlatan clairvoyant. Allegedly never fully privy to the details, he once described his role like receiving a radio broadcast that was continuously interrupted. So it was up to Addie to put the pieces together. Yet he managed to ferret out helpful facts during their murder investigations…through somewhat underhanded means.

"Rupert! Have you no sense of decency?"

"Probably not much. You know me better than anyone."

Faux modesty. In life, he was a famous Great War hero, his

exploits in his Avro aeroplane known throughout the United Kingdom, reported in huge font by all the newspapers. Rupert was brave. Fearless. Reckless. Peacetime bored him silly, and he took up with a string of mistresses who had understandably put Addie's freckled nose out of joint.

"Who's at this house party, anyway?" he continued. "Anyone I know besides good old Hugh and his missus?"

"How do I know?" Addie felt peevish. Rupert knew everyone. His social life was much more active than hers, particularly with a plethora of female "friends."

"Don't be so irritable. It's not my fault that I'm here."

"Oh, yes, it is!" Addie said with asperity. "If you'd behaved yourself when you were alive, you would go straight to Heaven and leave me alone for good!"

Rupert looked wounded. "At least I haven't wound up in the other place. Yet. These extra chances make all the difference. I have to say, though, that it seems like yesterday we were partners in crime. How long has it been? One loses track on the Other Side."

"Three months! And I'm not ready to get mixed up in another murder so soon." Or ever, if one was honest, despite the undeniable attraction of running into Inspector Hunter from Scotland Yard.

But he was very much off-limits at his own request.

"Dear me. You do live an exciting life. And how is your policeman?"

He would ask. "He's not my policeman. Anyway, I have no idea."

"What? I thought you two were getting chummy."

So had Addie. But when a man refuses to go any further than the most spectacular kiss in all creation, what was one to do without looking pathetic?

She raised her chin. "He has his career. And I have…my obligations to Compton Chase."

Her bravado didn't fool Rupert. "Believe it or not, I'm sorry to hear of your falling out. But who knows? The next murder might bring you back together."

No. Rupert had no decency at all.

After she threw a sponge at him, Rupert thoughtfully withdrew while Addie made up her face at the dressing table in her bedroom. She broke her promise to herself, her wits inevitably wandering to the future murder—who would the victim be? And why?

She felt gruesome speculating. In her opinion, at least from their behavior this afternoon, no one here deserved to die. Addie considered the guest list. Amanda and Marguerite Jordan were silly, but that was no crime—if it was, half the Bright Young People in Britain would be behind bars.

Hugh's attractive old army friends seemed innocuous enough. Patrick Cassidy was much too full of delightful Irish blarney to warrant a premature end. Addie shivered, remembering how easily he held her as he helped her mount her sneeze-averse horse. She could hear Beckett in her ear recommending him as a possible dalliance.

Evelyn Fernald and Simon Davies were older, but nowhere near decrepit and had years and years ahead of them.

Lucas hadn't arrived yet, but he was…well, Lucas. Much too nice to murder.

That left Hugh and Pamela. They'd already suffered so much. How dreadful to imagine someone killing either of them, or even more horrible, their child.

What about the staff? The butler in the buttery with a butter knife. Not that any death belowstairs would improve the situation. It was dashed difficult to get good servants nowadays, and Addie had great respect for those who toiled to make her life better.

Gracious. Maybe there was a mix-up wherever Rupert was stationed and he was sent in error. Accidents happened, didn't they? Even in the afterlife. Look what happened to Lucifer.

Beckett bustled in, full of gossip. Addie listened half-heartedly while her curls were tamed and coaxed into loose waves. But then something penetrated. "What did you say just now?"

"I shouldn't be carrying tales. It's wrong."

"When has that ever stopped you?" Sometimes Beckett needed a bit of prodding, but not very often.

"Maybe I misheard."

"Beckett! Out with it!"

"You probably won't believe it. It does seem far-fetched, him being so much older."

"Beckett!"

"All right, all right. They say downstairs that Lady Fernald is doing some barney-mugging with Mr. Davies, the society garden designer."

Addie wasn't shocked at all. "Good for them. Anyway, what do you mean, 'older?' They are much of an age, aren't they? Somewhere in their fifties or early sixties?"

"Not the old Lady Fernald. The young one."

"Oh!" Oh. Pamela! How awful. Poor Hugh.

But, really, it had been poor Pamela for years, hadn't it? It would be understandable if she sought physical comfort—she wasn't a living saint.

How awful anyway.

"Why do they believe this? And who is 'they' anyhow?" Addie wondered what sort of gossip her own staff got up to. They probably had a lot to talk about when Detective Inspector Hunter visited in April and then left the same day.

"The maids, mostly. Not her maid, Murray, though—the woman's defended her mistress like a bull terrier. But young Lady Fernald was seen going in and out of his room at all hours."

"Maybe Lady Fernald was consulting with him about the refurbishments."

Beckett rolled her eyes. "Lady A, you are as innocent as a newborn lamb. I'm glad you've got me to tell you what's what. They can't be talking about plants and parterres at two in the morning. It's unnatural." She gave Addie's bob a spritz of perfume. "There. You do look a treat."

"From the neck up. I'm still in my slip. What do you advise I wear?"

"The dark green watered silk is ever so elegant. The emeralds, of course. All of them. Don't be stingy—you want to outshine everybody."

"I do?"

"You have your reputation to uphold. You can't let your little riding mishap interfere with your glamorous feminine wiles."

Beckett was a big fan of the moving picture shows and had ambitions for Addie. Addie was fairly sure any feminine wiles she once possessed, glamorous or otherwise, had atrophied.

"Very well. Light me up like Broadway." They had recently spent five glorious months in New York, and the Great White Way was a sight to behold.

In an hour—after Beckett made "improvements" to Addie's maquillage—she was downstairs in the drawing room with a sherry in her hand, surrounded by four good-looking gentlemen. Lucas had arrived to complement Mr. Cassidy, Captain Clifford, and Mr. Bradbury. He knew them all, and the chatter flowed around her, not that Addie was especially flattered to be in the middle of it. It was more by default. The twins weren't down yet, nor was Pamela. Evelyn Fernald and her sister-in-law,

Iris Temple, who had a grace-and-favour cottage on the estate, were across the room talking to Simon Davies. It was as if a line of demarcation was drawn between the Old Guard and the New.

Hugh rolled in with his valet, Jim Musgrave, and surveyed the scene with a sunny smile. There was a lot to smile about— handsome guests, and an even handsomer drawing room, its salmon-silk walls designed to showcase Pamela's Dutch floral and fruit still lifes. On a new pink-veined marble mantelpiece, a pair of famille rose vases filled with apple blossom branches scented the air. A flowery needlepoint rug was underfoot, completing the effect.

Addie remembered the room as originally being dark, dim, and dreadfully Tudor, with armor and dead animals on the walls, but that was before Pamela. Her feminine hand was everywhere evident, with comfortable pastel upholstered furnishings and pillows, gilt tables, and pretty knickknacks scattered about. Briefly, Addie wondered how Evelyn had taken the changes to her late husband's ancestral home—it was always difficult to please two mistresses, although Rupert managed, hadn't he?

Hugh was not present at luncheon, so Addie greeted him with the warmth he always inspired. He had the world in the palm of his hand before the kaiser decided to poke his cousin, King George V, in the eye. Remarkably, chlorine gas-damaged lungs and a bullet lodged in his spine had not diminished his spirit.

"You're as gorgeous as ever, I see." She bent to kiss him.

"I try. I must keep up with this lot." He pointed to the assembled gentlemen. "Look at them, Addie! Don't they remind you of a Leyendecker advert for Arrow shirts? All the manly men, right here for your delectation. I think Jim does well by me, don't you? And I can't believe I actually beat Pam to the punch. Well done, Jim. Bonus for you."

It was a running joke between the Fernalds that Hugh was usually late, and not just always by necessity. Naturally, it did take him longer to get ready, but he was a stickler when it came to estate matters and could often be found up to his eyelashes in his study poring over account books when he was supposed to be elsewhere. But that was probably why everything was so perfect here—the property was beautifully run.

The long speech caused Hugh to erupt in a cough, and his valet gave him a handkerchief. "No need for a bonus, Sir Hugh," Jim said. Hugh had saved his life, and the valet had not forgotten it.

The men suddenly straightened up, and Addie turned. Pamela had arrived. Addie could be encrusted in emeralds right down to her toenails and she'd still fall short. Hugh's wife was the most dazzling debutante of the 1911 season, and the ensuing years only honed her beauty. She was as kind as she was attractive, so Addie really couldn't hate her. The woman sent flowers and fruit from her succession houses for months after Rupert died, which brightened Addie's own spirits.

Pamela's dress was simplicity itself, the kind of expensive simplicity that came out of the Parisian atelier of Madeleine Vionnet, if Addie was not mistaken. She was a vision in silver satin cut on the bias and clinging to her trim figure in all the right places, a spray of diamonds in her wavy dark hair the only jewelry besides her wedding rings. Addie now felt like a Christmas tree about to go up in flames.

"Hello, darling! Everyone," Pam said, beaming. "Addie, I do hope you've recovered."

"What's amiss?" Lucas raised his eyebrow in concern.

Addie needed to smooth that eyebrow down pronto. She didn't want to be teased mercilessly by her childhood friend for falling off a horse. "Not a thing. Do fetch me another drink, won't you?" She hadn't even swallowed half of what she had, so she drained the glass hurriedly and handed it over.

"You can't fob me off forever. I'll find out," Lucas told her. "I always do."

"I know," said Hugh with a broad grin, "all the embarrassing details, but I'll respect a lady's wishes."

"You always do." Pamela squeezed her husband's shoulder.

Addie experienced another pang of envy, but perhaps the next sherry would soothe her.

When they went in to dinner, the crystal, china, and sterling on the long polished table sparkled and shimmered even more than the Jordan twins, who came down in matching ice-blue sequined gowns and a considerable number of aquamarines. Addie was still trying to figure out which was Margie and which was Mandy, looking for a freckle or a wayward white-blond curl that might help her. She was fairly sure their cottony bobs owed something to their London hairdresser's familiarity with bleach but was not about to ask. Addie was certainly not above a little artificial enhancement herself, as Beckett would be proud to affirm.

Interspersed with tall candles, Pamela's magnificent cream-colored orchids were placed in Canton ware cachepots along the center of the table. Each of the endless courses was delicious and served in seamless style by the Fernalds' butler, Trim, and his footmen. Wine and conversation flowed generously throughout the evening, and Addie felt a little jealous again. Pamela was the consummate hostess. The last time Addie tried to throw a proper dinner party, her ex-neighbor and her gardener both wound up dead. Truth be told, Addie was afraid to entertain again. Dead bodies depressed one's appetite.

Once again, she remembered Rupert's warning, which dimmed her enjoyment of the evening. She tried to relax, studying the fine landscapes and portraits on the walls, but reality kept intruding. Which of the well-dressed, well-fed people around this lavish dinner table would soon meet their Maker? Would it be tonight? Her heart fluttered in distress.

"Are you quite well, Lady Adelaide? You've gone a bit pale," Owen Bradbury asked.

Oh, dear. He spent most of the evening in the clutches of one of the Jordan girls, and Addie was sorry he noticed her now. On her other side, Simon Davies did his best not to let her feel ignored, but he was now deep in conversation with Pamela. Mindful of Beckett's gossip, Addie didn't try very hard not to eavesdrop, just in case she heard something to corroborate the prevailing theory.

She attempted a smile. "I'm fine, really. Just warm. This whole month has been intemperate."

"Oh, don't tell me you want to discuss the weather like any other proper marquess's daughter seated next to a stranger. I expect much more of you after Hugh's singing your praises all these years."

Addie found herself being charmed. "Oh? And what did he say?"

"That you were a hellion as a girl—the scourge of the neighborhood. You bossed him around, along with your friend Waring, and they loved every minute. I know you had a bad... bit of luck lately. My condolences on the loss of your husband."

"Thank you. It was very unexpected." Addie took a sip of the dessert wine. Her throat felt suddenly dry.

"I didn't know him, but knew of him, of course. Everyone in England did, I wager. That sort of fame, well, it's tough on a fellow. One feels one must always outdo oneself, if you will. Keep the heart racing. Gosh, that doesn't sound right. I'm sorry."

"I think what you're trying to say is that Rupert missed the thrill of flying. His cars became a substitute, and he certainly raced." Right into a stone wall.

"That's it exactly!" Mr. Bradbury looked relieved. "You have a superior understanding, Lady Adelaide. I'm so glad we meet at last."

He was not as handsome as Rupert—or Inspector Hunter—but Beckett might approve of him too.

Would Addie?

"I know you served with Hugh. Tell me more about yourself, Mr. Bradbury."

Her mother always advocated this strategy, not that Addie wanted to write Mr. Bradbury's biography. Like most men, he had no difficulty whatsoever talking about himself and touting his accomplishments. Heir to his cousin, Baron Hurst, who was saddled with six daughters. Great girls, really, but fortunate for him, what? Important job at Coutts. Flat near Kensington Gardens. Addie hoped she looked like she was paying attention. She would have much preferred to listen to Mr. Davies and Pamela, but it was not to be.

At the head of the table, Hugh tapped his spoon against a glass. "Hear ye, hear ye! Welcome to our humble abode!"

"Humble!" Captain Clifford snorted. "Only place better in the kingdom is Windsor. And we've seen humble, for our sins."

"And never want to see it again," Mr. Bradbury chimed in. "Bloo—uh, blasted trenches. Mildewed tents too. Sorry, ladies."

"With thanks from our guest of honor and his compatriot," Hugh chuckled. "All hail the Four Musketeers! Long may they live and love wherever they are and keep out of the bloo—uh, blasted trenches and mildewed tents!"

"Amen!"

"Trim, pour us the Montrachet 1911, the happy year I met my wife. We'll drink to old friends and new."

The wine was poured, and more toasts to the Four Musketeers were offered, Bradbury, Clifford, and Hugh becoming more animated with every glass. The twins' incessant giggling grated on Addie's already tender nerves, and she admitted to herself she wouldn't mind if one—or both—got the chop, as Rupert said. Addie wondered if Hugh was counting D'Artagnan as the fourth Musketeer—it had been a long time since she'd read Dumas and she couldn't recall the plot very well. If she had much more to drink, she'd never care if père or fils authored the tale.

Chapter Three

Sunday afternoon

"Let's call it a day, Addie, my dear." Lucas leaped over the net like a damned gazelle and threw his arm around her, nearly knocking her over.

"You could have said that half an hour ago and put us both out of our misery. I'm sorry not to give you much of a challenge, Lucas."

It was such an uneven match that Hugh gave up watching on the sideline and went back into the house. Addie stopped herself from throwing her expensive racket over the treetops in a fit of pique. She would donate it to the church rummage sale, where someone less fortunate financially and more coordinated might benefit. Experience should have taught her not to take on her old friend, who had a deadly forehand.

"How is Pip?" she asked Lucas. They really hadn't much chance to talk since he arrived. He'd been a victim of one of the twins at dinner too.

"She's doing better. She sends you her love." He paused. "I say, Addie. You've been a brick about all of this."

Not too terribly long ago, Lucas wanted to marry Addie, even proposed. Now he had an understanding with Philippa Dean, a pretty, much younger redhead. It was a shame Pip was in mourning, for the sooner Lucas married her, the happier Addie would be. She loved Lucas like a brother, which boded ill for the marital bed.

"Nonsense. Pip is perfect for you." In fact, Addie considered herself their fairy matchmaking godmother. "Have you set a date?"

"Her mother thinks anything before September would be scandalous. It won't be a big wedding, due to the family's situation. I don't care about the frills and flowers. I hope Pip doesn't."

Young brides generally had quite a different idea about weddings than their grooms, but Addie believed Pip to be a sensible girl. She would be a viscountess, a big step up from being a self-made hotelier's daughter. She'd have plenty of opportunity to splash out in the future.

"Will you wed at the hotel in Brighton?"

"I've put my foot down there. Your cousin Ian has given us the use of Broughton Park's chapel and will hold the reception afterward for a select few. You'll be invited, of course."

"How is he?" Ian inherited the marquessate when Addie's father died.

"Good. You should visit while you're so close this week and see what he's done with the old place. I can drive you over."

Addie had no interest in doing so. Broughton Park was encased in amber in her mind. She didn't want to see any improvements, no matter how necessary they'd been.

"I know Mama is anxious to show me what she's done to the Dower House this spring. Perhaps I'll go soon."

"There you are. Another weekend sorted."

Addie stopped and sank on a stone bench overlooking the

parterres and the spouting fountain. "That's just it, Lucas. I don't want another social weekend or social week or social month. Maybe I've lost all my manners."

He sat down beside her. "Impossible. Your mother would turn in her marchioness card. She raised you to be the epitome of proper womanhood."

"And I'm a bit sick of it, to be honest. I don't really know what to do with myself now that Rupert's gone." She took a quick look around, half-expecting him to jump out of a rosebush. "It's been well over a year, you know."

"I know," Lucas said softly.

Of course he did. He'd been counting the months until they could marry without raising any eyebrows, and now the poor man was doing it again with Pip. Addie hoped for his sake he'd get his heir as soon as possible. Another honeymoon baby in the neighborhood if God was good.

"I don't want to travel. Our trip to New York was wonderful, but I got homesick. Missed Fitz, even if he's an entirely unsatisfactory dog. He'd go off with a stranger if they waved a strip of streaky bacon in front of his nose."

"Who wouldn't? Bacon is temptation itself. Even I'd consider it. But seriously, take the little mongrel with you when you go on holiday."

"Oh, it's not about the dog. I need...something." Beckett would say she needed a lover, but thank God Beckett wasn't here to do so.

"What about all your charitable work? And you've done wonders with Compton Chase—that's not an easy place to manage with all the old things you still employ."

"Mr. Beddoes may be an old thing, but he keeps the accounts straight and all I have to do is sign my name."

"I hope you read the paperwork first," Lucas cautioned.

She did. Most of the time.

"I want to feel useful. Life is too short to float through."

Lucas frowned. "You cannot get a job."

"Why not?" Apart from the fact she had no discernable skills. If she worked in an office, Addie supposed she could answer a telephone well enough, but type with all of her fingers without hitting the wrong keys, not to mention ruining her manicure? Doubtful.

"For one thing, you'd be taking it away from someone who needed it to support themselves and their families. Someone who didn't have your advantages. Moreover, whatever you'd earn in a month wouldn't be enough to buy you a decent hat to actually wear in public."

She hadn't thought about that angle; Addie did like expensive hats. She laughed. "I suppose you're right. I'd better primp and get ready for tea and pointless conversation."

"It won't be so bad. I'm here to rescue you now." He gave her a quick kiss on the cheek, and they parted ways.

"Well. He seems happy."

She suppressed the shriek that always threatened to burst forth when Rupert appeared out of nowhere.

"I knew you were here somewhere," she mumbled. No one was about, but a gardener could be trimming a hedge within earshot even if it was Sunday.

He picked a thorn out of his sleeve. "I'm pretty nearly always at hand, you know. It's part of my mission. All you need to do is summon me."

"I don't want to summon you. I want you gone. To wherever—at this point, I don't care."

"You might one day. Summon me, that is—I can't force you to care about my welfare after my various transgressions," he said, unperturbed. "I'm making up for them by being helpful now."

As he hadn't much been in life.

"Ouch. I heard that."

"Stop reading my mind! It's one of the worst things about this awful arrangement. My mind is my own." Addie glared at her late husband, who gave her a beatific smile.

"How fondly I remember our misunderstandings! You were so passionate. So fierce. All that flying footwear and the odd ashtray."

Fortunately, as she hadn't worn her spectacles often when married, she'd never scarred Rupert's handsome face. And his reflexes, after avoiding German aircraft for years, were excellent.

"They were hardly misunderstandings. I understood you only too well," Addie said. It took her a while, but eventually she realized Rupert was most unsatisfactory.

Much like her dog.

"You'd better get ready. And I don't mean donning a pretty tea gown to look at Pam's rare orchids in the conservatory," Rupert said. His expression was serious.

"You mean…"

He nodded. "I do. The details are sketchy but be on your guard. I have a very bad feeling." He patted her hand and was gone.

Beckett was waiting for her in her room, a white cut-lace dress laid out on the four-poster bed. "I'll run you a bath. You look a fright, Lady A," she said, which was only the truth. The afternoon had been hot and she'd run her feet off.

"Never allow me to play tennis again with Lord Waring. Unless it's mixed doubles and he's my partner and can do all the work." Addie flopped down in a chair and unlaced her canvas tennis shoes, kicking them aside. "I want to go home." She suspected she was a last-minute replacement and wished Pamela had flipped past the C page in her address book.

The last thing Addie needed was to be mixed up in another murder.

Beckett scooped up the shoes and wrinkled her nose. "If you don't mind me saying so, you haven't been yourself lately. You used to enjoy a good house party."

The good old days, when guests were kissing instead of killing each other.

"Aren't the people nice?" Beckett continued.

"Oh, they're all right." But someone definitely wasn't, and someone wasn't going to be.

After a quick bath, Beckett helped Addie dress. The maid insisted on piling on the rouge, as Addie was nearly as pale as Rupert. Worry did tend to rob her of color, but worry alone wouldn't solve the murder. She needed to go downstairs, as disinclined as she felt. She was experienced now, knew correct procedures thanks to her acquaintance with Mr. Hunter. If she couldn't stop the murder, she might still help.

Addie was halfway down the grand Tudor oak staircase when she heard the first of the screams.

Then shouting and more screams.

Here it comes.

She headed for the conservatory, nearly slipping on an ancient rug on the flagstone hallway in her haste. Where was bloody Rupert to catch her?

The conservatory was a late Victorian addition to the house, its elaborate lace ironwork famous and noted in several architecture books. Its glass doors were open, and Pamela's fancy orchids were everywhere.

The scent and heat of the room hit Addie at once. An impressive array of treats had been laid out on a horseshoe-shaped table in front of the central fountain, with small linen-draped wicker tables and chairs dotted about. But no one was eating; a group of guests and servants were all at the rear of the room. A woman was sobbing, and efforts to make her stop were ineffective.

"What's happened?" she asked a young maid at the edge of the cluster, white as Addie's dress.

"It's Lady Fernald," the girl whispered. "I think she's dead."

Evelyn or Pamela? She really didn't know how the staff kept them straight. Addie tried to see over shoulders or under feet to no avail. She tapped a gentleman's arm, and Owen Bradbury turned, his face drained of color.

"Who is it?"

"Pam. I don't know what Hugh's going to do."

Oh, no. Addie's heart seized. She'd known Pamela since they were in their teens, and while they weren't true bosom bows, it was a great loss, nevertheless. Poor Hugh. Poor John. Bradbury's face blurred in front of her.

"Has he been here?"

He shook his head. "Not yet. Hugh's always late, y'know. Has a lot to deal with to get out and about. My God, we even joked about it last night."

Hugh will deal with even more, Addie thought, wiping her tears away. "You should find him. Tell him. He mustn't come down to this."

"You're right. Denny, come with me. Someone has to tell Hugh."

Captain Clifford stepped back, rumpling his fair hair. "Christ. What a cock-up."

Not the reaction Addie would expect after the discovery of a body, and she filed it away. The two men left to find Hugh. His suite of rooms was on the other side of the house, and presumably they'd catch him before he made it this far.

Addie wriggled her way through and identified the housekeeper Mrs. Lewis as the sobbing woman. She knelt over

Pamela, who looked for all the world as if she was taking a nap on the herringbone brick floor, if one napped in public in pink floral chiffon. A broken glazed flowerpot lay nearby, its contents spilled, the orchid's roots exposed. There was no sign of blood, just the earthy odor of damp soil and something less pleasant.

Addie raised her voice over the crying. "Someone should call a doctor."

"Too late to do any good," Patrick Cassidy said in his soft Irish accent, "but you'll be right, Lady Adelaide. Trim, where's the nearest phone?"

"I'll take care of it, sir." He left to do so.

"Who found her?" Addie asked.

Mrs. Lewis looked up, her tears streaking through a light dusting of powder. "I did. The maids and I brought the tea things in at ten minutes to four, just as my lady asked. I don't know what made me check back here when we finished setting up the tables." The woman shuddered. "She was lying dead all the time we were working."

"Did you move her?"

"Of course not! But Mr. Cassidy came in and heard me—I was—I am—so upset. He checked her pulse. And then the other gentlemen came in with the Misses Jordan. One of them fetched Trim."

Addie turned to the two maids. "Don't let anyone else into the conservatory. Close the door and explain there's been an accident. One of you tell Trim to call the police too."

Margie Jordan grabbed her sister's hand. "The police! But why?"

"Lady Fernald was young and in excellent health. There might be foul play." She couldn't very well tell them it was Rupert's idea.

Mandy Jordan giggled nervously. "Foul play! What, are you some sort of female Sherlock Holmes now?"

Along with my late husband, the next best thing, Addie wanted to say. At least she tried to secure the scene and keep the rest of the guests out.

But she failed. A crashing noise heralded Evelyn Fernald, who swept into the room in umbrage. One of the maids came running after her, looking apologetic. "What's this about an accident? Is it my Hugh?"

Addie took the woman's arm and gave it a gentle stroke. "No, Evelyn. It's Pamela. She's—she's passed away."

"Passed away? Pamela? Don't be ridiculous!" Then she spotted Mrs. Lewis, still crouched on the floor. "Ruth, get up this instant! We have a houseful of company that must be attended to! Why—" The rest of her question went unasked as she herself slid to the ground.

Addie hoped she didn't break any bones; bricks were unforgiving. Her own mother, the Dowager Marchioness of Broughton, taught Addie how to faint with grace, and it appeared that Evelyn went to the same etiquette school. Mrs. Lewis hopped up as quickly as she was able, and being an old-fashioned sort of housekeeper, waved a vinaigrette from her chatelaine under her employer's nose.

Evelyn was unresponsive. Addie allowed as to how the woman should probably not be moved until the doctor checked her out as well.

"Mr. Cassidy, perhaps you can man the conservatory doors against any other comers. Margie, Mandy, Mrs. Lewis, you might be more comfortable waiting somewhere else."

Addie was left with the two bodies and a blinding headache about to get worse.

"Told you so. Poor Pam. I hoped against hope it was

someone we didn't know." Rupert inspected the buffet tea table. "Profiteroles, my favorite." He popped one in his mouth.

"How can you eat at a time like this?" Addie kept her voice down in case Evelyn woke up.

"I can't let a spread like this go to waste. It isn't every day I get to indulge. In fact, I can't remember the last time I had a decent meal."

"But...but you're dead," Addie sputtered.

"Exactly. All the more reason to have some fun while I can." He sniffed a tiny triangle. "Curried chicken. I say, that reminds me of your Indian policeman. You'd best give him a call, or they'll send out some idiot with ugly boots who'll probably arrest you."

"Me!"

"Why not? True, you have Beckett as an alibi for some of the time—and me too, not that I can count. Best to keep me under wraps unless it's an absolute emergency."

Addie wouldn't reveal Rupert's existence to anyone.

"Who did it?"

"Damned if I know. You know how it is with me; the glass is only half full. And I wouldn't want to deprive Inspector Hunter of apprehending the culprit after a very thorough investigation. The man lives for that kind of thing. Puzzles. Conundrums. Impossible missions. He's racking up more commendations than one can shake a stick at, although I don't see why one would shake a stick at anything."

Addie could. A stick would have come in very handy dealing with Rupert for the five years of their marriage.

"I heard that. You've turned quite violent in your old age."

A very big stick.

Chapter Four

Monday

What were the odds? Pretty much incalculable. Dev was not a betting man anyway. When the call was patched through to his flat from the Cirencester constabulary late yesterday afternoon, he knew the news wouldn't be good. But he hadn't anticipated Lady Adelaide Compton being smack in the middle of another suspicious death investigation.

In a few minutes, he would see her again, so he steeled what was left of his heart.

Dev tried to put her out of his mind. He was highly unsuccessful, but he couldn't go around kissing marquesses' daughters and live with the consequences. The caste system in the United Kingdom was as strict and as real as in his mother's native India. If Lady Adelaide temporarily suspended society's rules, he could not. In his experience, the rich could get away with literal murder. She could afford to skirt propriety, experiment, and be daring.

Not he.

He never should have accepted her invitation to visit

Compton Chase in April in the first place, but a month had passed since their collaboration, and he missed her. He also wanted to reassure her that he didn't hold her responsible for his own brush with death.

Dev worked through his discomfort until the pain receded. His superiors offered him leave, which he refused. One didn't take unnecessary time off and hope to be promoted; his father taught him that. Harry Hunter was renowned for never taking a sick day either in the army or at the Yard, and he expected his son to follow in his footsteps. They were big shoes to fill, but so far Dev had managed.

He did not speak to either of his parents about his infatuation with Lady Adelaide. He didn't want to hear the practical lecture from his father or see the sympathy in his mother's eyes. So he spent what little free time he had lately reading and studying the Ancients, trying his best to ignore the modern world around him.

A car from Fernald Hall was sent to meet the first train. Dev's sergeant, Bob Wells, sat up front, chatting with the chauffeur in hopes of gleaning any servants' gossip. Bob was good at that, leaving the posh people to Dev. Over the past ten months, he met more exalted folks than in his previous thirty-four years and was still figuring out how they ticked.

Dev read through his notes. Hugh Fernald was a baronet badly wounded in what turned out to be a hopeless battle, saving the lives of all his men bar one. Fernald's Fury. The newspapers heralded the man's bravery through gassing and grievous wounding. Dev remembered the headlines as he recuperated in a field hospital from his own less-publicized fury. The man was a national hero.

His wife, Pamela, was found on the floor of their conservatory by the housekeeper, still warm to the touch and showing no physical signs of any violent attack. The laboratory had not yet determined the cause of death, but poison was suspected.

There was a young son, John; the victim's mother-in-law, the "other" Lady Fernald; an aunt-in-law who lived in a cottage on the estate; eight houseguests; and a full complement of staff on the premises. Unlike many other country houses since the war ended, Fernald Hall was not run on a shoestring. Dev had yet to work a case where "the butler did it," so he concentrated on the guests but did not rule anything or anyone out.

Except for Lady Adelaide. Unless she'd undergone a massive personality shift, he did not expect to add her to the list of suspects. According to the Cirencester police, she attempted to protect the scene, forbade anyone from leaving the property, and asked pertinent questions of the other people at the house party before the police had a chance. The word "interfering" was used, and Dev could easily picture her ruffling feathers with her usual charm and determination.

And she asked for his help specifically. He wasn't sure if he should feel flattered or foolish. One thing he was sure of—he would not kiss her again, no matter how much he wanted to.

The Bentley turned down a long drive lined with evergreens. Despite the morning's sunshine, the car was enveloped in darkness for a bit, then emerged onto a circular drive. The impressive Tudor house was mostly stucco with elaborately patterned black beams, massive chimneys, and the odd architectural brick and Cotswold stone element denoting "improvements" over the centuries. A butler and two footmen stood on the steps. In the open doorway, a man in a Bath chair and his attendant awaited their arrival.

"There's Sir Hugh," the chauffeur said, pulling up directly in front of the house. "Poor bloke's had enough trouble. We all hope you get to the bottom of this quick."

Dev concurred. His last few cases had dragged on forever—there was always a surfeit of suspects and precious few leads.

"We'll do our best," Bob said.

It might help that they were to be put up at Fernald Hall for the next couple of days. Dev accepted the baronet's offer despite his misgivings. Lady Adelaide would be impossible to escape, and escape he must, for both their sakes.

They exited the Bentley, the butler organizing the footmen to take their travel cases. Dev extended his hand to Sir Hugh. "Please accept our condolences. You have my word we'll work as hard as we know how to discover what happened."

The man's firm grip was a surprise. "As I told you on the telephone, it must have been an accident. Pam would never have gotten into anything—well, she knew her plants, and she never, ever touched drugs. They haven't found a reason? The coroner's office, I mean?"

"Not as yet." There was a backlog at the laboratory, and it wouldn't help to let Sir Hugh know they didn't drop everything for his dead wife in the past twelve hours.

"And I suppose we can't rule out natural causes," Sir Hugh said, more to himself than Dev. "I know she was young, but strange things happen, don't they?"

"They do. But from what I gather from my colleagues in Cirencester, it looked like an overdose of some kind to the attending doctor."

"As I said, Pam never used drugs! Why, she barely finished a glass of wine with dinner. Never even took aspirin. Natural remedies only, and she knew what she was about. My wife had everything to live for—our son, her gardens..." Sir Hugh coughed. His manservant placed a reassuring hand on his shoulder while he pulled himself together.

"Let's get you inside, Captain," the man said.

"My valet, Jim Musgrave. Formerly my batman, now my nurse. I don't know what I'd do without him."

Musgrave flushed. "Stop your nonsense now."

"Let me introduce my sergeant, Bob Wells. I don't know what I'd do without him, either, although we didn't serve together." The injury to his foot was nothing compared to Sir Hugh's sacrifice, but the war had left its indelible mark, no matter what social strata one belonged to. "If you could ask your guests to convene in a suitable place, say, in half an hour, I can introduce myself and begin the questioning."

"I suppose the library's best, but these are our friends! Nobody would want to hurt Pam," Sir Hugh insisted. "The doctor has got the wrong end of the stick, I'm sure of it."

"I hope you're right. We'll do our best to make this process as painless as possible." Dev knew no matter what he did, someone was bound to object. Several someones, if his previous experiences proved true. He was often stuck between a rock and a hard place, with both suspects and superiors clamoring for his head. So far, he'd held onto it and his job.

He and Bob were shown to a pair of rooms in a no-man's-land upstairs between the staff quarters and the grander guest suites. The floors were carpeted with sisal rugs, the simple brown furniture serviceable, a white-tiled bathroom connecting the two rooms. Fluffy towels had been laid out on the beds, but there were no fresh flowers or biscuit jars or bowls of fruit that might have welcomed "real" guests. Sir Hugh's housekeeper had visibly firm ideas as to where London policemen fit into the order of things.

Dev splashed water on his face and unpacked the few possessions he'd brought. It wasn't as if he'd be dressing for dinner or a cricket match, so he didn't need much. But he was wearing a newish suit, replacing the one that had met an unhappy encounter with a bullet a few months ago. Despite his mother's valiant attempts at darning, that jacket would never be suitable for a baronet's house.

While the air outside was heavy with heat, the house remained cool, even this room on the top floor. A hardship in the winter, no doubt, but Fernald had the money to keep frostbite away with blazing fires and electric heaters. Dev gazed out his window and admired the formal Elizabethan gardens and sweep of lawn below. Everything he'd seen so far indicated that Fernald Hall was a prosperous, well-run establishment. He wondered if the mistress's death would change that.

There was a knock on the door. Bob must be anxious to get started. But when he opened it, it was not his trusty sergeant.

"Lady Adelaide." Further words eluded him.

"May I come in? I know it's bold of me, bothering a gentleman in his bedroom. My mother would have a fit if she found out. You might get Bob to come in and chaperone if I make you uncomfortable."

There was something in her tone that mocked him. By God, he should drag Bob in here. Or erect a barbed-wire fence. Hang up bulbs of garlic. Splash some holy water about. Make the sign of the evil eye. Chant something incomprehensible like the Holy Rollers and fall to the floor babbling in tongues.

Alas, nothing could diminish her unsuitable attraction.

"That won't be necessary." He stepped back, and she headed for the only chair in the room. He returned to the window. It was a very long way down, but still tempting.

"How have you been, Inspector?"

"Busy. And you?"

"I wish I could say the same. This murder has perked me up." She crossed her legs and swung a foot.

So, she was as nervous around him as he was with her.

"Lady Adelaide! We have not yet established that Lady Fernald's death is murder." Granted, it was an unusual, unattended death. And because of Lady Fernald's place in society and her husband's reputation, custom dictated it deserved scrutiny.

"Piffle. I wouldn't have called for you if there was a question in my mind. I thought I might fill you in before you interrogate the suspects."

"Guests, Lady Adelaide."

She waved a jeweled hand. He noted she was still wearing her wedding rings, sparkling diamonds and sapphires he'd never be able to afford to give her if he lived forever. "A question of semantics."

"What makes you so sure this is murder?"

Lady Adelaide gazed off into a corner. "I suppose you'd call it a hunch. After what's happened lately, I'm learning to trust my instincts."

Just as Dev trusted his. The odd feelings he got doing police work were inexplicable, especially if he tried to reveal them to his bosses. They'd think he was barmy if he talked about prickles up and down his spine or suddenly acute hearing. But most good coppers operated on some form of instinct; whether it could be chalked up to experience or something less tangible was a matter for debate.

"Tell me then."

Lady Adelaide's foot continued to jiggle. She was wearing sensible oxfords, perfect for tramping through the countryside. She had not dressed as a femme fatale, for which he was grateful. Seeing her in glittery evening clothes would test his resolve.

"Talk belowstairs is that Pamela was having an affair with Simon Davies. I have no idea whether that's true or not, but the rumor alone might cause someone to poison her."

"Let me guess—Beckett is your source."

"Naturally. I expect you'll want to talk to her."

Dev hoped Bob wouldn't mind—Beckett was always good for a laugh. She might be just a maid, but there was no "just" about her. "Was Lady Fernald's husband aware?"

Lady Adelaide shrugged. "I have no idea, and I'm not about to ask him and presume on our friendship. He has enough to worry about."

"You don't think he killed his wife?"

She looked at him with scorn. "Of course not! He loved her, would do anything for her. Why, he just bought her three horses."

A betrayed husband was always a prime suspect. Hell, one didn't even have to be betrayed. Husbands killed their wives with alarming frequency for all sorts of reasons. Burnt toast. Mismatched socks. A sharp retort. The horses could be a cover-up for his nefarious intentions.

"Besides," she continued, "as you know, he has great difficulty getting around. He wasn't anywhere nearby when she was found, and his valet can vouch for him."

"Not if they were in it together," Dev replied, enjoying the shock on Lady Adelaide's face.

"People like Hugh..." she trailed off, realizing her mistake. In Dev's opinion, almost everyone was capable of murder if pushed far enough.

Chapter Five

Addie tried to inform Inspector Hunter of the particulars as she knew them but felt as if she cast her pearls before an especially handsome swine. It wasn't her fault if it took him twice as long to get the lay of the land. He didn't even pull out his notebook—which she presumed was a brand new one after what happened to the old one—to take down what she said when she barged into his room.

Of course, he was very smart. She caught sight of the books on his bedside table in his stark little room. Philosophy and religion. She'd shoot herself if she had to read such dull stuff. But then, Inspector Hunter had been shot at least twice that she knew of, so perhaps his mind was affected with the vagaries of existence. One wanted to look at the Big Picture. It was probably good training for all the tedious and technical things he dealt with in the course of an investigation. Venality. Immorality. Pure evil.

Human nature was the very devil, wasn't it? And the devil was in the details.

He didn't ask her to sit in with him while he questioned Hugh's friends, either. In fact, he told her to take a walk and enjoy the day, and here she was.

Not that she could really blame him. Before Saturday morning, she hadn't met any of them except for Hugh's family and Lucas.

Addie kicked a rock out of her way. She headed for the new folly area through the tidy knot garden and wondered if it would be completed now that Pamela was dead. Simon Davies had aged a decade since yesterday, causing Addie to believe there was something to the gossip. But he did not seem like a Lothario to her; instead, he was courtly, almost fatherly.

Maybe Pamela just needed a wise older friend, and really was just going over horticultural designs in the wee hours of the morning, despite what Beckett said.

Rupert kicked the rock back, as if he was playing a ghostly game of football. "Penny for them."

"I don't have any thoughts," she said crossly. "I've been dismissed." And apparently saddled with her late husband, who had stuck to her like a barnacle when she'd left the house to clear her head.

Fat chance of that with Rupert around.

"Now, now. No gentleman likes to be told how to do his job, especially by a woman."

"I wasn't telling him how to do his job! And women are every bit as capable as men, I'll have you know. Perhaps more so. We're not starting wars and blowing up things willy-nilly."

"I know. We've made a muck of things for centuries. I'm sure you were only trying to be helpful. However, the good inspector has succeeded on the force for over a dozen years without you, my dear. You mustn't have hurt feelings."

"My feelings aren't hurt!" Addie lied quite loudly. Fortunately, there was not a soul in sight. The guests were indoors all waiting to be interviewed, and the staff was busy dusting and making up beds and getting a decent luncheon on the table, despite the fact their mistress was dead.

Rupert waggled his finger at her, a most annoying trait. "And, really, you know, a lady never goes to a gentleman's bedroom uninvited. What would your mother say?"

Addie had been trying to get her mother's voice out of her head for a good twenty-five years. Rupert's wasn't much better.

"Put your finger away. It's not as if I tried to seduce him. I was entirely business-like." Look at her! A veritable drudge. Long twill skirt, a loose lisle sweater set, her oldest shoes. True, she'd brushed her hair, but Addie looked like a governess.

Or someone's unmarried great-aunt.

"You carried a scurrilous tale. Servants' gossip," he sniffed.

"When did you get so virtuous?" Addie asked.

Rupert examined his fingernails. "I really don't know. It's come upon me very late, as I'm sure you would agree."

"Too late," she muttered. "I wish you'd figure out how to get into Heaven. These constant intrusions into my life are revolting."

"Revolting! That's unkind. Now I've got the hurt feelings. Does it mean nothing to you that I've kept you out of jail and saved your life from crazed killers? And you could have broken your pretty coccyx or worse if you hadn't landed on my lap yesterday, you know."

"You took your own sweet time with the murderers. I might have been killed!"

"I'll have you know I was very punctual. And you weren't killed, were you? Here you are, not a scratch on you, bum intact."

"Never mind about my bum!"

"One of your best features. You should be happy I've turned up. You'll have another shot at Hunter now. Another shot! Get it?"

And with this very lame joke, he disappeared from the grassy path.

"Revolting!" she shouted after him. Damn Rupert. Not that she wanted him to head to the nether regions anymore. Addie had to admit he was somewhat improved now that he was dead. He'd always been horribly handsome, and was still, if a little pale. Loaded with charm. The life of the party.

The last, at least, was no longer true.

She walked through an arched hedge opening and came upon three white-haired men leaning on shovels. This was the planned site for the folly. Once an old summer house she played in as a child stood there, but Pamela said it fell to pieces during the war and had been knocked down. Turf was turned up in a hexagonal, roped-off area, but the men stood outside it near a neat stack of painted splintered wood and a few mossy shingles. They stopped talking and lifted their caps when Addie stepped through the bushes.

"Good morning!" she said brightly. "What a lovely day!" She hoped they wouldn't think her callous. Their mistress was, after all, dead. She noted they all wore black armbands in her memory.

"Is it true there's someone from Scotland Yard up at the house?" one of them asked.

"Yes. A detective inspector and his sergeant."

"Better go fetch them then, Bert."

The man called Bert put his shovel down and pulled a handkerchief from his back pocket, distributing the dirt on his face more evenly. "Are you sure, Barry? What about Sir Hugh? He'll need to know."

"And so he will, eventually, if he doesn't already."

"Barry! Shut up!"

Addie's senses were on alert. She tried to peer around the men into the overturned earth. "What is it you've found? Buried treasure?"

"A body, my lady. A soldier, by the look of him. Go on, Bert. We're not getting any younger. And don't bandy it about everywhere, not to that busybody butler Amos Trim nor nobody. The coppers won't like it. Just tell whoever's in charge, and you do the shutting up."

Bert disappeared through the hedge. For an elderly man, he was sprightly.

A few spots rolled in front of Addie's eyes, but she willed them away. Now was no time to be missish and faint, even if she knew just how to do it without anyone getting a glimpse of her French knickers.

She was amazingly lucky so far. Despite helping the police in two murder investigations, she did not see any of the bodies. And there had been six! Six! Half a dozen souls whose lives were cut short by two murderers. After getting a very quick glimpse of the seventh—poor Pamela—Addie had scuttled away yesterday as far across the conservatory as she could waiting for the doctor, until Rupert came for tea.

She now debated whether she should peek into the trench the men had dug and decided against it. She had no forensic knowledge, and might disgrace herself by fainting, falling into it, or worse, losing her breakfast.

"Is it, um, a fresh body?" Addie tried not to breathe in too hard.

"No, ma'am. And I bet I know who it is."

"Really?"

Barry turned to the other man. "Charlie, you remember that fellow who came to visit on leave after Sir Hugh was invalided home? The one who deserted? There was a hue and cry and the muckety-mucks were all over the estate for a day or two asking a thousand questions. They even interviewed me."

"Aye. You're not sayin' that's him."

"I'll bet you it is. Should be easy enough to tell—he's still in his uniform."

"Did you go through his pockets?" Addie felt somewhat grisly speaking up.

Barry gave her a withering look. "'Course not. He's still half-buried anyway. We're gardeners, not gravediggers."

"The grounds are truly lovely." Addie wanted to make up for her faux pas.

"We do our best. Been at it here for forty or more years, the three of us. Wait, I remember you—you're the Merrill girl from over to Broughton Park. The older one."

"That's right. I used to visit Sir Hugh when we were children. Mr. Dunn, right?"

"One of 'em. Haven't seen you lately."

"No. I was out of the country for five months." And before that, in mourning, but she really didn't want to get into that with Mr. Dunn, who had once chased her with a rake after she'd jumped into a pile of leaves and scattered them across the county.

"Well, you've grown up."

"Yes."

He gave her a look. Yes, he remembered. "Still getting into mischief?"

He didn't know the half of it.

She was saved from responding by the emergence of Inspector Hunter from the boxwood. "I understand you've found a skeleton?"

"Over here. Watch your step. The ground is uneven, and there's some loose debris under the dirt. A nail or two too."

Mr. Hunter climbed over the rope and dropped into the beginnings of a foundation hole. He stood, hands in pockets, his face impassive.

"You discovered him just now?"

"Young Lady Fernald had asked us to get started on the folly last Friday, and we thought it was the least we could do for her. Had her heart set on the improvements, she did."

"There was a building here before, wasn't there?" Addie asked.

"Wood rot got it, and Sir Hugh's mother had it knocked down. Nothing was salvageable, not even the screening. Tears you could drive a lorry through. We burned up the worst of it at the harvest bonfire, and the odds and ends was used to help fill the hole."

"When was that?" Mr. Hunter's notebook was out.

"Fall of '16," Barry said promptly. Of the three Mr. Dunns, he seemed to be the one in charge. "I remember especially 'cause a friend of Sir Hugh's went missing after his visit here right before that—a lieutenant. Can't remember his name, but there was a scandal. Desertion, they said. Upset Sir Hugh something fierce, said the fellow would never do such a thing."

Addie tried to recall if she'd heard anything about this missing friend nine years ago and drew a blank. She was in London most of that year, volunteering with her mother on various committees. She liked to think she made a difference in the war effort, but her work was insignificant compared to those who'd trained as nurses and hello girls.

"And you think this might be the man?"

"Stands to reason, don't it?"

"I agree it's quite a coincidence, and I don't much believe in them. I think you're done digging for the day. It goes without saying that you must not touch anything else. And please don't mention your suspicions about this fellow's identity to anyone, the family or the staff. It might impede the investigation. Can one of you stay here until the team from Cirencester shows up?"

"Sure. We'll all stay. Have our lunch."

Addie spotted the metal lunch pails in the shade of the hedge and shuddered. The thought of a picnic next to a dead body, newly buried or not, was not on her agenda today or any day in the future.

"Lady Adelaide, I'll walk you back to the house."

She nodded. Her wandering about the estate was over. In no time the place would be crawling with policemen, and after yesterday, she knew she was not their favorite. She noted their scowls and heard the muttering about "women" pronounced in a certain way, as though her sex invalidated her brains. Why, she probably investigated more deaths than any of them! The Cotswolds had way more missing sheep than murders.

"Did you know of this incident? The missing lieutenant?" Mr. Hunter asked.

"I've been trying to think. So many of our friends were killed, I stopped reading the papers. But no one I knew just up and disappeared when home on leave. Hugh will know, and his army friends Captain Clifford and Mr. Bradbury. They were all very close. Did their training together and were in the same unit."

"Clifford is still serving?"

"Yes. He's about to be posted to India. This week was supposed to be a fun farewell for him. In his honor." Saturday evening's dinner had been filled with toasts and ribaldry, most of which Addie had not understood.

But now she did. "The Four Musketeers! That's what they called themselves, only it didn't make sense to me, since there are only three of them in life and fiction. The lieutenant must have been the fourth friend."

"Someone didn't like him much," observed Inspector Hunter, and Addie couldn't argue.

Chapter Six

Shot through the head. There was no chance that the soldier fell asleep in a hole in the ground and was accidentally covered over with building detritus. Someone placed him there nine years ago and went about their life.

The lieutenant's body—if that's who it was—was a complication Dev did not need. He hadn't even begun his interviews. One death at a time, he reminded himself, though they were probably connected. As he told the gardeners, he didn't give credence to coincidences. Philosophically, Dev believed everything in life was interrelated—one false word could cause a civilization to topple half a world away.

Lady Adelaide was unusually quiet as they walked along the crushed stone paths that cut through the formal knot gardens. Everything was extremely orderly, and Dev realized he'd prefer a touch of wildness amongst the pruned roses and weedless beds. The late Lady Fernald had green fingers for certain, but the effect was an almost make-believe kingdom.

Artificial. Too perfect.

"You knew Pamela Fernald well?"

"I've known her since we were both eighteen. We were

presented at court together in 1911." She paused, plucking at a spill of yellow roses that climbed a trellis. "My, that seems like another lifetime. We bumped into each other at all the parties and were friendly but not friends. But then she and Hugh married at the start of the war, and I got to know her better. I've known him since we were children—Broughton Park is only a few miles from here."

"How is Lady Broughton?" Dev was grateful the woman was not here; she made him unaccountably nervous. "And your sister?"

"Oh, they're as ever. Driving each other mad. Cee needs to find an occupation."

Dev thought it interesting that Lady Adelaide did not suggest marriage for her younger sister. It didn't solve everyone's problems. Once burned, twice shy, he supposed.

"Prior to coming here, you hadn't heard any rumors about the Fernalds' relationship?"

"No, I told you. Rupert and I only saw them a few times a year when they invited us to one of their dinner parties or Saturday-to-Mondays. They don't—didn't—generally go out, and what with me being in mourning and then away, we haven't socialized for ages. Were you even listening before?"

He had tried not to, but ignoring her was proving to be impossible. And probably bad for the case to boot. "I know you want to help."

She blushed. "Of course I do! Why wouldn't I?"

"You have a childhood friend to protect. That might cloud your judgment."

"You can't possibly think—oh, you can! And do! I'd swear on my husband's grave that Hugh is innocent."

"I'm not jumping to any conclusions—I hope you know me better than that. But with an old friend of Sir Hugh's probably buried on the estate and his wife poisoned, there is definitely something untoward going on."

"If anyone can get to the bottom of it, it will be you. And I'm here if you need me."

Just what he didn't need, again. "Your belief in my abilities is admirable, but this is another dangerous situation. Please stay out of it."

"All right."

He didn't believe her for a minute.

Dev made the necessary calls and spoke to Mrs. Lewis, the housekeeper. He returned to the library, a dark, cavernous room holding hundreds of leather-tooled books behind glass doors, finding members of the house party in various stages of restlessness. Well, he had information that would galvanize their attention.

"Thank you for your patience. I'm afraid I have more bad news. The gardeners have discovered a body on the property."

Lady Adelaide had chosen to sit next to her friend Sir Hugh and touched his shoulder. There were gasps all around and a sea of ashen faces.

"Who is it?" Lord Lucas Waring asked. Dev was somewhat annoyed to find the viscount present but knew the man no longer had designs upon Lady Adelaide. He read the surprising engagement announcement in the Times. But if a woman had the prerogative to change her mind, so must a man. Oddly enough, Waring was now planning to marry a girl Dev had met during a case a few months ago. Even being a detective, he had no clue how that came about.

"We don't know yet. Until we do, I'd appreciate it if you all would refrain from speculating."

Clifford and Bradbury exchanged a glance. "You're sure it's human remains?" Clifford asked.

"Quite. And not a Roman." Nearby Cirencester, then Corinium, had been the second-largest Roman city in Britain and was now a treasure trove of significant ancient artifacts and earthworks. Farmers were still turning up tile fragments and coins in their fields, expecting to strike it rich.

"Where is…it?" Lady Fernald asked.

"The area where a new folly is to be built. The men began digging this morning."

"Hugh, now that Pamela is gone, perhaps we shouldn't…" Simon Davies didn't finish.

Fernald touched his temple and shut his eyes briefly. "I don't know, Simon. I can't think about the plans now. But if Pam wanted the changes, I think we should honor her wishes. It's the least we can do in her memory."

"We can discuss it later, darling, though I've always thought a new folly truly was a folly," his mother said. "We already have the belvedere. Now, I hope you know I'm not criticizing—Pamela's taste was exquisite—but perhaps she was a trifle over-ambitious. Inspector, what about my daughter-in-law? Have you anything new to tell us? You were interrupted."

"The laboratory has yet to determine the cause of death. But all indications lead to a fast-acting poison." The room was so quiet the proverbial pin could drop. "As for the timeline, that's where I'll need your help. I understand Lady Pamela Fernald was attended by her maid in her suite between three and three thirty or so. She was discovered in the conservatory around four. I'd like to speak to each of you about your whereabouts between those hours yesterday afternoon."

"You think one of us killed Pamela?" one of the Jordan twins asked. Dev wasn't sure which. Both were confirmed flappers with their plucked eyebrows, kohl-rimmed eyes, and crimson lips, and far too young to be mixed up in murder. But Dev knew anything was possible amongst the Bright Young People nowadays. One or both of them could have poisoned Pamela for no more reason than a dare.

"I didn't say that, Miss Jordan. Your observations might be helpful to the investigation."

"Maybe she took something herself. Made a mistake," the other twin said. "Everyone takes drugs nowadays, don't they? Everyone amusing, anyhow. Why, we—" She caught herself, realizing she was about to confess her social sins to a policeman.

"Never," Fernald said. He clutched the arms of his pushchair, knuckles white. "You and your sister didn't know her all that well. She'd never do something stupid. She—she loved John too much."

In Dev's experience, no one really knew anyone well, sometimes not even themselves. He saw too many criminal acts that shocked those closest to the perpetrator. And he noted that Fernald didn't claim his wife loved him too much. Could she have taken her life, or simply experimented with something out of boredom that led to her death?

Dev checked his watch. "The housekeeper told me a buffet lunch will be laid out in the dining room between noon and two o'clock. Sir Hugh has lent me his study next door for our interviews. Mr. Davies, I'd like to begin with you if I may."

Dev looked to the reactions of those present. Had they heard the rumors too? But no one seemed concerned about where Dev had chosen to start.

The older man nodded. "I'll help in any way I can."

They adjourned to the wood-paneled room next door. It, too, was lined with books, and estate ledgers were stacked on Sir Hugh's desk blotter. Dev set them aside and took out his notebook. Davies pulled a chair up and sat.

He looked directly into Dev's eyes, something Dev wasn't

used to. Most people were too nervous speaking to him, their gazes darting everywhere else. Dev knew better than to think that sort of behavior showed guilt; even the innocent were nonplussed by the police.

"This is a terrible business. I've known Pam since she was a child."

"Oh?"

"Her mother and I were…ah, close." Davies's sharp cheekbones bore a telltale flush.

Were they cousins or lovers? "In what way?"

Davies studied his hands now, less eager to make eye contact. They resembled a gardener's more than a gentleman's, gnarled, knobby, and sun-browned. "Iris—Mrs. Temple—told me what the servants' gossip is here, and it's shameful. Pam was, at times, distraught. Perfectly understandable with all her burdens. She's had almost a decade of sacrifice. Hugh's a fine lad, but not the man she married. She came to me for advice quite often, and not at bankers' hours. I assure you, there was nothing inappropriate between us. I loved her mother, and looked upon Pam as the daughter I wished I had."

"I take it Lady Fernald's mother is dead?"

"Her father too. The Barlows were on a P & O liner bound for India when it struck a mine. The Maloja."

"Do you recall when?"

"All too well. February 1916."

An eventful year here, and for him as well, as Dev's injured foot reminded him every damp day. "Why was Lady Fernald distraught?"

"She trusted me in life. I'm not going to breach her confidence in death."

Dev stopped himself from rolling his eyes. This was no time for Davies to be pigheaded about his word as a gentleman. "May

I remind you this is a police investigation, Mr. Davies? Keeping secrets will not help me discover how Lady Fernald died."

"I don't believe Pam's concerns have any bearing on what happened to her."

"Why don't you let me decide that?"

"I'm sorry, but no. I'll be happy to tell you where I was between three and four, though. In my room, in my bath. I had been repotting orchids in new majolica containers all afternoon in the conservatory—Pam wanted her guests to be impressed. She meant to do it earlier in the week herself but was too busy."

"Can anyone vouch for you?"

"No. I didn't bring my valet with me. I hadn't planned on staying quite so long at Fernald Hall, but Pam's ideas for the gardens became ever more complex by the day. I wish to God I left sooner."

"So you saw or heard nothing suspicious?"

"I'm afraid not."

Dev wondered if the man would tell him if he had.

Chapter Seven

Addie picked at a sandwich, then decided to go upstairs to the schoolroom to see John. She spoke to him briefly last night. He'd been naturally solemn, shocked about his mother, concerned about his father. As an only child, he was—or had been—close to both his parents.

Pamela's cousin Juliet, something of a poor relation, served as John's governess for the past five years but was about to be replaced by a male tutor so John could be better prepared for boarding school in the Michaelmas term. Addie wondered if the tutor would still come and the boy still go. Hugh might need his son close after the devastating loss of his wife, and keeping John's familiar routine might be preferable.

From what she had heard from Rupert and others, Britain's public schools were barbaric. Flogging and bullying and worse could not possibly produce well-adjusted youth, though Addie would be the first to admit to not understanding the male perspective at all. Her men friends seemed to enjoy reminiscing about the various horrors they experienced, just as they now sometimes did with their war exploits when they were amongst themselves. Females were presumably too weak—or sensible—to comprehend.

Juliet was several years younger than Addie and trained at a teacher's college. She came into the household after struggling at a rural school on the Borders, and was profoundly grateful to Pamela, so much so that in Addie's opinion, she allowed herself to be taken for granted. Not by John, who showed affection for her, but by Pamela, who treated her with an indifference that Addie found slightly off-putting. Sometimes Juliet was invited to dine with the family, expected to make up numbers when there was an overabundance of men; other times she remained firmly upstairs. But Addie did not see her downstairs at any of the activities these past two days.

She knocked on the closed door and heard the scraping of chair legs on the wooden floor beyond. John opened it a few inches and gave her a wobbly smile. His dark eyes, so like his mother's, were suspiciously bright.

"May I come in?"

"Of course. Juliet," he called, "it's Lady Adelaide."

He loped off to her quarters in case she hadn't heard. Juliet had an apartment adjacent to the large sunny schoolroom. It consisted of a bedroom, bath, sitting room, and tiny kitchen. John's own bedroom was down the hall.

He came back, composed. How brave he was. "She'll be a few minutes."

That was fine—Addie came to see him, not Juliet. While they waited for her, she gave John a quick, awkward hug. "I've been thinking about you. What are you working on?"

A table was spread with maps, some so tattered they looked as if they'd factored into Sir Hugh's schooling, or even possibly his grandfather's.

"India. You know my Barlow grandparents were going there before they drowned. Juliet's got a job near Bombay when Mr. Stewart comes. Mummy fixed it up."

"Does she? What a long way away!" Addie liked travel as much as the next person, but India was a continent too far. She tried to imagine Juliet in the jungle surrounded by colorful wildlife, and failed. Juliet never struck Addie as an adventurous person at all. A classroom of rough northern children defeated her in her first teaching job; John by comparison was an angel.

"Juliet says there's an Indian detective from Scotland Yard downstairs."

"There is. But I don't believe he's ever been to India. His father was in the army and he married an Indian lady."

John swept the maps up and put them in a large folder. "I'd like to go one day. I don't suppose Papa would allow it."

"Maybe you can go when you're all grown up and don't need permission. I'm sure he'd miss you, though. Especially since..." Addie stopped.

"You mean because of Mummy. He'll be lonely for the rest of his life."

Addie nodded. "It's very hard when someone dies." Even when that someone made you miserable and drove you around the bend, like Rupert. "But time is supposed to heal all wounds." A cliché and not precisely accurate.

"Is he all right?"

"Your father? Haven't you seen him today?"

John shook his head. "I know he's busy. There are even more policemen in the garden now. We watched them from the window."

Addie was stunned that Hugh had not sent for the boy. "He has a lot to deal with at the moment, I suppose."

"I know. Juliet says I mustn't fuss."

Suddenly Addie was angry. "I should think fussing is natural. You had something dreadful happen."

"Men don't cry."

"They jolly well do! When my father had to put down his favorite hunter, he wept buckets and was not one bit ashamed, and that was just a horse that died, not a human. And my husband told me once that when he was in his plane, sometimes the sky and clouds and earth were so beautiful, he was moved to tears. He joked it made for tricky maneuvering with everything so bleary."

If only Rupert flapped around in Heaven right now. She wondered if her father the marquess was reunited with his horse. Did animals go to an afterlife? Another question for Reverend Rivers, if she was allowed to go home to Compton Chase.

"Juliet says we might go riding later when the policemen go."

"They may be a while." Addie walked over to the window. From this vantage point, she could see everything for miles, including the cars and ambulance that were parked on the grass beyond the hedges. A slew of men surrounded the ropes, and several were inside digging carefully.

John stood next to her. "What are they looking for?"

How much should she tell him? "The Dunns found some bones. Old ones."

"A body?"

Addie nodded. "I don't want you to worry. Nothing else terrible is going to happen." She hoped.

Juliet entered, flustered. "So sorry to keep you waiting, Lady Adelaide. I was washing up our lunch dishes. I hate to leave them about dirty and sticky before one of the kitchen maids remembers to collect them. Sometimes they forget all about us up here."

"That's all right. I just came upstairs to check on John. And you, of course."

"We're fine." Juliet angled her head toward the window. "Why are they still out there?"

"Lady Adelaide said the police have found a body!" The boy sounded more than a little pleased. Children were savages, even well-brought-up ones like John Fernald.

The governess blanched. "A body? Don't be silly, John."

"No, I'm afraid it's true. The gardeners discovered—someone. I don't think it has anything do with Pamela, though."

"I should hope not! We've had enough nonsense."

Cock-up. Nonsense. Two words Addie would not normally associate with unattended deaths. She must remember to tell Inspector Hunter.

Juliet worried the hem of her white blouson. The family resemblance to Pamela was uncomfortably clear—same dark eyes and hair, fair complexion, neat figure. But where Pamela had been an acknowledged beauty with fashionably short marcelled hair, Juliet was merely pretty enough, her own hair in an untidy bun.

She lacked Pamela's confidence and spirit, too, which was understandable. Her father was a drunkard who abandoned his family to genteel poverty, while his brother, Pamela's father, made money hand over fist. Addie knew well that money, while not everything, was certainly something. She tried to give away as much of hers as her man of business would allow, and then had to listen to her mother's lectures about her improvidence.

Addie changed the subject. "I understand you have a position in India."

"Yes. Well—things are uncertain now, I suppose. Pamela was determined to hire Mr. Stewart to replace me." Juliet gave a dismissive sniff at her rival.

"Stewart. The name is familiar. Do I know him?"

"He's the youngest son of a solicitor in Stroud. Since graduating from university last year, he goes around Gloucestershire and Oxfordshire polishing up boys before they go off to public school. He has a reputation."

"Good, I presume."

Juliet sighed. "Oh, yes. He's very much in demand. The boys love him, and he's so handsome their mothers do too."

Addie hoped that went over John's head. He was still looking out the window like a preadolescent vulture.

"Please let me know if there's anything I can do for you or John. I'm not sure when Detective Inspector Hunter will let us all go home, but you know I'm not that far away. Maybe you both can come for the day and look over my late husband's car collection." She bet John would like that.

"Thank you. This has been a terrible shock."

A shock, yes. But Juliet did not seem particularly sad that her glamorous cousin was dead.

Chapter Eight

"Huh. That was interesting."

Addie clutched the hand railing. Rupert was lounging on the landing as though he were sunbathing at the Côte d'Azur. If she hadn't been minding her steps, she might have pitched forward over his long legs and met her own untimely fate.

"Stop doing this, turning up without warning! If you were a cat, I'd bell you. I could have fallen down the back stairs and broken my neck."

"Someone would have found you eventually, although the maids do give Miss Barlow a wide berth. I wonder why she's not popular."

"Been eavesdropping?" It was one of Rupert's singular accomplishments.

"Singular? Come now. I'm more useful than that. Look at what I've accomplished in the past."

He was reading her mind once more, loud and clear. "Are you going to physically materialize again?" Rupert had turned up more or less in the flesh in the nick of time on their last adventure, frightening a murderer out of his wits.

"I'm not sure. That was an emergency and took a lot out of

me—supposedly you're the only one I'm assigned to grace my presence with."

Addie snorted. She could do without being graced with Rupert's presence for the rest of her life.

Rupert ignored her. "Generally we ghosts focus on moving objects about, and believe me, that's arduous enough. You'd never believe how much air can resist an ordinary object. There's a formula."

Addie was not science-minded and didn't really care about formulas. Formulae? See, she didn't even know the correct plural word. She sat down on a carpeted stair tread. "So, who is guilty?"

"For which death?"

"Don't be tiresome. I'm not choosy—either one. I know you know more than you're telling me. I bet you've been lurking about all morning and afternoon gleaning lots of fascinating facts with your devilish mind-reading."

Rupert put a finger to his lips. "Shh. No summoning the D-fellow, if you please. So far, I've avoided him and his minions, and I want to keep it that way. One would so hate to incinerate."

She gave him a very weak punch, chilling her knuckles. "What have you found out?"

"Ungrateful girl. What's in it for me? I know you'll run right off to earn points with your precious inspector."

"Now that you've turned over your new leaf, aren't you obliged to do the right thing just because it is the right thing? And as I said, he's not my inspector! There's no reason for you to be so jealous."

Unfortunately.

"As if I could be. I left all that sort of silliness behind." Rupert didn't meet her eyes, and that gave her a perverse sense of satisfaction. She knew he cared about her, which was rather ironic after all he put her through. "All right. I did pick up a valuable nugget."

"Out with it!"

Rupert smirked. "It's rather enjoyable keeping you in suspense. My pleasures are so limited lately."

"Good! You had enough pleasures to last several lifetimes before you crashed the Hispano Suiza."

With his French mistress.

The latest one. There had been another Frenchwoman in his past, as well as several ladies from the United Kingdom and beyond, a veritable female League of Nations. Most of them had shown up at his funeral. Rupert had been an international ambassador of adultery.

He nodded in guilt. "All right, all right. We've established I'm a dog."

"That is an insult to dogs. Tell me what you know."

"When Michael Ainsley went missing, Bradbury and Clifford were also present, lieutenants all. They somehow wangled leave together and came to cheer Hugh up in his bed of pain. Even your buddy Lucas dropped in for a drink a time or two."

"Who's Michael Ainsley?"

Rupert waggled his usual finger. "Come now. Use that beautiful head of yours."

Light dawned. "Oh! You mean the soldier who deserted. Except he didn't! He was buried on the grounds."

"Well done. So, one of them might know something. The two or three of them might know something. And I suppose you could throw Hugh into the mix, although I gather he was pretty badly off when they visited. Half out of his head sometimes. Pamela had her hands full, plying him with leaves and twigs and what-not, beyond what the sawbones prescribed to keep the pain at bay." Rupert tapped his square chin. "She was quite a witch, you know."

"Rupert! Don't be so misogynistic!" While she and Pamela

were not best friends, she was always pleasant and thoughtful. All the flowers she sent a year ago after Rupert died brightened up the dregs of Addie's winter.

"I'm not referring to her personality, you goose. I mean she was very knowledgeable about the old ways. Herbal remedies. You saw her bottles and jars the other day. Tinctures and salves and so forth."

Addie had, shelves lined alphabetically, the labels in Pamela's neat handwriting. "You don't mean she dabbled in poisons, do you?"

"Might have."

"Did she poison herself?" The idea seemed absurd. Pamela was a perfectly perfect hostess all weekend. There were no signs of depression or agitation that Addie noticed.

"I didn't say that. I agree—it seems unlikely. She was made of stern stuff. Had to be, with Hugh's situation." He paused. "I knew Pam rather well, you know."

Addie covered her spectacles with her hands. "Oh, God. Not another one."

Rupert shrugged. "She was lonely. It didn't last very long. She felt a bit remorseful, and maybe I did too. Pam was fond of you, you know."

Addie didn't want to hear the details and tried to control her urge to push Rupert down the stairs. It wouldn't do any good. Or any harm, for that matter—he was already dead, damn him.

That explained the masses of hothouse flowers, didn't it? Gladioli of guilt.

Another betrayal, but she was accustomed by now. There was no point in being upset—it wouldn't help solve the case. "Does Michael Whosis have anything to do with Pamela's death?"

"I feel strongly that he does. Call it sixth sense, if you will. Your inspector has a touch of that, you know."

"He is not my inspector," Addie repeated. "I suppose intuition is handy when you deal with the worst of humanity."

"Indeed. It's also very useful in wartime. One gets used to trusting those odd feelings. I can't tell you how many times I knew when Jerry was about to make himself a bother and took action accordingly."

Rupert sounded as if he'd like to relive those awful days. Men. Really, they were incomprehensible, dead or alive.

"So, getting back to the present, you suspect Owen Bradbury and Dennis Clifford?" She didn't bother to include Lucas—Rupert was always negative about her old friend.

"I didn't say that either. I did catch them in a heated confab on the terrace after lunch, though. Perhaps you can exert your feminine wiles and discover something."

Another person giving her wiles too much credit. She'd never been an accomplished flirt to begin with, and most of the young men she'd unartfully practiced on were in graves across France.

"Captain Clifford called Pamela's death a cock-up. I thought that was strange."

"Well, there you go. Find out what he meant by that." Rupert checked his third-best watch, the one the undertaker had tried to discourage her from burying with him. Rupert had collected watches as he had cars, so half a dozen were still in a leather case in the safe at Compton Chase. She really should send them to his parents in their seaside manor house in Cornwall.

"I've got something I must do," Rupert said with a mysterious air. "Good luck, my dear." He vanished from the landing.

Addie wondered how far Inspector Hunter was in the interview process. There were the houseguests. Evelyn Fernald. Hugh's Aunt Iris. He probably wanted to talk to John and Juliet Barlow too. Pamela's maid. Jim Musgrave. Beckett. Sergeant

Wells would talk with the rest of the staff, if this case was any-thing like the one that had occurred at Compton Chase.

If Rupert was right and the two deaths were connected, that would eliminate those who weren't here nine years ago. That surely meant Margie and Mandy Jordan—they were still in pigtails and pinafores in 1916, their pigtails probably brown. Presumably, Patrick Cassidy was in Ireland or in uniform some-where in Europe. Addie crossed Lucas off her mental list because he was Lucas, even if he'd come over to Fernald Hall for dinner or drinks that fall. She hardly thought he'd commit a postpran-dial murder. As for the rest, she'd be discreet in her inquiries and make sure Mr. Hunter was unaware of her assistance.

Of course, if the discovery of the soldier's body had nothing to do with Pamela, then all bets were off. They could be deal-ing with two killers, possibly even more if the murderers were working in teams.

She couldn't help but shiver, although it was a perfectly warm June afternoon.

Making her way down the back stairs, she encountered the maid, Mary, going up, the same girl Addie had asked to keep people from the conservatory. Mary nearly tripped and set the box she was carrying on a step to regain her footing.

"Pardon, Lady Adelaide, I didn't expect to see anyone. These old books are heavier than I thought. Mrs. Lewis should have sent a footman up."

A good thing Mary hadn't tripped over Rupert—or was that impossible? Did one walk through Rupert? Addie picked up a volume and opened it. *A School History of England*. Oddly enough, it was written by a teacher in the New York City Public Schools and had been printed over twenty years ago. She flipped through the illustrations and colored maps of countries that didn't exist anymore.

So no Great War within, which made the book almost a fantasy. A fairy tale.

The war had changed everything.

"Poor John. He's got a lot of reading ahead, doesn't he?"

"Mr. Stewart had the books sent over. I don't know how they expect the poor boy to concentrate—he's just lost his mother." Mary bit her lower lip. "I know it's not my place. But I think it's wicked he's to be sent away, I don't care what anybody says."

"I think I agree with you." Unless his father somehow killed his mother.

Addie needed to speak with Hugh.

Chapter Nine

Bob handed him the packet. Frugal that he was, the Cirencester coroner had crossed out a dozen names before Dev's on the battered brown envelope. Would he expect it back so it could be used a fourteenth time? Dev unwound the red string from the clasp and pulled out a sheaf of papers. Bob waited patiently while he scanned the report quickly, then went back to read it at length.

Good God.

Aconitum, commonly known as aconite. Also monkshood or wolfsbane. Pamela Fernald had probably ingested liquid obtained from boiling the plant's roots. The effects would have been sudden and irreversible. Numbness, nausea, difficulty breathing, paralysis of the heart. He'd check with the gardeners as to where the plants were located on the property and if any had been recently disturbed.

Aconite had been used for centuries by hunters to poison arrows. Anyone who was a plantsman would know how deadly all the varieties were. Even touching the leaves could be dangerous.

And the coroner's biggest bombshell: Pamela Fernald had been about four months' pregnant.

A substantial motive for suicide. Unless her husband was not as impaired as everyone believed him to be. Dev knew couples could get creative in the bedroom, but frankly couldn't imagine asking Sir Hugh if he was still capable of engaging in any form of intercourse.

Some questions were not meant to be asked amongst civilized men. He could feel his own blushes rising, and cursed Lady Adelaide for bringing him here.

"What's it say, guv?"

"A plant-based poison. Aconite." Dev kept the rest of the medical examiner's report to himself. He trusted Bob implicitly but needed some time to think.

"Something she grew here?"

"Very probably. The gardens and greenhouses are full of all sorts of things. The question is whether she poisoned herself or someone else did."

"There wasn't a note. And there usually is." Bob picked up a photograph of Pamela from Sir Hugh's desk. Dev had stared at it long enough during the interviews.

"Not that anyone's found yet." The Cirencester police had been all over the house Sunday afternoon and evening. It was possible they'd missed something, though.

Dear Hugh, I'm sorry I was unfaithful.

But if she ended her own life, she also ended a child's. It didn't square with the little he knew about Pamela Fernald. She was a nurturer, whether it was taking care of her son and husband, or her plants and horses.

"A real beauty, wasn't she?"

"Indeed she was." That kind of beauty was almost a curse. Harmony. Symmetry. Pamela Fernald's face would have been at home on a caryatid, perfect waves of hair framing a perfect face. Dev had been reading the Greeks lately—in translation, as he'd not benefitted from a classical education and hardly knew a gamma from a delta—and was reminded of Helen of Troy and all the trouble she caused.

"'Course, Sir Hugh is a good-lookin' chap too. Must have been quite the couple before he was wounded. Like cinema stars."

Dev didn't follow films, though he knew most women of his acquaintance adored them. Too much drama and peril for him—there was enough in his job. "What did Jim Musgrave have to say?"

Bob sat down and pulled out his notebook. "That his master was taking his afternoon nap during the time in question. He swims most every morning, then usually exercises with weights after lunch. All that tires him out, so he goes down for at least half an hour. Sometimes he reads rather than sleeps, but Musgrave says he put Sir Hugh into bed on Sunday afternoon. He'd been out in the sun watching his guests play tennis and was hot and a little cranky."

Cranky enough to kill his wife? "What time?"

"He said well before three—he wasn't sure of the exact time."

"Where did Musgrave go afterward?"

"His room, right next door to Sir Hugh's. And no, no one saw him. There's a connecting door, so he didn't have to go out in the hallway. He had a few winks himself before Sir Hugh rang for him to help him get ready for the tea party at about ten till. Cutting it close, according to Musgrave. Young Lady Fernald didn't like them to be late all the time and they both joked they were going to be in the doghouse when they got to the conservatory. They were just about to leave the suite when the captain and Mr. Bradbury stopped them."

Cutting it close was right—Dev supposed Musgrave could have poisoned Pamela somehow and nipped back into his room in time for Fernald's summons, but it seemed unlikely. Why would he want to kill his master's beloved wife?

Unless he knew her secret.

Or unless Sir Hugh did and ordered the man to. But loyalty should only go so far.

"Did any of the servants notice anything?"

"Too busy to see straight, I'd say. Trim and Mrs. Lewis run a tight ship here. Sir Hugh is a generous employer and well-liked. He has their sympathy and respect, and they work hard for him."

"And Pamela Fernald?"

"They didn't dare to speak against her to me. But you already know what the rumor was."

"And according to Simon Davies, there was nothing to it." Someone had to be the father of Pamela's baby, however.

"How are you making out, sir?"

Dev glanced at his own notes. Besides Davies, he'd questioned four of the guests with remarkable speed so far. The Jordan sisters knew nothing of value, both of them regretting that they came to a house party in the country when they could be in London at the Thieves' Den or the Southern Belle belting down bourbon and dancing their nights away. Even two deaths were not exciting enough for them.

Pretty idiots.

Dev reminded himself not to overlook any possibilities. Their motive might be murky to him at present, but it didn't mean they were innocent.

Patrick Cassidy was a relative stranger, although Sir Hugh bought horses from him before. He only met the Fernalds in person when he arrived five days ago, and he noticed nothing Sunday. He was out riding and working with one of his horses most of the day until he cleaned himself up for tea.

Iris Temple had few words to say that weren't platitudes,

the barest minimum, which raised Dev's antennae. Usually a murder investigation incited some curiosity, but she exhibited none.

She was an elegant woman of a certain age, still blond and profoundly attractive. A longtime widow, she lived in a grace-and-favour cottage on the estate. Mrs. Temple was there alone until she walked over, discovering the conservatory doors closed and a commotion in front of them.

Her late husband was Lady Evelyn Fernald's brother, making her Hugh's aunt by marriage. She claimed to be a best friend as well as a sister-in-law and was, so far, discretion itself. Evelyn got along perfectly with Pamela. Everyone did. She was a beautiful young woman, loyal wife, loving mother.

Dev now knew not all of that was true.

He had yet to speak to Bradbury, Clifford, or Sir Hugh's mother. And of course, there was also the ever-present thorn in his side, Lord Lucas Waring.

Something about the viscount set Dev's teeth on edge. While he knew that the man was engaged—to Philippa Dean, of all people—it was not so long ago that Waring had aspirations to wed Lady Adelaide. How had she taken his change of heart? The man was inconstant and had questionable taste besides.

Ah. Enough. Pip Dean was a sweet girl, and deserved happiness if it could be found with Waring. Their relationship was none of his business, and he could not see how it had any bearing on this case. He needed to stay clearheaded, which was always challenging around Lady Adelaide Compton. She befuddled him, and befuddlement was not his usual state.

"I'm getting nowhere. But fast, at least." Dev grinned at his sergeant.

"Is that because they know nothing? Or won't tell you anything?"

"A little of both, I think. What are the servants' impressions of the guests?"

"As I said, they're pretty much too busy to have impressions of anything. Everyone has visited Fernald Hall before for one event or another except for the Irish horse breeder. But here's the best news, and I hope you won't mind I saved it for last. Captain Clifford and Mr. Bradbury have been coming here since the war. They were here the time when that lieutenant disappeared." Bob looked chuffed, and so he should.

"One thing at a time," Dev said, though he was obviously intrigued.

"I know, sir. But that's handy, ain't it?"

"See if you can get me a list of who else was present back then. Trim would probably know—he's been here since the Conquest and seems pretty sharp." The butler had a quiet word with Dev when he brought in coffee, assuring him of the staff's full cooperation.

The coffee was cold now, which was just as well, as the wood-paneled study was quite warm. Dev got up from Sir Hugh's desk and pushed the windows all the way up. The scent of fresh-cut grass and roses wafted through the room, and he stifled the urge to take a turn around Pamela Fernald's too-perfect garden to clear his head.

"And do me another favor, Bob—see how they're progressing at the folly site." That case had not yet fallen into his lap, but Dev expected it would sooner or later. If he could kill two birds with one stone, all the better. "But don't step on any toes," he added. Local police were often overly sensitive about their patch and had no reason to like Londoners swanning in to solve their crimes.

"Sure enough. Who do you want to see next?"

Upright Waring was an unlikely culprit, but it might be fun to torture him a little. But not yet. "Let's get Bradbury in, Clifford after—might as well do it alphabetically. Then Lady Fernald, I suppose. Say, if I may be nosy, how does Francie get along with your mother?"

Bob shook his head. "Chalk and cheese, guv. Chalk and cheese. And now that little Joan is crawling about, they fight over everything. Is she old enough to toss her bottle and drink from a cup so she can spill milk down her front? Who will pick her up when she's crying? Or should anyone pick her up at all so she can cry herself to sleep? Sunday lunches are hell, if you want the truth. I'd rather be at the Thieves' Den dancing with one of the Forty Dollies picking my pocket, and you know I don't much like jazz."

The members of that girl gang should not be trifled with, so things must be dire indeed. Poor Bob. But according to what Dev heard so far, Pamela and Evelyn Fernald were on good terms.

Dev's own mother was anxious to be a mother-in-law. He thought she should be careful of what she wished for.

"I'll go fetch Bradbury, then check on the digging." Bob shut the study door quietly and Dev was left with his new notebook, pages empty and waiting for the worst.

Chapter Ten

Addie knocked on the door of Hugh's suite, then knocked again. When she was nearly ready to give up, Jim Musgrave opened the door, minus his jacket, his sleeves rolled up.

"He's taking his afternoon rest, Lady Adelaide. You can come back later if you like." Hugh's valet looked intractable, but Addie felt strongly that Hugh should be disturbed and held her ground.

"It's important, Jim. I've just been upstairs to see John."

"The boy's all right?"

"Not really. I mean, he's fine physically, but is naturally sad. Could I speak to Sir Hugh for just a minute or two? I promise I'll try not to upset him."

Any more than he already was.

"Come in then. You'll have to wait while I make him decent."

Addie was left in the handsome small parlor. It was very masculine, with dark-blue patterned wallpaper, wide leather chairs and a well-worn oxblood Chesterfield sofa. She wondered if Hugh was moved from his chair to sit on the regular furniture to entertain family and friends here—it was a very cozy space.

She'd never been invited in before and was struck by the portrait of Pamela over the carved fireplace mantel. In fact, Pamela was everywhere, photographs both posed and candid inside polished silver frames scattered throughout the room. Pamela under a huge flower-bedecked hat in the garden, matching her surroundings. Pamela at her presentation to the king, feathers pinned to a headband with diamond clips. Pamela holding John as a baby. There were a few of Hugh, too—Pamela and Hugh on horseback before the war. Pamela and Hugh on their wedding day. Addie had attended and tossed rice along with everyone else.

They were truly a golden couple in Addie's social circle. How would Hugh manage without her?

Addie picked up the one photograph on the tabletop that differed from the rest, and not only because it was not encased in silver. Four young men were immortalized—Hugh in his pushchair looking frail yet jaunty, younger versions of Captain Clifford and Owen Bradbury, and a face she didn't recognize, although it looked slightly familiar. No doubt it was the poor lieutenant. He wore the wide grin of a man who didn't have a trouble in the world and enjoyed being with his best mates. Who could imagine he'd be killed so soon after this picture was taken?

"The Four Musketeers," Hugh said softly. He rolled himself in and was dressed in a black silk robe over pajamas. Jim Musgrave was not with him. "Sorry I'm not in tails and top hat."

Addie set the onyx picture frame down. "And I'm sorry to interrupt your nap."

"I wasn't sleeping anyway. Can't. Jim tried to give me some powders, but I told him I'd sack him if he kept after me so. He can be a dreadful bully." Hugh gazed up at her, blue eyes solemn. "He said your visit was important. What's happened? Another body in the bushes?" he asked wryly.

"No, thank God. It's John." Noting the alarm on Hugh's face, she said hastily, "He's perfectly fine. Well, that's not true—he's asking after you. I know I'm sticking my nose in, but I think you should spend some time with him today. The police in the garden have aroused his curiosity, and...worried him."

Hugh gazed off into a dark blue corner. "I know you're right. Frankly, I wasn't sure I'd be strong enough for him. I—I feel like a complete coward. My emotions are not quite what they should be." The tremor in his voice confirmed his words.

Addie was compelled to give her old friend a hug. His shoulders were still broad, and she knew he exercised every day to maintain his upper body strength. Tears came to her eyes.

"You mean they're not under rigid control? Hugh! You've been a hero to us all for years, even before the war. No one would think any less of you if you gave in to your heartbreak. Your wife has died. Believe me, I do know how you feel—the shock of it anyway. Rupert and I were not blessed with the love you both shared, so it must be even worse for you." Addie would go to the stake before she told Hugh about Pamela's affair with her late husband.

"She was exceptional, wasn't she? Putting up with me after everything." He drew a breath. "I know she wouldn't want me to feel sorry for myself. She never let me get away with the blue devils, always had a way to jolly me out of them. I was lucky; she proved that to me every day. But now..."

"I think John needs a good cry. You both do." Addie might even join them.

Hugh's mouth twisted into an almost-smile. "Yes, Herr Doktor Freud."

"You may tease me all you like. You know I've never been able to keep my mouth shut when I'm in the right."

"You were a martinet when we were children."

Addie smiled. "Some things never change."

"Remember the time you made Lucas wear your straw hat?"

"He was meant to be Huckleberry Finn. And I took the pink ribbons and flowers off! Goodness, I got quite a spanking from Nanny for that hat's desecration. Hugh, promise me you'll send for John this afternoon. He can't go outdoors because of the police."

"God, are they still here? How long does it take to cart away a body? I wonder who it is. Some old vagrant, I suppose. Not that that makes it any better."

Inspector Hunter said nothing about the uniform, and Addie was certainly not going to mention it. She gave Hugh another hug, and then he rang for Musgrave.

Good deed done, it was time for fresh air. Addie wouldn't wander in the direction of the police activity beyond the formal garden, but she was in luck—a classic stone belvedere at the end of the east lawn's reflecting pool was empty and shady. She brought a book from Hugh's library, a murder mystery of all things, borrowed Saturday night to help her fall asleep. She once gave them up for good after she was mixed up in one—a murder, not a book—but had since relapsed. Unfortunately, she was only on Chapter Ten, and she was almost entirely sure she knew the identity of the killer. It was all she could do not to sneak a look at the last few pages to confirm her suspicions.

Of course, she was wrong before in real life. Twice. Never in a million years would she detect the killers in the cases in which she'd assisted. The only gratifying thing? Inspector Hunter, who had far greater experience than she, had difficulty until it was almost too late.

She brushed her curls behind her ears and removed her glasses. While she had trouble seeing things far away, she didn't need them for reading. Much to her mother's disapproval, she'd been wearing spectacles this past year, and was simply amazed she could see each leaf on a tree.

Each long dark eyelash of a certain policeman.

She shook leaves and lashes out of her head, leaned back against the cool gray stone, and opened her book. She got as far as five sentences when she wondered again how the questioning inside was proceeding. It was late afternoon now, almost tea-time, and Mr. Hunter (she did not allow herself to think of him as Dev very often) had been at it all day. She hoped she'd be allowed to leave tomorrow; he certainly wouldn't accuse her of anything. Addie was responsible for him being here, after all.

Still, that would be quite the red herring, wouldn't it? The murderer arranging for the investigator? The plot had promise.

But Inspector Hunter would never believe she was capable of killing anyone, and she agreed that under ordinary circumstances she wasn't. True, she had fleeting naughty thoughts in the past of exterminating Rupert by pillow or hammer, which had ultimately proved unnecessary. However, she lobbed enough breakable objects at his head and wished him to perdition during their five years of wedded unbliss. Addie had, in short, behaved like a fishwife, not the cosseted, conventional first daughter of the Marquess and Marchioness of Broughton.

Her life was certainly calmer now, with the exception of Rupert's occasional reappearances and the dead bodies he heralded. Calm, and, if she was honest, a little boring.

Not that she wanted to exercise her brain with murders. Crossword puzzles were a far safer substitute.

Resolutely burying her nose back into her book, she didn't notice the arrival of Patrick Cassidy until he slid next to her on the bench. She was so preoccupied he could have snuck up and murdered her if he was so inclined.

She needed to be much more alert if she was of any further use here.

"Good book?" he asked.

"Not really." She shut it. "What's going on up at the house?"

"Your policeman is with Lady Fernald now. Only Lord Waring is left."

"He's not my policeman!" It seemed she was constantly denying this. It was too annoying.

"Well, you asked for him. I thought you and he were particular friends." The way he said it made Addie blush, and quick to deny it.

"He investigated an incident at my estate last summer. And then something else in Town this spring when my sister was the victim of an accidental poisoning. We are merely... acquaintances."

"Ah. So you attract villains and mayhem clear across the country. I'm keeping company with a dangerous woman. A femme fatale. What's to become of me in your presence? Will I be unmolested, or meet my own dreadful demise?" He gave a dazzling smile, looking very much as if he'd like to be molested.

"I'm sure you're safe. Or as safe as anyone can be when bodies are being dug up," Addie said, a bit tartly.

Mr. Cassidy's russet eyebrows knit. "Will there be more than the poor fellow behind the hedge, do y'think?"

"I hope not. I'd like to go home."

He sighed. "Aye, so would I, and now it looks as if Sir Hugh will not be buying my horses after all, what with his lady wife gone."

"Oh! I hadn't thought of that. Timothy Hay is for John, isn't he?"

"Aye. A horse to grow into. And I spent the weekend trying to break him of the bad habit of throwing his rider off. I've sold the Fernalds a few horses before over the years, but this was the first time I was able to come along with them. We've had a steady correspondence, Sir Hugh and I."

Patrick Cassidy looked prosperous enough that the loss of the sale of three horses would not break him. He wore a Harris Tweed jacket and deerskin trousers, a paisley ascot at his throat. Addie was sure if she looked with her spectacles back on, she'd see her reflection in his expensive polished boots. A signet ring whose design was nearly worn flat was his only adornment. All in all, he was the epitome of a country gentleman.

"I don't relish another trip across the Irish Sea with those high-strung beauties," he continued. "I don't suppose I could interest you in purchasing one or two? I'll give you a good deal."

Addie simply looked at him, and he smiled again.

"Aye, you're no horsewoman. But I'd be happy to teach you. Throw in some lessons for nothing. It would be no hardship to spend more time with you, my lady. None a'tall."

"I'm too old," Addie said reflexively. Bones became brittle as one aged, and Addie was fond of hers the way they were. And she was much too old to fall for Cassidy's flattery.

"Bunkum. You've stables?"

"Not really. My husband's cars have taken the space over. He had quite a collection. I really should sell them."

"No fancy motorcar can replace a good horse."

"Bunkum indeed." Addie jumped a foot as Rupert appeared on her other side. "And why sell my beautiful automobiles? They're practically works of art. Handmade, every one of them. You don't need the money. You manage the estate very well. For a woman."

Clenching her fist, Addie murmured an indistinct sound. She was doomed.

"Get rid of this redheaded stranger. I have news." In reality, Patrick Cassidy had lovely dark auburn hair, which flopped across his tanned forehead, just begging to be brushed back.

What could Addie say to make the Irishman go away? She

was raised to be polite. All of the innocuous excuses her mother provided her growing up were obvious lies. She didn't have a headache; one didn't read with a headache. Feel faint. Have a touch of nausea. And Mr. Cassidy, being a gentleman, would only offer to walk her back to the house if she used any of them.

"You might try passing gas. That works a treat."

"Rupert! I mean, my husband Rupert would probably haunt me if I sold the cars. So, I'll have to decline your generous offer."

Mr. Cassidy gave her another of his too-charming smiles. "A sophisticated woman such as yourself can't believe in ghosts."

"You'd be surprised."

"Did Cassidy not go to Sunday School? We're in the Bible, you know," Rupert interjected.

"My old granny was one for telling tales of the dead. Superstitious, she was. She was convinced she saw my brother walk after he passed."

Addie felt a cold finger poking in her spine. She glared quickly at Rupert, then turned to Mr. Cassidy. "I'm sorry for your loss. Perhaps your brother had unfinished business."

"Aye. I wish he'd shown himself to me."

"How did he die, if you don't mind me asking?"

"Isn't that the question of the century? Perhaps if we knew, his spirit could be at peace."

"That's not how it works," Rupert snapped. "Come on, Addie. Give him the old heave-ho. This is important."

She lurched up. "I've just remembered something. I need to…"

"Meditate," Rupert suggested. "All alone. You're thinking of turning to an obscure eastern religion for solace and comfort in your tragic widowhood. Omm, and what not."

"Speak to my maid," Addie said in desperation. "It's urgent. Could you send her out to me? I've, uh, twisted my ankle."

"Have you indeed? I could carry you back to Fernald Hall if you like."

He looked perfectly capable of doing just that. She couldn't help but notice his muscular body and the strong, brown hands capable of controlling the most difficult of horses. "No, no! Just tell her to bring wrapping. Ice. Perhaps a stick. And an aspirin. A big one." The bigger, the better to get rid of the insistent throbbing in her head named Rupert. "Take your time. There's no real rush." She sounded like a ninny—either it was urgent or it was not.

"Nonsense. Are you in great pain? Do sit down. You should have said."

"Not at all. It's a trifling twinge, but Beckett will know what to do. It's—it's an old childhood injury. It flares up when one least expects it."

Like Rupert.

Addie hoped Beckett wouldn't beat her with the stick once she found out the truth. She was probably enjoying a flirtation right now with one of the footmen. Her heart supposedly belonged to Addie's gardener, Jack Robertson, but they weren't formally engaged yet.

Addie felt an odd squirming sensation as a concerned Mr. Cassidy took a perfectly healthy ankle in his callused hand and gently rubbed it. "Oh!" she said, suddenly inspired. "Tell her I have the exact same symptoms as Lady Grimes."

Since Lady Grimes was an entirely imaginary friend of Addie's, she hoped Beckett understood this was no true emergency. Lady Grimes was a useful fictional excuse and was summoned when Addie needed to prevaricate. Her maid would assume that Mr. Cassidy made himself too familiar—which he had—and Addie sent him off with a flea in his ear.

Ignoring her instructions, the man jogged off at a rapid clip across the grass. Addie turned to Rupert, who was also staring at her ankle with a most unwelcome gleam in his eye. For heaven's sake. Ankles were the least attractive part of one's body, besides elbows and nostrils. Men were ridiculous.

"What is it? For all I know, Beckett will organize the footmen to bring a litter and Pamela's disgusting liniment."

"She's too smart for that. Your Lady Grimes is a genius idea—I wish I'd thought of something similar myself when I was alive."

"And no doubt you would have tricked me with whomever you dreamed up. Just like Bunbury in *The Importance of Being Earnest*."

"One of my favorite plays. Do you remember—"

"What do you want?" Addie tried not to shout but was unsuccessful.

"All right. I'm glad you are sitting down." Rupert looked… nervous. She wasn't used to that.

He cleared his throat. "I know how fond you are of him, but I warned you, didn't I?"

"What on earth are you talking about? Or should I say who?" Addie asked, exasperated.

"I told you all along he was not as innocent as he seemed, and my instincts were correct."

Addie had a sinking feeling. "You don't mean Hugh murdered Pamela! How could he even accomplish it?"

"What? Oh, no. I mean maybe, but I'm not privy to that information yet. But your precious former suitor Lucas Waring and Pamela were lovers. I heard him talking to his solicitor in Stroud on the telephone, all whispery and hush-hush, swiveling his head about like a top as if he was afraid to be overheard. He's worried, and so he should be. Addie? Are you all right? You've gone as pale as I am."

Well, she felt faint now. And more than a touch nauseous.

Chapter Eleven

Lucas was the last of the preliminary interviews for today. He was alone in the shadowy library, staring at his hands. He looked up briefly—and bleakly—when Addie entered, shutting the door in Rupert's face.

Not that a closed door denied him entry—a ghost—or at least Rupert was able to appear at will just when they weren't wanted. But she begged him for privacy. What she hoped to discover would only be hindered if he was his usual interfering self, making her talk to two people at once and making no sense to either of them.

Addie bumped into Beckett on the way back, armed with a first aid kit and a strong, probably flirtatious footman, just in case she misunderstood the Lady Grimes reference. Addie claimed a miraculous recovery for the footman's benefit, and asked Beckett to wait in her room for further instructions. The maid grumbled but didn't ask any questions. They'd have a good gossip later.

"Still waiting?"

"He's been with Lady Fernald over an hour. He can't imagine—well, I suppose he can. Hunter has probably seen everything. We're all guilty of something, aren't we?" Lucas smiled, but it didn't reach his eyes.

"Are you—are you worried?"

He shifted in his leather chair. "Why should I be?"

"Um…" How awkward was this? Very awkward. But Lucas did not kill Pamela. He just couldn't have. "I know. That you and Pamela…" The words got stuck in her throat.

"Me and Pamela? What are you talking about, Addie?"

Had Rupert got it wrong? He disliked Lucas for no reason Addie could fathom, and she wouldn't put it past him to besmirch Lucas's character, even as he was supposed to be improving his own posthumously. "That you were more than friendly neighbors. That…you were having an affair with her."

Lucas went snow-white. "Who told you? Who else knows?"

Addie ignored the first question. "I don't know—I assume you both were very discreet. But you must tell Inspector Hunter. Don't try to lie to him."

"Jesus." He buried his head in his hands. After a minute of silence, he gathered himself. "Please don't tell Pip. I ended it with Pam before I came up to London to see you when you came home from the States in March. I thought we'd get engaged at last, and I didn't want any complications. Clean break and all. Pam understood."

"Did you love her?"

"Don't be silly! I loved you, Addie, or thought I did. But then I met Pip, and—and—"

Addie clasped his hand. "It's all right. My feelings have never been hurt. We don't suit, except as friends. Did Pamela love you?"

He shook his head. "She loves—loved—Hugh. Always has. It was just physical. An escape for both of us. I know I wasn't the only one over the years, but she wasn't indiscriminate. Not like

Kathleen Grant. Nothing like her. She wanted to protect Hugh and John from any scandal and was very careful."

"Who were the others?"

"I don't know. She'd ride over to Waring Hall, maybe once a month. We...we never talked all that much." Lucas had the grace to blush. Addie wondered if he and Rupert had far more in common than she ever expected.

"Did Eloise know?" Eloise was Lucas's older cousin, who kept house for him until her recent marriage.

"God, no. She would have read me the Riot Act. A traditionalist, is Eloise. Infidelity is definitely de trop in her eyes, no matter what the circumstances. Pam would come when Eloise was involved with one of her charities. She went up to London for meetings, you know, and we took advantage of her absence."

"What did your attorney advise?"

Lucas looked shocked. "You overheard? I was sure there was no one about. This just gets worse, doesn't it?"

"Only if you don't tell the truth."

"The truth? Stewart told me to keep my mouth shut unless I want to dangle from a silk rope. No one knew about my relationship with Pam. I'm sure of it."

She'd seen that mulish expression on Lucas's face since they were six years old. "You shouldn't be. There was servants' gossip about her." They just picked the wrong man.

"I'm certain my people don't know, so why should Pam's? Nothing ever happened here. We met in an empty cottage on my estate. And Hugh is my friend. I can't have him know."

"You might have thought about that before you slept with his wife." Addie sounded judgmental even to herself, but she couldn't help it. She might be worldlier now, but Rupert's infidelity had wounded her, perhaps beyond repair.

"It meant nothing to either of us! It was like...scratching an itch. I'm not a monk, and poor Pam—to expect her to live the next fifty years like a nun—you understand, don't you?"

In fact, Addie almost did. This conversation might have knocked the stuffing out of her a year ago, but she knew better now.

Not that she could approve.

She sighed. "I can't make you tell Mr. Hunter, but I wish you would."

"Well, I won't! It has nothing to do with Pam's death. How could it? I didn't kill her."

"But someone did, Lucas. The sooner the person can be brought to justice, the better. What if this person found out about the two of you and wanted to put a stop to it? What if he comes after you next to punish you?"

"What—what—what do you mean?" Lucas sputtered, looking distinctly ill. Addie was prevented from saying any-more, as Devenand Hunter entered the library from the hallway, as crisp and fresh as when he stepped out of the Bentley this morning.

How long was the detective outside the door? What did he overhear? They spoke in hushed tones, but Addie had a feeling his hearing was superhuman.

If Lucas didn't tell him, should Addie? She'd betray her oldest friend and possibly cause his arrest. If she didn't, she withheld evidence from an investigation, possibly punishable by her arrest. The nausea settled in.

"I hope I'm not interrupting anything important."

"No, not at all!" Addie sounded idiotically bright. "How are the interviews going?"

"You know I can't discuss anything with you, Lady Adelaide." He was so stern, and she barely overcame her desire to stick her tongue out at him. "Thank you for your patience,

Lord Waring. I hope you haven't been inconvenienced by the delay."

"No. But I'm afraid you'll be disappointed, Inspector. I really haven't got anything much to contribute." Lucas got to his feet, appearing determined to be stupid.

"Do you want me to go in with you, Lucas?" Addie asked.

"What, are you my nursemaid now? I'm sure I can withstand the thumbscrews." He gave Mr. Hunter a wary smile.

"I hope it won't come to that, my lord. Lady Adelaide, if you will excuse us?"

Oh, Mr. Hunter was being ever so proper. Addie preferred him flushed, his chiseled lips reddened, his lush dark hair rumpled. She would relive that kiss for the rest of her life, but remembering it was not anywhere near as satisfactory as repeating it.

Could she replicate it? What if she went around kissing strange men? Patrick Cassidy was a potential victim of her lust—tall, fit and attractive; he appeared interested in her. She might cross paths with Owen Bradbury or the captain, if they weren't too enamored of the vapid Jordan sisters.

No. None of them would do at the moment. She watched as Lucas and the inspector went through the hidden door to the study, then took note of her surroundings. In the waning sunlight, dust motes swirled from the open leaded-glass windows. Floor to ceiling were an inordinate number of books. Neither Pamela nor Hugh were at all studious, so other Fernalds over the centuries must have begun the impressive collection.

Addie's own education left a great deal to be desired—she was sent to an excellent school but, as a young woman, wasn't expected to learn much. Even though she had all the time in the world now, she didn't think she could immerse herself in the sciences. Astronomy, perhaps, because who didn't like to look at the stars?

She should ask John's handsome new tutor for book suggestions. Go on a self-improvement plan like Devenand Hunter. Her sister, Cee, read all sorts of worthy tomes, too, although Addie wondered if she actually understood the books she toted around. Addie suspected they were more for show to irritate their mother.

After her poisoning scare in March, Cee read medical textbooks. Mama despaired, but Addie thought the subject matter might have more to do with Dr. Paul Kempton than intellectual vigor or the desire to pursue a career in nursing. The young medic was solicitous during Cee's recovery, and he wasn't completely without society credentials—his father was an earl.

Cee's love life was certainly more interesting than Addie's. Oh, well. Passion was overrated. Just ask Rupert. Under its influence, one ran straight into a stone wall.

Chapter Twelve

Monday evening

There were no flowers on the table tonight, orchids or otherwise, just a lopsided arrangement of hothouse peaches and grapes in an epergne. Hugh, understandably, had not come to dinner. Evelyn Fernald presided in his place at the head of the table, her nod to Pamela's death being a plain black satin gown and a distinct lack of celebratory diamonds. Her dark hair was swept up in a neat chignon revealing silver streaks at her temples. She was a handsome woman, her pale complexion smooth and owing nothing to cosmetics. Addie wondered why she never remarried, but then again, she had reason to know there were no guaranteed happily-ever-afters.

Last night, members of the house party dined on trays in their rooms while the constables clumsily searched through the house for clues. Tonight, Beckett discovered the guests were all expected to dress for dinner despite the depressing circumstances. Addie had heard the Royal Family always traveled with a set of mourning clothes, but alas, she expected a normal week-long house party. Her most circumspect dress with the least amount of beading and sparkle was the dress she wore Saturday night. It was having a reprise, but the emeralds were left behind in her jewel case. Addie refused Beckett's assistance with her makeup, as no amount of powder and paint could conceal her worry.

Ending the very long day as it began, Mr. Hunter was meeting them all in the library after they finished eating. The hope amongst the guests was that those who wished to leave could do so tomorrow morning, though Addie wasn't counting on her freedom. The discovery of a second body was bound to complicate things.

The others looked as uncomfortable as she felt. Conversation around the table was hushed at first, with the exception of the odd giggle from one of the Jordan twins. Addie wondered where the detective and Bob were right now—with the servants, or ensconced in their own private parlor? Would they be dining off the same menu of poached salmon, new peas, and Cornish game hens, or having something more mundane? Mr. Hunter had a very healthy appetite and would eat whatever was put in front of him, and sometimes what was put in front of you.

Her own appetite was absent. Seated between Owen Bradbury and Simon Davies again—a sure sign Evelyn was too distracted to bother moving the place cards—Addie worked at being congenial, and mostly pushed her servings around the gilt-edged plates. Mr. Davies ate very little himself but attempted to carry on a neutral conversation. He reminded Addie a little of her late father. His mustachioed lip remained stiff despite the two dead bodies discovered on the premises.

Across the table, Hugh's aunt, Iris Temple, tried to catch his eye on numerous occasions, but the gardening expert was oblivious, politely speaking to Addie, and then his partner on the right, Mandy Jordan, his head turning like an automaton on a timer.

Evelyn and Captain Clifford discussed conditions in India with quiet earnestness. Sitting opposite Evelyn at the other end of the table as the most elevated titled male guest, Lucas was definitely not his usual jolly self. With the burden of trying to keep the twins on either side entertained, he looked as if he'd rather be descending into a Welsh coal mine without a canary.

Only Patrick Cassidy appeared to be in his natural element, charming Iris when he wasn't flattering Margie outrageously. Pamela's name never came up in any of the bits and pieces of conversations Addie overheard, which struck her as very odd.

At Evelyn's instruction, Trim and the footmen served coffee and tea in the dining room to the whole party. The men would have to do without their port and cigars.

Evelyn tapped a cup with her spoon, silencing the desultory conversation.

"I must apologize for the dreadful situation we find ourselves in. I imagine all of you would like to go home. My son was much too broken up to join us this evening, but he tasked me with telling you that should the police require it, your extended stay at Fernald Hall will be met with every courtesy and amenity we can provide. We hoped for an entertaining week for you, but now…" she trailed off.

Margie Jordan gasped. "You mean that horrible inspector is making us stay?"

Addie was sure Mr. Hunter had not behaved horribly, but she held her tongue.

"He mentioned something about the inquest. Now with that body being found this morning, you may be inconvenienced for an extra day or two. He'll explain it all tonight."

"We don't know anything about anything! We told him so!" Acting like a spoiled child, Mandy folded her arms over her flimsy white sequined gown. She had not decided to be circumspect or glitter-less.

"We didn't kill Pamela," Margie added. "We don't know about poisons."

Addie agreed—the twins weren't fonts of knowledge, and probably never would be. As the youngest daughters of a baron, they'd floated by so far on their money, looks, and youth, which could get one relatively downstream in 1925. How old were they? Nineteen or twenty? Addie could barely remember being that young.

"And of course, you are invited to stay until after the funeral," Evelyn said, rising. "As soon as we can arrange it. When they— when they release the body." For a second, her voice cracked. Addie admired how very hard she tried to hold herself together and make this impossible situation bearable for her guests.

The group shuffled down the oak-timbered hall as if their feet were mired in molasses, clearly not eager for another encounter with Scotland Yard. No matter how innocent one was, talking with the police was unsettling. Every word uttered sounded like a lie to one's own ears, so how might it sound to a suspicious stranger? They had reason to worry—Addie knew just how sharp Inspector Hunter was.

Which was why she wanted to avoid him. She'd not yet decided what to do with Lucas's confession. On the one hand, it was absurd for anyone to think Lucas would poison Pamela Fernald. Their affair was over, and he was now engaged.

On the other, what if Pamela had threatened him somehow? Philippa Dean was a naive young woman, no matter how modern she tried to be with her shingled red hair and dark lipstick; she might not like the fact that her fiancé had engaged in a years-long adulterous affair with a friend's wife. It went against common decency, no matter how they justified it. Addie only had Lucas's word that the relationship ended. She never had reason to doubt him before, despite Rupert's continual disparagement, but—

Oh, dear. Once trust was breached, it was impossible to feel the same way she had.

Hugh had come from his suite, along with Jim Musgrave, and they waited at the open doors. Hugh had made an effort, wearing a black velvet smoking jacket over an open-neck shirt. Each of his guests murmured a greeting as they entered. Both twins had kissed his cheek and made a show of weeping into their lace-trimmed handkerchiefs, bottling up the doorway. They were making his tragedy their own.

Addie found herself very annoyed with their drama. Not because they made her feel old. Or frumpy. She wasn't jealous. Really. She didn't wish them harm, but she did wish them away. Perhaps Inspector Hunter would allow them to go back to London and dance their innocence away.

All the electric lamps were on in the library, plus several lit candelabra, but the light was still swallowed up by the size of the room. Lucas avoided her, taking up an entire window cushion by himself. He was about as far away from Mr. Hunter and Bob Wells as he could get. She avoided them too, sharing a leather love seat with Iris Temple.

"This is most inconvenient," the older woman said, smoothing her already smooth blond hair. It was rolled up tight with jet-tipped hairpins, exposing an enviably unwrinkled neck. She had not succumbed to the short hair craze, nor had her sister-in-law, Evelyn. Addie once debated long and hard about it herself, but finally relented.

"I'm glad you're here to support Evelyn. I'm sure she appreciates it," Addie said diplomatically.

"Yes, well, we are family, after all. But this will mark the second night I've not slept in my own bed. When one reaches my age, one will understand. I'm afraid I'm a total creature of habit, selfish to the bone."

"But you're just down the lane. Surely the police won't object to you going home."

"Who knows? They might think I'll abscond. I'm as good a suspect as any."

"What do you mean?"

"You've heard the servants' gossip, I'm sure. Pamela had a little crush on Simon and was always after him for one thing or another. And Simon and I—well, we have an understanding. Do you think that's silly at our age? Don't tell me if you do—it will make more sense to you in thirty years. Perhaps I was jealous, crept into the conservatory, and strangled her to death." Iris smiled rather grimly.

"She wasn't strangled."

She waved a jeweled hand. "However it happened."

Addie knew Evelyn much better than Iris, but it was difficult to picture either of them putting a period to Pamela's existence. Murder just wasn't done in their circle. It would be like her accusing her mother, the Dowager Marchioness of Broughton…

Um. Perhaps under special circumstances, Addie's mother was capable of murder. She was a formidable woman, despite her diminutive size.

"I'm sure the police will figure it out."

"I do hope so. The sooner the better. I miss my cat, silly as it sounds."

Addie realized she missed Fitz too, and wondered what mischief he'd gotten into in her absence. No doubt it was best she did not know. They waited while the others found seats and settled in. The inspector was standing before a large globe, and Addie was reminded of the outdated maps in the schoolroom.

Borders changed and entire countries disappeared at the politicians' whim. One could never keep up with world events, or events closer to home, for that matter. Addie did not really know the men around her at all.

"Thank you again for your time," Mr. Hunter began. "We have some news."

There was an uneasy rustle throughout the room.

"As you are aware, the gardeners discovered a body this morning. We have tentatively identified the remains as Lieutenant Michael Brandon Ainsley, who was charged with desertion after failing to return to his regiment during the war. We know why now."

"I knew it! I knew he wouldn't do such a thing." Hugh looked almost happy. "Denny, Owen, you said it too! By God, this is the best news I've had all day. Sorry, Inspector, I imagine that sounds odd, but he was our friend. But to think he died here all those years ago—how?"

"We have yet to determine whether his murder—"

"Murder!" Evelyn Fernald interrupted, her voice unusually shrill. "You can't know that."

Mr. Hunter's lips thinned. "I beg to differ. He was shot in the head." Nearly everyone gasped, Addie included. To think she had been within a few feet of poor Lieutenant Ainsley this morning. "Even if he took his own life, he didn't bury himself. Someone on the estate knew...or knows...what happened in the autumn of 1916." He paused, letting his words sink in amongst his stricken audience.

"It's too soon to tell if this has a bearing on the death of Lady Pamela Fernald. I'm inclined to believe it does, despite the difference in the methods used and the time elapsed. Today, you were questioned about your relationship with the deceased and your whereabouts the afternoon she died. I'm asking for your patience to undergo further interviews tomorrow. Sir Hugh and his mother are cooperating in the fullest and are making their home available for as long as you'd like to stay, for which I am most grateful."

"I'm to leave for India next week," Captain Clifford said.

"I don't foresee that to be a problem as yet."

Unless Clifford turned out to be the murderer, Addie thought.

"What about Michael's family? Who is going to tell them?" Hugh asked.

"We're looking into that now," Mr. Hunter replied.

Hugh shook his head. "He's been here all this time. I can't believe it."

"Someone knew." Mr. Hunter swept his dark gaze over the assembled guests, and even Addie felt guilty.

Chapter Thirteen

Dev was both tired and hungry. His handwriting was beginning to resemble a drunken spider's web, so his notes in Hindi were practically unreadable. Which was as it should be, except for the minor detail they were supposed to be legible to him. His private code was meant to protect his notes. Now they were just giving him eyestrain.

He looked up from his papers as the housekeeper, Ruth Lewis, knocked on the open library door.

"It's awfully late, Mr. Hunter. Can I get you anything before I retire?"

He didn't want to be a bother and said so.

"Nonsense. I know you haven't eaten supper; your Mr. Wells told me so. I can make up some sandwiches if you like."

Dev smiled. "Only if I can eat them in the kitchen and save you the trouble of bringing them in here. If you let 'civilians' into your kitchen, that is."

"I like to think Mr. Wells has been right at home, despite all his questions."

"Yes, he told me how kind and helpful you and the rest of the staff have been. We have to be thorough. We really are sorry for your loss, you know."

"Lady Fernald was…so pretty and lively. Was good to all of us. I don't know how the master is going to cope. They were as close as can be."

One woman's opinion. Dev rose and blew out the candles on the desk, and Mrs. Lewis followed suit throughout the rest of the room. She checked the window locks, turned off the electric switch, and now the library was only illuminated from the light in the hallway.

"Follow me. I warn you, it won't be anything fancy."

Dev was so hungry he'd eat a bowl of lukewarm gruel if she chose to serve it to him.

The kitchen was vast and whitewashed, and he sat at a work-table while Mrs. Lewis bustled about, energetic even at this hour. Without asking, she fetched him a bottle of beer from the buttery.

"You'll be wondering why we have no cook. We did once. A French chef he was, hired by Sir Hugh's mother when she came here as a bride thirty-odd years ago. Lots of wine and fancy sauces, and a temper that would peel paper off the walls. We were all terrified of him, but he was sweet as pie for Lady Fernald. He surprised the lot of us when he went home to fight in 1915, being as old and ornery as he was." She spread butter and mustard on two slices of whole meal bread and topped one with a slab of ham, a slice of cheese, and a spoonful of chutney. Dev tried not to drool as he watched.

"We never knew what became of him. Blown up in some wasteland, no doubt, poor man. I took on his duties—it was meant to be temporary until he came back, yet here I am. The food got much simpler, but no one complains. Lady Fernald—the elder Lady Fernald—organizes the maids' schedules and runs the house with me, more or less. Young Lady Fernald was more interested in outside the house—the stables and gardens and so forth." Mrs. Lewis passed him the plate.

He tried not to snatch it from her hands. "Thank you. This looks wonderful." And tasted even better than it looked. After swallowing a large mouthful, he said, "You must be exhausted from all the company and the extra work of a house party."

"I don't mind. None of us do. It's hard for Sir Hugh to get out and go up and down stairs in other peoples' houses. It wouldn't do for him to become a hermit, a young man like that, never having any fun or seeing any friends. My girls are hard workers and I have plenty of help. The master and mistress only entertain like this a handful of times a year. Gives us something to look forward to." She shook her head. "Gave, I suppose. Sir Hugh won't want another gathering like this for a long time to come."

"How long has this week been in the works?"

Mrs. Lewis wiped down the workspace. "A good month or more. Two couples sent their regrets—I'm sure when they hear the news, they'll be glad they didn't come."

"Do you have their names?" Just because they didn't accept the invitation didn't mean one of them didn't somehow manage to gain entry and kill Pamela Fernald. It was the longest of shots, but Dev would leave no stone unturned.

"I don't. Sir Hugh's mother would know. She and his wife planned these things together."

"Thank you. I'll ask her tomorrow. They got on well, did they?"

Mrs. Lewis folded her cloth with deliberation before she spoke. "Well enough. Are you married, Inspector?"

"I haven't had the pleasure." Yet. His mother was constantly introducing him to suitable brides, but Dev had not succumbed.

"They say too many cooks in the kitchen spoil the broth. Young Lady Fernald was a canny one—not sly or sneaky, mind. I don't want you to get the wrong idea. But she let her mother-in-law think she was in charge. Deferred to her in most things.

They had Sir Hugh in common, you see—his comfort and happiness was paramount."

"You were here when he came home injured."

"Yes." She shook her head. "It was awful. We did our best, all of us, but you can only do so much."

"Do you remember when Lieutenant Ainsley went missing?"

"I do. Those boys were here on leave for two weeks before they were to go back to the front. Sir Hugh hadn't been home long, perhaps two months. He was still very badly off—his lungs were damaged too, and he coughed his head off. Could hardly catch his breath to string a sentence together. Couldn't sleep for the pain in his back. And…" She paused, remembering. "Some days he was so confused he didn't even know he was home."

"It must have been difficult for you," Dev said with sympathy. It was obvious Mrs. Lewis was still affected by Sir Hugh's past trauma.

"Oh, we were the lucky ones, weren't we? But when those three young men came, the master forgot his troubles and laughed with them—oh, he laughed until we wondered if it would hurt his insides somehow. Cheered him up, they did, though his mother didn't approve, she was so worried he would overdo. But their presence made life seem less of a misery for him, and the servants too. It had been so quiet here before, like a church. Or a funeral parlor."

"What was your impression of the lieutenant?"

"Really, I can't recall. The three of them blended in together back then, just active, healthy young men. They drank a fair bit, and who could blame them? Ate whatever I served and asked for more. They were happy to be safe for the time being."

One of them hadn't been safe at all. "So, you can't think of anything in particular?"

"Oh! He liked to dance, Lieutenant Ainsley did. Brought his

own records with him when he came to stay. They're still here somewhere, I suppose. There was a wind-up gramophone in the drawing room and they all took turns with Lady Fernald—Pamela—after Sir Hugh went off to bed."

"Thank you, Mrs. Lewis, for the information and the delicious food."

"You're welcome. Don't hesitate to ask for what you need—we all want this to be over and the murderer hanged."

Dev would bet not everyone in the household shared that opinion. "If you and Mr. Trim could get me a list of those on staff who were employed here in the autumn of 1916, I'd appreciate it."

He finished the last of his sandwich and beer while she continued to tidy the already immaculate kitchen, then brought the plate to the soapstone sink. Wishing the housekeeper a good night, he went up the staircase to his room.

There was no light under Bob's door. His sergeant must be enjoying an uncomplicated night's sleep, no cries from a teething baby to disturb him. Now that he'd eaten, Dev felt recharged and was not yet ready for bed. He took off his jacket, tie, and waistcoat, turned up his sleeves, and settled into the chair to read.

No convoluted mysteries or light comical skewering of society for him. He was a serious man…or trying to be. He found his place in Plato, adjusted the lampshade, cleared his mind, and began to read.

He didn't get very far. There was the lightest of taps on his door.

Sighing, he got up, not even wondering who it would be.

She was determined to drive him to the very edge, wasn't she?

Doubly determined, for she was wearing a dressing gown in

a very becoming shade of apricot, which matched the freckles across her aristocratic nose. But while it was a dressing gown, it had buttons that were firmly fastened up to her stubborn chin, and sleeves that ran to the length of her wrists, which he found somewhat disappointing.

She was still her proper mother's proper daughter, even if she was in his bedroom for the second time today.

"Go away," he whispered. Bob had good hearing, although his steady snores were audible in the hallway.

"I need to talk to you," she whispered back. "I'm having a crisis of conscience."

Dev stepped back, and Lady Adelaide swished into the room. She took the chair he'd recently vacated, picking up his book before she sat down.

"Plato? Doesn't he believe in the immortality of the soul? That we go on forever?" She frowned. "I don't even know how I know that, but I do."

"You're not here to discuss philosophy with me, are you?" Although once or twice they talked about reincarnation.

How would Dev choose to come back? It was out of his hands, he supposed.

He took the book from her and put it back on the bedside table. There was nowhere for him to sit but the bed, so he remained standing.

"Well, sort of. I, uh, have an ethical dilemma. What would you do if a friend—um, an acquaintance—told you something that would get him—or her—in terrible trouble if people found out he—or she—lied about it and thought the worst, even though you know he—or she—is innocent?"

"What did Lord Waring tell you?"

She blinked behind her spectacles. "Honestly. You really are a detective, aren't you?"

"You should know that by now. Lady Adelaide, if you have information that will assist us, you are required to disclose it."

"You wouldn't arrest me if I didn't, would you?"

He wouldn't, no, and she knew it. Subverting the course of justice was a punishable offence, but he had no appetite to lock up Lady Adelaide anywhere except in his bedroom.

God help him.

Chapter Fourteen

Addie had been unable to sleep. After tossing and turning, she had removed the silk netting and pins from her hair, brushed her teeth again, put on the merest touch of lip rouge and powder, and set off through the mostly pitch-black corridors of Fernald Hall. Every now and again she encountered a sputtering electric sconce, but then was steeped in gloom. If anyone spotted her, she was prepared to reverse direction and go to the kitchen for some warm milk, which, quite frankly, would be a revolting end to a revolting evening.

Fernald Hall, much like her home, Compton Chase, was built over several centuries, and she was careful not to trip over the corridor steps that warned of a "new" addition. It was much easier to find Inspector Hunter's room this morning, and a little voice in her head—well, her mother's—told her she should turn tail and go back to lie awake all night.

Addie ignored the voice and found herself standing in front of Detective Inspector Hunter's door. Some robust snoring came from the right. She certainly did not want to wake up Bob Wells, even though she sought his boss out— ostensibly—on police business. She valued Bob's good opinion, and he probably would not think much of her wandering about in her robe.

She'd rapped with one knuckle. Inspector Hunter had not been happy to see her. Yet here she was, sitting in the only chair in the room—quite uncomfortable, not just from the hard chair, but in innumerable ways.

She didn't think he would send her to jail for not disclosing what she knew, but no doubt he had his ways to intimidate a witness. Bright lights. Bad food and worse coffee. Cigarette smoke blown in one's face. Sleep deprivation.

She already had the latter.

She didn't want to betray Lucas. But if the police discovered the relationship between him and Pamela Fernald and that he was not honest, he'd become their prime suspect. They'd say he killed her to smooth his way to his upcoming marriage.

During their interrogations, everyone claimed to be in their rooms changing for tea between three and four. The twins had each other as an alibi, as Addie had Beckett, but the rest were on their own Sunday afternoon without valets or maids. Any one of them could have met with Pamela and given her something to drink, disguised in a teacup or a flask. As far as Addie knew, nothing had been found at the scene, so the poisoner had probably taken the receptacle with him.

Or her. Addie gave some thought to the women at Fernald Hall. Evelyn, whose maid had the afternoon off. Iris, within walking distance. Margie. Mandy. Pamela's maid, Murray.

And Juliet. Had she been interviewed? She didn't fit in belowstairs or above.

Changing the subject from her possible incarceration, she added, "Have you spoken to Juliet Barlow?"

"I did. During your dinner. And the boy too. Together. I tried to make it as painless as possible. Why, is she having it on with Lord Waring?"

"Good heavens, no! I just wondered."

Mr. Hunter folded his arms across his chest. He was in his shirtsleeves, and his bare brown skin contrasted with the bright white of his shirt. "Why don't you get to the point, Lady Adelaide? It's late."

"I told you about the rumors concerning Pamela and f-fidelity." Fidelity was a tricky and too-personal subject. Addie was embarrassed, since Inspector Hunter knew far more than he should about her own unhappy marriage.

He nodded but said nothing. The silence lengthened.

Addie noticed a torn fingernail and tried to wear it down with her thumb. "I know she was devoted to Hugh, despite everything. They married when they were both twenty-one, just as the war began. Hugh enlisted at once, and she's been with him through thick and awfully thin since. Everyone admires—admired—her for her devotion. It can't have been easy."

"I expect not."

"She—she—I learned she had an affair. Affairs, really." She knew of at least one other, with Rupert, who was probably causing someone trouble right this very minute. It was a wonder he hadn't crawled out from Mr. Hunter's ascetic single bed to torment her by waggling his tongue and making funny faces as he sometimes did to amuse himself and drive her crazy.

Inspector Hunter lifted an eyebrow. "With Lucas Waring?"

Addie swallowed. "He broke it off in March because he thought he and I were going to be married. So it's practically ancient history. But I thought you should know, even if Lucas thinks it's none of anybody's business. He didn't kill her, of course, but one might think he did for some reason."

"What would some reason be, Lady Adelaide?"

Addie's face grew warm. "He's engaged now, and Pip wouldn't like knowing that he had that sort of relationship, I don't think—she's a traditional, middle-class girl, even if she tries to be something of a flapper. But it's not as though Lucas and Pamela had a grand passion—from what he said, it was like—like—a dentist appointment. You know, once a month at a fixed time."

"You must have very healthy teeth," Mr. Hunter said wryly.

Mortification. "You know what I mean! It wasn't as if they were slipping into cupboards or attics or wine cellars at the drop of a hat and ripping off their clothes. They were…civilized."

"According to him."

"Yes, according to him! I can't very well verify it with Pamela," she said crossly.

"Who else knows about this?"

"Lucas says no one. He's quite certain. But I'm not. This is the country, and even the trees have eyes. Someone must have seen them over the years, and if they told you and you found out and thought he lied, it wouldn't look good for him."

"But you didn't know."

Addie shrugged. "As you must realize by now, I've been an absolute simpleton for ages. It's rather sad." She was determined to put her innocence behind her, but certain people weren't being cooperative.

Which was one of the reasons—pathetic, really—that she was sitting here in her pretty silk robe, unchaperoned, in an attractive man's bedroom.

Inspector Hunter wasn't moonstruck with lust, however. Had he forgotten their kiss? Maybe it had meant nothing to him. He must have lots of kissing opportunities in London.

"You are convinced he had nothing to do with Pamela Fernald's death?"

"Absolutely. You know Lucas. Sort of—I know he's not your favorite human being, but he's simply not a murderer. Your instincts about people are good."

He met her eyes. "Sometimes."

"And I have the hugest favor," Addie said. "You mustn't tell him I've told you this. We've been friends since we were six. I'd be very…unhappy if I were to lose his good regard."

Lucas would want to kill her if he knew she was here tattling. But wanting and doing were two different things, weren't they?

"Perhaps I learned about it from one of the trees."

"Exactly! I think he'll feel so much better if he tells you. But he's worried about Hugh finding out, so you'll have to be discreet."

Inspector Hunter raked a fall of dark hair from his forehead. "I know you think you are helping your friend. And the police," he added as an afterthought. "But I'm afraid your revelation only makes it look worse for Viscount Waring."

Addie sat back. "What do you mean?"

"I can't tell you. I haven't even had the opportunity to talk to Bob yet."

"Can't or won't?"

"Both. Lady Adelaide, you should go."

Addie felt a sense of dread. "You cannot in good conscience suspect Lucas of anything more than being a man. Pamela used him, don't you see? Well, I guess they used each other. Given the choice, most men would choose to sleep with a lonely, beautiful woman."

More mortification. Addie hoped that Mr. Hunter didn't think she was fishing for compliments or accusing him of being less than manly. She wasn't that lonely, and she knew she really wasn't that beautiful. "Oh, this isn't coming out right at all. I shouldn't have come."

"Probably not."

Addie wanted to punch something, but the arm of the chair was not upholstered, and she'd only hurt herself. She rose with as much dignity as she could muster and walked to the door. "Good night, then."

He opened the door, stepped out into the hallway to check for activity, and nodded that the coast was clear. "Good night. Sleep well, Lady Adelaide."

No chance of that. Addie picked up her robe and practically ran away. The clocks throughout the house began to chime one o'clock. The house was so well organized there were only a few straggling gongs in less than thirty seconds.

"Slow down, Cinderella. What's the rush?"

"Oof. Sorry." Addie had pitched into Patrick Cassidy's arms in the dim hallway. He was still wearing his evening clothes, his tie loosened, his russet hair slightly disarranged. She hadn't seen him as she rounded the corner, anxious as she was to put the whole Hunter debacle behind her. She should have, though—he was carrying a small torch to navigate the dark corridors.

"I see your ankle's mended."

"Uh." She knew herself to be a terrible liar, which had been very convenient for her parents.

"Soaked it in Epsom salts before dinner, did you?"

A lifeline. "Yes! My maid Beckett is brilliant when it comes to indispositions."

"I told her to. Irish, isn't she? Maeve, she said her name was. Pretty little thing. I enjoyed our brief chat. Reminded me of home. But I can't be homesick so soon, can I? Especially with you English roses about."

What was Beckett doing making a conquest of Mr. Cassidy? There was no point in chastising her—Beckett pretty much did as she pleased. And Addie had to admit that the fellow was quite flirt-worthy, an Irish charmer.

Not that she really wanted to flirt with him or anyone, despite Beckett's prodding. Her latest forays into flirtdom had ended in abject humiliation.

"Can't sleep?"

Hot milk, hot milk, hot milk. "I was trying to find my way down to the kitchen. I thought some hot milk might help. I—I didn't want to wake Beckett."

"You're going in the wrong direction. Here, let me walk you downstairs, just in case that ankle gives way again."

Addie didn't even try to discourage him. Glumly, she took his arm and followed his beam until they got to the pristine white kitchen. Allegedly injured, she sat at the pine table in silence while Mr. Cassidy found the milk and a pan and a pinch of cinnamon. He seemed to know his way around a stove, handy and fairly unusual for a man.

"Vile stuff, this is," he said cheerfully, stirring the liquid with a wooden spoon and adjusting the heat. "My old granny swore by it, but I'd just as soon have a brandy."

So would Addie, and she said so.

"You're in luck then!" He reached into his dinner jacket pocket and brought out a small silver flask. "Do y'want it straight, or poured into the milk?"

"Neither, thank you. I really haven't a head for spirits, although brandy can be delicious. It would probably just make me more awake than I already am, though. What's keeping you up?"

"Ah, this and that. I'm worried about the horses. It seems crass to hold Sir Hugh to the sale."

"Have you spoken to him? John is just as horse-mad as his mother was, and perhaps he'll keep one or two. Or even all three."

"The man has more important things on his mind. I'll not

intrude." He poured the milk into a white mug and delivered it. "Cheers!" He raised the flask to his lips, then thought the better of it and capped it.

"You're right. I shouldn't stimulate myself at this hour. Wouldn't want to lose my head. It's enough of a thrill to be across from a lovely woman. Here we are, all alone, everyone else just where they should be."

Oh, dear. Addie did not feel particularly lovely and wished a few other guests or servants might wander into the kitchen to act as duennas. The buttons at her throat were strangling her, too, though at least she wasn't giving Mr. Cassidy any ideas with a risqué negligee.

He had ideas anyway, sliding next to her on the bench within striking—or kissing—distance.

Addie drank as much of the horrible warm milk as she could without retching. She let Mr. Cassidy do all the talking, just as her mother advised in her many attempts to train Addie to appear to be a dutiful, docile young woman. The dowager marchioness knew one must eventually reveal one's true colors, but one had to catch a man first, lulling him into complacency before the feminine hammer dropped.

Addie didn't want to catch anyone tonight and tried to figure out how she was going to escape Mr. Cassidy's clear admiration. She couldn't fake another injury, could she?

Hallelujah! She was at the bottom of the mug. She rose. "Thank you so much. You've been very gentlemanly."

He popped up too. "Aye. Despite what you may have heard, we Irishmen can be civil when we've a mind to. Or rough, if that's your pleasure. May I walk you back to your bedroom?"

She could swear she saw his eyebrow waggle. "No! No, thank you. If we met anyone in the halls, they'd think we were up to, um, something."

He leaned in closer, his breath tickling her ear. "And would that something be out of the question, Lady Adelaide?"

Yes.

No.

Maybe.

And then Lady Broughton, the dowager marchioness, asserted herself again and Addie's mouth opened. "I don't wish to give you a false impression, Mr. Cassidy. I am not that sort of woman."

"Now that," he said, "is a crying shame."

Chapter Fifteen

"That was a close escape. I was prepared to deck him if I had to, to defend your vaunted virtue." Rupert cracked his knuckles, which made no sound at all. "The cheek of him! Thinks he's God's gift, doesn't he? He's nothing but a jumped-up groom when all is said and done."

Addie curled another short strand of hair and secured it. She was the only person she knew besides her sister, Cee, who had to curl her curly hair to make it straighter. Spitting the rest of the pins out into her hand, she wished they were mini-darts that could fly across her bedroom to lodge in the apparition who was now lounging in plain sight on her wrinkled counterpane. "Don't you get tired of trying to startle me?" She was quite proud she didn't scream.

"Would you rather I knock next time?" Rupert asked, tucking a pillow under his head. "You'd probably open the door and slam it in my face. You've done that a time or two."

She had, and it felt very satisfying. "Don't get too comfortable. I'm almost ready to go back to bed. Why are you here now?"

"Someone had to protect you from that Gaelic gigolo. You've

missed a hank of hair in the back. I do hope you're reconsidering and letting your hair grow again."

"I haven't decided." Even after two months, she was still getting used to her bob but wasn't going to confess that fact to Rupert.

"I realize I lost my right to tell you what to do—"

"As if you ever had a right! Honestly, Rupert, you're antediluvian. Women can make their own decisions about their own hair which grows out of their own heads, and anything else that concerns them, without a man's interference, thank you very much."

He looked slightly chastened, but only slightly. "Well, yes, I suppose. I didn't come to argue."

"Why did you come?" Addie repeated.

"As I said, I'm more or less your guardian angel. Should some bounder try to woo you with warm milk or a bad batch of brandy, I shall step in, never fear."

"Am I to thank you? I believe I can handle Mr. Cassidy—or anyone else—on my own."

"Never be too sure. You know how gullible you are."

"I was. I like to think I can recognize a worm when I see one." Addie stared hard at Rupert, but he was adjusting his tie and missed the implication.

Rupert stopped fiddling and sighed. "I'm the bearer of bad tidings again."

"Oh, joy." She slid the last pin in and covered her hair with the net. In her previous life—and his as well—Rupert would never have seen her in such a state, but her days of trying to appeal to him were very much behind her. "What is it now?"

"You know your inspector keeps his notes in some sort of code—and yes, I know he's not your inspector, so don't take on so. Try as I might, I cannot make head or tail of the squiggles, but he was careless, leaving a very official-looking envelope unsecured in his room."

"In his room! Don't tell me you were there when I spoke to him earlier!"

"I won't tell you. And anyway, you didn't suspect a thing, did you? I was very well-behaved in his little monk's cell, quiet as a mouse."

"Or a rat! Oh, Rupert, how could you! Isn't it breaking and entering?"

"I broke nothing, and I'd like to see them try to convict a spirit of a little subterfuge. Highly entertaining that would be."

"Why would you do such a thing?"

"He's not the only chap around with brains. I thought I might be more useful armed with information from the horse's mouth, as it were. Anyhow, when he went to have a long, hot bath to wash away his sins and do who knows what else after you flounced off, I looked through his things. Quickly, for I knew that Fenian fellow you bumped into was not where he was supposed to be, and I'm meant to be on alert."

This was getting completely out of hand. It was one thing for Rupert to step in in an emergency, but to sneak around and eavesdrop and rummage through one's private papers, especially if one was a bathing policeman? Addie was incensed for the poor inspector.

And for Mr. Cassidy. "I doubt Patrick Cassidy is a revolutionary."

"Perhaps not, but I don't trust him. He's hiding something—I feel it in my bones. Getting back to the point, I read the preliminary coroner's report. A lot of mumbo-jumbo, to be frank, but even little old me could read the pertinent words plain as day."

Addie knew he was expecting her to ask, "What words?"

So she didn't.

Rupert tapped his long white fingers with impatience, and finally gave up. "Pamela Fernald was *enceinte*."

"What?" Like all well-bred girls of her class, she'd studied French at Cheltenham Ladies' College and had been to Paris three times. Not lately, though.

"Indeed. Now your inspector—yes, yes, I know—believes Waring is the father of that poor little soul, which would give him every reason to poison Pamela. So your mission of mercy tonight has gone awry. If you were hoping somehow to deflect blame from Saint Lucas, you've failed in spectacular fashion." Rupert looked quite pleased at this turn of events.

Addie's heart thumped about, causing her to feel light-headed. "But he broke it off!"

"The timing makes the scenario still plausible, I'm afraid. Despite the closed bathroom door—thank heavens—I could still read a bit of Hunter's mind. Expect Waring to be carted off in handcuffs tomorrow."

Oh, what had she done? The road to hell was paved with good intentions. Lucas would never, ever forgive her, and she'd never forgive herself. And poor Pip, her brother murdered, her fiancé an accused murderer! The girl's chance of happiness forever thwarted, just because Addie thought she knew best.

"I'll have to warn him. He can flee to the Continent."

Rupert chortled. "Waring? Are you mad? It's a matter of pride and honor now. If he felt less than manly growing vegetables during the war, imagine what his ego would do if you tried to make him run away in the face of a capital crime. No, he'll hang with his dimpled chin high."

"Rupert! This isn't funny!"

"I admit it's not, although I confess I am deriving some enjoyment from it. No one ever said I was a saint."

An understatement if there ever was one. "What can we do?"

"I don't know about you, but it's been a very, very long day—it feels like half a book. I plan on retiring."

Addie was still in the dark about Rupert's day-to-day—or night-to-night—existence. She watched him eat toast and drink coffee once—and that profiterole—but he didn't seem dependent on food or a regular night's sleep. Before she had a chance to ask him where he was going, he disappeared.

"Bloody hell! He's chock-full of advice when it's not wanted, and now the weasel has gone to ground. Oh, what am I going to do?"

Pacing was pointless. Addie had to act. If only she could present Pamela's poisoner on a platter. If only she weren't so alliterative in her anxiety.

She would talk to Lucas. She wasn't sure where he was billeted, but each guest's room had a card inserted in a brass frame with their name in exquisite calligraphy. Addie knew Juliet was responsible for them, one of the many extra duties she had.

Addie didn't have a torch like Mr. Cassidy, but there was a candle in a china holder next to her bed and a box of matches in the drawer. She'd better dress first, though two men had seen her in her robe already. Three, if you counted Rupert, but he'd seen it all before. However, Lucas was terribly old-fashioned.

Though perhaps she should reevaluate that opinion of his character after today's revelations.

For the second time this evening, she removed the bobby pins from her hair and brushed it into a becoming halo. She skipped the makeup—Lucas wouldn't even notice anymore, so besotted was he with his young fiancée—and slipped into a plain navy dress trimmed with white braid about the collar and cuffs. It was the closest she could come with the clothing she brought to look penitent for potentially causing him trouble.

Her glasses on her nose, she lit the candle and crept barefoot down the hallway, squinting at the doors in the flickering light. The Jordan sisters in two separate adjoining rooms. Captain Clifford across the hall. A room with no name affixed to the outside next to his. Quietly, she opened the door. There was no one within, a bare mattress proof that no one had been there for a while.

The corridor zigged right. Mr. Bradbury and Mr. Cassidy were on one side, Lord Waring on the other.

Addie did not want to encounter Mr. Cassidy again. She tapped the door as gingerly as she could and waited. Lucas was no doubt sound asleep at this time of night. Being a gentleman farmer, he kept country hours. Up with the chickens, he claimed, and Addie wondered how Pip, used to busy Brighton hotel life, would adjust to being a farmer's wife.

She turned the knob, and the door swung open. The bed was made up, the matelassé pillows marching in a row, no sign that Lucas had ever gone to sleep this evening.

Addie bit a lip and turned on the light. The closet door was ajar, its padded hangers empty, no suitcase on the shelf. A quick check in the bathroom showed there was no shaving kit or toothbrush. No crumpled tissue, no discarded magazine. All traces of Lucas's presence were gone.

Another weasel gone to ground.

Chapter Sixteen

Tuesday morning

Dev left the house hoping the fresh morning air would clear his head but encountered Patrick Cassidy as he came out of the stables. The man had been on an early ride—very early. The sun wasn't even up over the treetops, but Dev had been awake forever himself. After another nocturnal visit from Lady Adelaide—she was dressed this time, thank God, even if he had been in his bathrobe—he'd been on the telephone half the night trying to discreetly ascertain Waring's whereabouts and slept perhaps two or three hours.

Once awoken, servants at Waring Hall pleaded ignorance. They had not seen their master since he left to go to a farm equipment auction on Saturday, and he wasn't expected back until next Saturday. Catching her at breakfast a few minutes ago, her voice still froggy from sleep, Waring's fiancée Philippa Dean claimed she had not heard from him, but she certainly could be lying—he might be on his way to the Brighton seashore as they spoke.

Dev requested assistance from various branches of the

constabulary across the country to make inquiries, fully cognizant they needed to be careful. Waring was a viscount, awarded
honours for his service during the war. Thanks to him and his
agricultural knowledge, food production for the troops dou-
bled. He might now be a fugitive, or he remembered a pressing
appointment that made him sneak out in the middle of the night
like a thief, conveniently forgetting to inform the police.

It was all headache-inducing.

"Good morning! You're up bright and early. Going riding, are
ye?" Cassidy was wind-flushed, the picture of a healthy sports-
man. Did Lady Adelaide find the man attractive? Dev batted his
jealousy away.

"I'm afraid not, though it's tempting. Say, did you notice any
unusual activity in your corridor last night? Your room is opposite Lord Waring's, is it not?"

"'Tis. But I was late coming to bed. Couldn't sleep, and I
wasn't the only one."

"Oh?"

"Lady Adelaide and I had a bit of a midnight romp, if you
must know. She's my alibi and I'm hers in case you want to arrest
us."

Dev stiffened. "I beg your pardon?"

"Ah, not like that, Inspector. Good lord, don't bite me."
Cassidy laughed. "The poor woman was looking for the kitchen
and got all turned around. You know what it's like in these big
old houses. Or perhaps you don't—we weren't all born with silver spoons, were we? One needs a trail of breadcrumbs like that
children's story.

"Anyway, I fixed her some warm milk, watched her struggle
to swallow the nasty stuff, and then we went our separate ways.
There were no shenanigans, more's the pity. The ladies here
at this house party leave a lot to be desired. Either they're old

enough to be my mam or empty-headed twits like the Jordan sisters. Young Lady Fernald and Lady Adelaide were my only hope, and one of them is quite beyond my reach now."

Both of them, Dev hoped, although it was absurd for him to feel possessive. He had no say over what Lady Adelaide chose to do at midnight or any hour of the day. "So you didn't see Lord Waring on your evening ramble?"

"No, I didn't. Why, is he missing? Perhaps he didn't want to sit through another day of questioning. I admit, I'd like do a bunk myself, but here you've captured me." The man held his hands out as if waiting to be cuffed.

Dev tamped down his annoyance. Murder was serious business, even in Ireland. "Maybe we can finish up right now. Where were you in the autumn of 1916?"

"Not here, I assure you. Some muddy trench in France that I'd as soon forget."

Dev empathized. "Were you acquainted with Lieutenant Michael Ainsley?"

Cassidy looked startled, then twisted the gold signet ring he wore. "And if I was?"

"I'd wonder why you didn't mention it yesterday."

"Maybe I didn't think it was that important. I knew a lot of lieutenants. Before you could blink, they were either dead or promoted."

Cassidy was glib, but Dev sensed there was more to it.

"How well did you know this particular lieutenant?"

"Not well at all. He was an Englishman and I'm Irish. Like oil and water, chalk and cheese we were."

"Are you saying you didn't get along with him?"

"I'll not speak ill of the dead, Inspector. But I wasn't here, and I didn't kill him and bury him beyond the hedges. If that's all, I'd like to change and eat my oatmeal."

Dev couldn't hold him in the stable block indefinitely, so he nodded. The War Department would track down Ainsley's family, who would no doubt be relieved to discover that their relative's honor was still intact. Even after all this time, deserters and conscientious objectors were still vilified and jailed, and those suffering from shell shock were treated as badly, perhaps worse.

There was nothing cowardly about remembering and reacting to hell on earth. It was a bloody shame that those who hadn't fought at all had the last dismissive word.

He entered the cool, dark building, smelling horses, hay, and the result of combining the two. A young groom, barely more than a boy, was attempting to remedy the latter with a pitchfork, and didn't even look up. There were a dozen gleaming horses in their boxes, and Dev wondered which were the new Irish arrivals. He'd have to telegram Belfast to get more information on Cassidy and his business.

Dev had already checked the garage after Lady Adelaide came to him in the wee hours. Waring's Frazer Nash was gone, as he expected. No one heard or saw a thing, which struck Dev as doubtful. The viscount probably bribed whoever was about into silence. Bob would get to the bottom of it later. That mechanical horse was out of the barn for hours and Waring could be anywhere.

If he were Waring, where would he go? Brighton seemed iffy; he'd have to explain to Philippa Dean why he'd arrived on her doorstep so unexpectedly. His estate was too obvious, and, really, practically right around the corner. Dev would stop by there later today. His club in London? Friends? He would quiz Lady Adelaide at greater length this morning to see if she had any new ideas.

She was naturally upset last night when she discovered the

viscount disappeared. Tried to explain that it was she herself who frightened Waring, suggesting the possibility he might be the next victim because of his adulterous relationship with Pamela Fernald. It was a load of poppycock as far as Dev was concerned, but he supposed the idea could have merit in this topsy-turvy household.

Who knew about them? And how could Dev find out without blackening their names? Had Waring been present too when Ainsley and his comrades were here? It was times like this that made him yearn for his old days of foot patrol.

But his father was ambitious for him, and he couldn't argue with the old man—Harry Hunter was something of a legend at the Yard and at home. Dev eventually discovered he had a real a knack for police work, though every time Lady Adelaide Compton was involved—which was now three times too often—his brain went fuzzy.

He headed back to the house, mentally arranging the interviews. The Jordan sisters could be dispatched with immediately once they were awake, unless they were somehow trying to avenge a childhood crime. He didn't think either of them had the wits to plan anything more taxing than a tea party, if that. As aspiring Bright Young People, he wondered how they wound up in the Fernalds' more conservative orbit. Sir Hugh had scolded them last night for not knowing Pamela well, though they had been guests here before.

From what he gathered from Mrs. Lewis, Sir Hugh and his wife lived quietly, opening their house up perhaps a handful of times a year to week-long company, and inviting their neighbors for dinner once every few months. They hosted the occasional Friday-to-Monday but could hardly be called wildly social.

He now knew that Pamela got out more frequently than one supposed. Did she ride over to Waring Hall, or drive? It probably didn't matter—someone there must have realized what was going on despite Waring's insistence otherwise.

Dev would see the ladies first. Lady Evelyn Fernald. Mrs. Temple. Juliet Barlow was not working here when Ainsley went missing, but she might have some connection with him that no one knew. After speaking with her last evening, he was convinced there was no love lost between her and her dead cousin. About to lose her job and be shipped all the way out to India, had she decided to try to stay in the foulest way?

He entered the house through the kitchen door, found Bob tucking into a substantial breakfast and had a quiet word with him. Around them, a whirlwind of activity reigned. Mrs. Lewis was arranging individual trays for those who preferred to break-fast in their rooms—Sir Hugh, his mother, his aunt—and two footmen were tasked with pushing a cart loaded with covered chafing dishes to the dining room.

Dev hesitated a moment as to whether he should join his sergeant, then decided it might be interesting to catch the real guests in their element. He followed the two young men as they hefted the cart on a removable ramp over the steps up to the main floor without incident, then placed all the dishes on a massive sideboard under Trim's supervision. Meeting with his approval, they left.

The large dining room—really a banquet hall in Dev's book, with landscapes, needlepoint banners, and life-size portraits hanging on crimson walls—was deserted now save for the but-ler, who looked as weary as Dev felt.

"Good morning, Inspector Hunter. Mrs. Lewis says you'd like a list of people, guests and servants both, who were here when Lieutenant Ainsley disappeared."

"Yes. That won't be a problem, will it? I realize it was long ago."

"No, we keep meticulous records of the staff. And there's a

guest book, a kind of diary—several of them now—who was here when and where they slept, what was served, the entertainment provided. Lady Fernald, Sir Hugh's mother that is, never wanted to repeat a menu, you see, since so many of the guests returned year after year. The notes include preferences, and what shouldn't be served as well—Captain Clifford is allergic to strawberries, for example, so you won't see any here, not even Mrs. Lewis's jam for your toast. A pity; it's quite delicious."

Dev smiled at the butler. "I'm sure I can get by with marmalade, or plain butter in a pinch."

"Oh no, sir. Besides the marmalade, there's honey, damson plum jam, and apple jelly on the table. From the estate—our own hives and orchard, and the late Lady Fernald grew orange and lemon trees in the succession houses. You won't go hungry. Do you want to make up a plate to take to the study before you get started for the day?"

Dev noted the array of glistening spreads in cut-glass ramekins at each place setting. "If it's all the same to you, I'd like to eat here."

Trim was too experienced a butler to bat an eye. If he thought an Anglo-Indian policeman did not belong beneath the Fernald ancestral portraits that hung above him, one would never know it. He pulled out a chair for Dev at once. "May I pour you coffee or tea?"

"Coffee, please."

Dev sat in solitary splendor enjoying his coffee as Trim lit the candles underneath the silver chafing dishes. "Guests usually help themselves, but you need only ring for assistance."

"Thank you, Mr. Trim. I'm sure I can manage." Dev was hungry enough to devour one of the horses he'd seen in the stables and was pretty sure he could lift a lid and shovel some food onto his plate and into his mouth without help.

He was alone for perhaps five minutes before Captain Clifford and Owen Bradbury made their appearance. They too were experienced enough to be polite, Clifford especially so. Since he was about to be posted to India, it was obvious he thought he could practice his diplomacy on Dev, and the three of them made general small talk over the kippers and shirred eggs. They discussed the extremely dry weather—of course—Baldwin's government, the return to the gold standard, and whether that explorer fellow Fawcett would ever emerge from of the Amazon jungle alive.

"Speaking of jungles, where in India were you born, Inspector?" the captain asked somewhat baldly.

Dev tempered his retort; he was used to being seen as foreign. "Sorry to disappoint," he said with a thin smile. "I'm afraid I was born in Chelsea."

Clifford's cheeks reddened. "My mistake. I'm keen on learning as much as I can before I deploy. It's such a vast country, isn't it?"

"I've never been."

"I say, can we get the third-degree over right here, right now instead of swapping our curriculum vitae?" Bradbury broke in. "You know what they say, fish and company smell after three days, and it's now four for us at Fernald Hall. Even though I'd planned to stay the week, I'd like to get back to my own home."

"Wouldn't we all?" said Dev. "I'm sorry, gentlemen. The dining room is not the place for a confidential interview, and my notes are upstairs." He'd have to jot down his impression of Cassidy's statements as soon as he went back to his room. It was unlike him not to have his notebook tucked inside his jacket pocket, and he felt practically naked without it. It had come in much more than handy once.

He wiped his mouth with an embroidered linen napkin and rose. "If you'll make yourselves available after lunch, I'd appreciate it."

Ladies first, after all.

Chapter Seventeen

Addie racked her brain, what little there was left of it, trying to figure out where Lucas might have gone. What could he be thinking of? His disappearance only pointed to his possible guilt.

And it just wasn't like him to be irresponsible. To be dishonorable. Rupert sneeringly called him Saint Lucas. Was there even such an historical personage? Addie was certain if Lucas had been forthcoming with Inspector Hunter that they could resolve his role in Pamela's life without incident. But now...

So, Lucas was imperfect. Everyone was, except maybe for her mother, who possessed enough dignity and duty for the entire Kingdom. Perhaps, since Addie was so close, she should motor over to the Dower House and see how she and Cee were getting on. Inspector Hunter made it clear she was superfluous to requirements here.

And who knew? Mama or Cee could have some ideas as to where Lucas went, and they wouldn't blab it all over creation that he was missing.

Addie informed Beckett that she was taking her car to visit her family instead of going down to breakfast, and that if anyone wanted her, they need only phone. The dowager marchioness had made improvements to her manor house inspired both by her stay in New York and Addie's own renovations of Compton Chase last year. Electrical circuits and new plumbing might not be feasts for the eye, but there was apparently plenty of new paint and wallpaper too. Addie was remiss not going sooner, but ever since they came back from New York in March, it had been one thing after the other.

Four murders, for example. Cee's recuperation from her poisoning. Addie's inability to tie up life's loose ends and move forward.

She spoke briefly to Trim, who had her car brought from the garage to the studded Tudor front door. Imagine all that the door had witnessed, Addie thought. Pamela's death was just one of many in a property this old. It almost made her long to live a house in one of the new "garden cities" that were sprouting up everywhere. Everything was fresh and clean and lacking any unpleasant history whatsoever. No garderobes or chamber pots or established multigenerational mouse families or priest holes or blocked chimneys, all the dubious delights of antiquity.

Definitely no ghosts.

The drive through the familiar winding country roads was lovely. Hedgerows were lush with berries and birds, bursting with early summer bounty. Addie and Lucas had come this way with their nannies in pony traps for years to play with Sir Hugh, who'd been a baronet from the age of three. It must have been difficult for Evelyn, managing alone, raising Hugh to become the fine man he was. God knows, widowhood was not for the fainthearted, even without a dead husband to haunt one.

Idly, she wondered what Rupert was doing, half-surprised that he hadn't slunk into the passenger seat at the last minute. She hoped whatever it was turned out to be useful, although she couldn't approve of his current methods. Imagine! While Mr. Hunter was in the bath…Addie shook the image out of her mind with some difficulty.

She passed the main gate to Broughton Park, steadfastly keeping her eyes on the road. She couldn't help the pang she felt for the loss of her childhood home, but there was primogeniture, primed to prick the air out of one's female balloon. Her cousin Ian was a nice enough fellow, but rather boring. What he needed was a young wife to shake him up, like Pip would do to Lucas. Addie would give matchmaking some thought once her current situation returned to some semblance of normalcy. Marriage might not be for her, but she was open to its advantageousness for others.

She turned down a long, mowed lane. Her mother still used the front gate out of habit when she left the estate, so this road's maintenance left something to be desired. She had to concentrate on avoiding the rabbit holes, and a fox dashed across mere feet in front of her, causing her to stall the car. Far across the open field, Addie spied the crenelated roof of Broughton Park, and looked away.

The car was finally coaxed to life. Up ahead was the perfectly lovely Dower House, a much more modest dwelling, yet still worthy of the Dowager Marchioness of Broughton. Lush red roses obediently climbed the facade, and tubs of scarlet pelargoniums lined the wide slate walkway in precision order. Her mother must have come out with a tape measure when her gardener set out the jardinieres.

The door sprang open before Addie could get out of the car, and she was enveloped in her sister Cee's arms.

"You've got smut on your nose, and you look exhausted!"

"Thank you, Cecilia. It's nice to see you too."

"I'm only trying to be helpful, Adelaide. Have you come to

save me again? I promise I won't vomit this time." Last March, Cee had required some medical intervention when she was accidently poisoned at the Savoy, an anomaly, Addie hoped. The Savoy's reputation for its cuisine was very well-deserved. But one could die there without consuming food and drink—a few years ago an Egyptian prince was shot dead by his disgruntled wife.

"What do you need rescuing from now?" Addie laughed, hugging her sister tighter.

"Mama, of course. She's on the warpath. Again. She disapproves of Paul, you know, even if his father is an earl. He's completely out of the succession—he has five older brothers and who knows how many nephews, can you believe it? One would have to drown them all in a sack like kittens for me to become a countess, but I told her I don't care. I don't! What is more admirable than saving lives, I ask you."

Cee had a penchant for falling in love with peculiar ideas and unsuitable men, but Addie didn't think Paul Kempton quite qualified for that description. He was an engaging young doctor with all his hair and teeth, and a promising career ahead of him. One day he might have an exclusive office on Harley Street, especially if he was married to a marquess's daughter, and she said so, extricating herself from Cee's embrace and straightening her hat. She'd deal with the smut later.

"Tell Mama that. Do you know what her latest scheme is?" Cee shuddered. "She wants me to marry Ian."

"Our distant cousin Ian, the current Marquess of Broughton?"

How odd that Addie had been mentally pairing him up with a mystery girl just minutes ago. But Cee? That required further thought.

"The very same. Really, all she wants is to get back into that house and run things again. She must think I'm a pushover! I told her I'd rather die than marry him."

"Don't joke, Cee. Death isn't funny."

"Pish posh. If I have to stay buried in the country much longer, I will die and be glad of it." She looped her arm in Addie's. "What brings you here? I thought you were with the Fernalds for the week."

"Well, a real death, actually. I don't know if word has traveled, but Pamela died on Sunday afternoon."

Cee stopped in her tracks on the front walkway. "What? How?"

Addie was surprised that her sister wasn't aware—gossip usually spread like wildfire in this part of the world. "The police believe she was poisoned."

"Poisoned! Police? What kind of a mess are you in now? Is that gorgeous guy from Scotland Yard here too?"

"Hush. He is. And perhaps we shouldn't make too much of it in front of Mama."

"Oh, that's easy. She went down to London on the train yesterday morning. No wonder the phone was ringing off the hook. She must know—she knows everything. I thought it might be Ian and told Carstairs not to answer it."

Carstairs was her mother's very proper butler, and Addie imagined he was dreadfully conflicted respecting Cee's wishes. In Carstairs's world, all doors were opened and all calls answered with great dignity. He was almost as perfect as Addie's own butler, Forbes, whom she stole away from both her mother and her cousin when Ian moved into Broughton Park.

"Why would Ian be calling you?"

"Because Mama has put a bee in his bonnet. He thinks I have a pash for him! Crikey! He's got that gray tooth, you know." Cee stuck her tongue out, then swept it across her own remarkably white teeth as if to make sure they were all still there.

"It's toward the back, isn't it? Perhaps he can get it capped.

It shouldn't be disqualifying. He's nice enough." If, as she'd thought earlier, a little boring.

"You can marry him then."

"I'm not marrying anyone," Addie said, as Carstairs opened the front door, giving her a very correct bow.

"Good morning, Lady Adelaide. How nice to see you. It's been too long."

"I know. I should have called first. I'm sorry to have missed my mother. How have you been?"

"Well, my lady. Shall I have Cook send up coffee and cakes?"

"That would be lovely. I left Fernald Hall without stopping down to breakfast and I confess I'm starved."

Her mother's cook was more than up to the challenge, and Addie expected delicious things would appear shortly. She and Cee went into the sun-drenched morning room and settled into freshly upholstered leaf-green armchairs, admiring the garden view flanked by new gold-shot silk curtains.

"So, who's the mustache-twirling villain at Fernald Hall?" Cee asked. She was a touch too enthusiastic for Addie's comfort.

"I've no idea," Addie said, removing her gloves. "Plus, the three Mr. Dunns found the body of a soldier who vanished in 1916. So, that's two deaths in two days."

Cee clapped her hands. "Right up your alley! What does Inspector Hunter have to say?"

"Not much to me. He thinks both murders are related somehow. I'm really not so sure. I say, Lucas hasn't come by here today, has he?"

Cee frowned at the change of subject. "No. Should he have?"

"He left the Fernalds rather abruptly. I just wondered—he talked the other day about going to see you all and Ian."

"Well, if he's at Broughton Park, I wouldn't know. I'm not spying there through binoculars like Ian does here."

"Cee! What a thing to say!"

"He does! He has a telescope on the roof too. I'm afraid to sunbathe in the garden."

"You'll only get freckled anyway. Coco Chanel may design beautiful clothes, but she's ruining her skin." The French designer had caused a sensation after getting sunburned on a cruise a few years ago, and modern young women everywhere were throwing off their hats and clothes with abandon in order to resemble farmworkers.

"Oh, you're such a spoilsport. You sound just like Mama."

Addie was irked by the criticism but knew it was true. She had a tendency to summon her mother's spirit when she least wanted to, although it warded off Mr. Cassidy with some success.

She listened to her sister complain about their mother and Ian for the next five minutes, until Carstairs entered with a heavily laden tray that could have fed several famished sunburned farmworkers. And then she listened some more, as her chewing was preventing her from taking much part in the conversation. Once she had eaten more than her fill, she told Cee that she was going to phone Ian.

"You can't! Well, if you do, tell him I'm not here. Or that I've got measles or something dreadfully contagious."

"We've already had measles. You were six and I was twelve. We were as red as postboxes head-to-toe."

"He won't know that. What do you want to talk to him for?"

"I wonder if he has any idea where Lucas went."

Cee returned her coffee cup to its saucer with a clatter. "Gosh, you don't think he killed Pamela, do you? Not your Lucas." She paused. "Well, he used to be."

Even her sister gave Addie men that didn't belong to her. "Of course not. But he needs to come back to Fernald Hall. Mr. Hunter is questioning everybody with no exceptions."

Just then, the doorbell rang. Cee leaped up. "I know it's him! I've got to hide."

"Who's him?"

"Ian! I bet he was peering through his telescope like a...like an eagle and saw you drive up."

Addie supposed it was possible, if unlikely. Surely their cousin had better things to do. "Eagles don't require telescopes, Cee. But go out the garden door and then inside through the back hall. Lock yourself in your room. I'll tell him it's your time of the month."

Cee's expression was a sight to behold. "Adelaide Mary Merrill, you will not! I don't want him thinking of any part of my body, especially not down there! Honestly, you are a horrible sister even if you let me vomit all over your fingers."

"Go, go. You're wasting valuable time."

Cee rushed out into the garden and Addie stopped herself from laughing. She knew what it was like to be pursued ardently by a man one wasn't truly interested in. She'd had a near-miss with Lucas, and now—

Now, she was the pursuer, and the man wasn't interested in her.

Carstairs appeared in the open doorway. "Lady Adelaide, the Marquess of Broughton is here. Are you and Lady Cecilia receiving?"

"Of course! Bring another cup, please. But my sister is feeling somewhat indisposed at the moment and has gone upstairs."

"What a shame. May I bring her anything?"

Addie hated to lie. "I don't think so. She'd just like some peace and quiet for her...for her headache. Do I still have a smudge on my nose?"

"I wasn't going to mention it, but yes. No, a little to the left."

Addie examined her napkin. Motoring in the countryside could be a dirty affair, even if one was not held at knifepoint.

Chapter Eighteen

Ian Alexander Percival Merrill, the eighth Marquess of Broughton, entered the morning room with a smile, and Addie looked in vain for the objectionable gray tooth. Perhaps he'd already attended to it. Lord knows, there was plenty of money to see as many dentists as one could stand, and periodontists besides. Broughton Park and its home farm were prosperous thanks to Addie's late father, and Ian seemed to know what he was doing as well. He wasn't going to squander his opportunity as many young men sometimes did.

He was of a height that made Addie stand on tiptoes to kiss him on the cheek. "Hallo, Cousin! It's been ages."

"It has. I hope I've done nothing to offend you."

She felt a stab of dismay. Ian wasn't an offensive sort. He was sensitive to the Merrill women and their needs when her father died and was generally a nice human being, if somewhat shy and serious. Addie's father thought him a worthy successor. "What makes you think such a thing?"

"You know you have an open invitation to Broughton Park, yet you haven't come. It's been five years."

They'd seen each other at county events and parties, and he

had come to her, but he was right. She hadn't walked through the door of her old home since her mother moved to the Dower House.

"Oh, Ian." She swallowed. "It's hard for me. If you ever have a daughter"—he colored, but she went on—"she might feel just as I do when she has to leave. It's very bittersweet."

"I didn't throw you out. You were already a married woman with a home of your own," he reminded her without rancor.

"I know it doesn't make any sense, but so few things do nowadays." Addie gave him a half-hearted smile. "How are you?"

"Well enough. I understand Cecilia took ill?"

"It's nothing to worry over. A...a slight bout of indigestion." Or had she said headache before? Lying simply was not her forte. She gestured toward the tray. "I've asked Carstairs for another cup. Cook outdid herself on the elevenses, and Cee might have eaten a little too much." Her sister would punch her if she found out what Addie said. Ladies were never supposed to overindulge, and never, ever finished everything on their plate.

"I can't stay, I'm afraid. I'm on my way to Town and wondered if your mother or Cecilia had any requests."

See? A generally nice human being. Not bad-looking either, with a full complement of the Merrill fair curls, if not as handsome as Devenand Hunter.

But then, who was?

"How considerate. Mama is already there. Perhaps you'll run into her. I don't know when she plans on coming home." Addie's mother often stayed in Addie's flat on Mount Street when she visited the metropolis but must have made other arrangements this time.

"I'll be on the lookout. Is there anything you need?"

Answers to so many uncomfortable questions. "Thank you, but no. I'm not even home at the moment—I'm at the Fernalds.'"

"Oh? One of their famous house parties? Should I be insulted that I wasn't invited this time?"

"I don't think so—you've dodged a bullet, so to speak. You haven't heard that Pamela is dead?"

Ian's chocolate biscuit dropped to the floor. "No! When?"

It wasn't like her neighbors and their servants to be so circumspect with gossip, but seemingly Pamela's death was still a secret. "Sunday afternoon. Lucas and I are both guests and have been up to our ears in interviews with an inspector from Scotland Yard. Murder is suspected. You haven't seen him, perchance, have you?"

"The inspector? Why should he want to talk to me? I wasn't even there! I know nothing."

"No. I mean Lucas."

He shook his head. "Waring can't have done it—totally out of character. Stake my life on it."

"I agree, but he's gone off somewhere and that doesn't look good."

"I'll be sure to tell him if I run into him." Ian looked down at his watch. Her father's watch, actually, and Addie felt another pang. "Look at the time. I'm going to miss my train." He bent down to give her another quick kiss and left.

Cee bounced into the room as soon as Ian's car was out of sight. "What did he want? Did he tell you he's carrying a torch for me?"

"He hardly mentioned you," Addie said, amused to see Cee's face fall. "He was on his way to Town and wondered if he could bring anything back to you and Mama."

"Bootlicker."

"Cee! I think he's being kind. A good neighbor. But imagine the adorable blond children you'd have." Addie ducked the flying pillow with ease. Cee never wore her glasses, so her aim was off completely, being almost as nearsighted as Addie. "What exactly is wrong with Ian?" she asked her sister.

They hadn't grown up together like Lucas and Addie had; he wasn't like a brother to Cee. True, as the heir, he'd been a frequent visitor to Broughton Park. He and the Merrill sisters shared a great-grandfather, but not a great-grandmother, which made them half-second cousins. Not too close; not like Cleopatra and her brothers, which was entirely far too propinquous.

"Please! Not you too! Has Mama been brainwashing you?"

"I haven't spoken to her at all about Ian. How long has she been harboring this idea?"

"Ever since we got back from New York. She says I'm an old maid, doomed to be alone forever."

"Well, there are plenty of us in Britain." A whole generation of young men never returned from the war to become husbands.

"You're not an old maid, you're a widow."

"Same difference—there's no man in my life." One couldn't in good conscience count Rupert.

"But you did have your chance, even if it went all wrong. Sometimes I don't think I'll ever get mine." Cee sighed somewhat dramatically.

"You're not on the shelf yet. What about Paul? I'm sure we can bring Mama around."

Her sister looked out into the garden. "He's very busy, you know."

Ah. Perhaps he was not quite as keen about his former patient as she was about her former doctor. "What will be will be." One couldn't force things. Addie helped herself to one last wild strawberry tart.

Cee threw herself down in a chair. "Let's change the subject. Tell me all the grisly details about what's going on at Fernald Hall."

Addie proceeded to do just that, including mention of Lieutenant Ainsley, his alleged desertion, and the recent discovery of his body. Cee had no recollection of the first—she'd been away at school—but sat goggle-eyed as Addie related most of the events since Sunday.

"Gosh. Some house party. Poor you."

"Poor Hugh." She didn't tell her little sister about Pamela's pregnancy—how would she have come by such information? Addie couldn't very well attribute her knowledge to Rupert's snooping.

"Is the inspector still as dreamy as ever?"

Cee didn't know about the Weekend of Folly and Failure in April. "I guess so. He's been too busy to pay me much attention, and that's just as it should be," she fibbed.

"So, who did it?" Cee asked again. "You're practically a professional by now. You must have a theory."

"I really don't," Addie said. "Pamela was well-liked by everyone. Maybe it was an accident—that's what Hugh claims, that somehow she ate or drank something she shouldn't have."

Could she have killed herself? Addie didn't want to think so. Pamela wouldn't do that to Hugh and John, even if she was having another man's child.

Lucas's? Oh, what a mess.

"Do you have to go back there?" Cee asked. "It must be frightfully grim."

"Inspector Hunter is still interrogating people. I don't know when he'll let us leave."

"He can't suspect you!"

"Am I too nice?"

"You are, you know. It's annoying. One wants to rebel against your good sense, but one can't ignore it, even if one wants to."

"I'll remind you of those words the next time we have a spat."

"I'll deny I ever said them." Cee picked up a piece of short-bread and rubbed its thistle design. "Did Ian say when he was coming back from London?"

"He didn't. When do you expect Mama to return?"

"She left all of a sudden—I was still in bed half-asleep when she came in to tell me, and she was very mysterious. I don't even know where she's staying."

"How odd. That's not like her."

Cee waggled a penciled eyebrow. "Maybe she's meeting a man!"

Addie considered it would be a good thing if she was. Her mother was still youngish—only in her early fifties—and attractive and shouldn't be interred along with her husband. Addie presumed her father was not haunting her mother. As opposed to Rupert, he'd lived a relatively blameless life and should have gone straight to Heaven when his time came.

"I need to go. If you hear anything about Lucas, could you ring Fernald Hall and let me know?"

"All right. But I don't expect to." Cee gave her another hug and walked her to the door.

Addie was tempted to wrap up a few more strawberry tarts in a napkin but practiced self-discipline. She put on her gloves and started up her shiny green Alvis two-seater. Bumping along the drive, she tried to enjoy the sun on her shoulders. It really was a lovely day, spoiled, however, by the tragedies. It seemed shallow to contemplate country walks or croquet or badminton, which no doubt would have been on the menu for the guests today if nothing horrible had happened. Addie decided when she got back, she'd try to lose herself in her book. Fiction was always more fun than fact.

Chapter Nineteen

Tuesday evening

When she got back from Broughton Park, Bob told her she could leave tomorrow, and Addie held onto that plan like a bright and shining beacon. She skipped drinks in the drawing room, not looking forward to making more irrelevant small talk, or worse, the kind of existential maunderings death always unearthed. One became obsessed with one's own mortality, wondering if one would even be mourned when the Grim Reaper arrived.

No matter how well-lubricated the other guests got beforehand, dinner was another awkward affair. Hugh joined them tonight, resplendent in his dinner jacket. Evelyn, in black velvet this time, had dug into her pearls, and was modestly accessorized. Addie eschewed her green gown for the purple dress she meant to wear Sunday night, along with her amethysts. The twins gleamed under the lights as usual; Iris Temple was distinguished in trailing dark gray chiffon; and the gentlemen were suitably attired. If one dropped in from Mars, one wouldn't have any inkling the party's hostess died two days ago.

There was one unexpected face at the table: Juliet Barlow,

who wore a severe black jersey dress with a diamanté clip at the shoulder. Hugh asked her to join them to even out the numbers. Unfortunately, Lucas was still missing, so they were still odd.

The elephant in the room. No one said anything about his absence, which made it worse somehow. The murderer was breathing a sigh of relief, since all fingers pointed to the vanished viscount.

She was alliterative again, but there was a certain ring to the appellation. It would make a good mystery title, wouldn't it? The Vanished Viscount. Or The Viscount Vanishes? Maybe when this was all over, Addie would try her hand at writing the sort of book one could curl up with in bed, a mug of tea on the bedside table, and a dog at one's feet. The heroine would be a nearsighted duke's daughter with a naughty Airedale. Might as well elevate her consequence while she was at it. Enlarge experiences all around.

There would be no ghosts.

"You're smiling, Lady Adelaide. It can't be from the convivial company—the house is like a morgue," Captain Clifford said quietly.

"I just had a silly thought. I'm sorry I'm not holding up my end of the conversation." Margie was on her left, busy competing with her sister across the table to capture Owen Bradbury's regard. Why should the girl bother talking with another woman? An older one at that.

Addie had been measured and found wanting.

"I don't mind. It's hard to fathom why they're going through the motions—the Fernalds, that is. I'd be as happy with a toasted cheese in my room. More comfortable too, out of my monkey suit. Even my uniform is less irritating."

"This isn't a very cheerful going-away party for you, is it?"

Clifford took a sip of wine. "It doesn't matter about me. It's Hugh I worry about."

Addie glanced down the table. Juliet had been seated between the captain and their host, who was at the head, Bradbury opposite at the other end. Hugh had Juliet's full attention, her facial expression solicitous, her words soft, her hand occasionally brushing the arm of his dinner jacket. Addie wasn't the only one ignoring Dennis Clifford.

Evelyn protected Hugh on the other side. Simon Davies was between her and Iris Temple, so there would be no need for furtive looks and signaling tonight. Next came Mr. Cassidy, then Mandy Jordan. The twins were having better luck with Bradbury than they did last night with Lucas, and Cassidy was a bonus bachelor.

"Did you know Hugh before the war?"

"A little. Bradbury and Ainsley knew him better than I; they went to Eton together. They took pity on this Harrow boy and had my back. Their friendship means the world to me. Saved my life, literally."

"I can't imagine what it was like." Rupert told her a tale or two but had been mum with the specifics. Of course, he wasn't in the trenches like the Four Musketeers; he'd been flying high, far away from the mud and blood, strafing and dropping bombs with what Addie hoped was accuracy. "Will you be sorry to leave your friends and England behind?"

Clifford shrugged. "For King and Country. The army is my life. I have no family to miss—my parents have passed, and I haven't been lucky enough to find a helpmeet. We—Michael and Owen and I—envied Hugh, despite all he's suffered, if you can believe it. We were a little in love with Pam." Addie had difficulty hearing him over the chatter and clink of forks against china, but his face said it all.

Was Clifford one of her admirers? Was Pamela "a little in love" with him?

"It's a dreadful shock about Lieutenant Ainsley," Addie said, fishing.

"The whole week so far has been shocking. Let's talk about something less gruesome. Are you a fan of moving pictures? Looks like I'm going to miss the latest Charlie Chaplin next week. I wonder if they have theaters in India."

Curses. Foiled again. "My maid is completely addicted. Last month all she could talk about was the plot to kidnap Mary Pickford in Los Angeles. One would think she was family." Addie rattled on about Beckett and her movie magazines, which were frequently strewn all over Compton Chase. Clifford seemed gratifyingly amused, but she did all the talking.

Breaking her mother's rule. So much for finding out more about him.

Addie switched gears. "I haven't seen that detective all day. Do you know how he's getting on?"

"That detective? I thought he was a friend of yours."

She felt a blush coming on. "We've...ah...met in the course of two investigations. I wouldn't say we were friends."

His eyes were pale gray, and sharp. "Then the rumors aren't true."

"What rumors?"

"Oh, someone mentioned something. I must have misunderstood." He said it with such a smile that she was meant to be reassured.

She wasn't. Addie knew a woman's reputation was everything, even if she was anxious to compromise it a few months ago. Why were men allowed their flings? Look at Rupert, rutting around the countryside, still accepted everywhere.

Except in her bed. In the last year of her marriage, she lived like a nun without the shorn head and wimple.

"He has been nothing but professional," Addie said a bit grandly.

"You lucked out you weren't here when Michael disappeared. What a cock-up the local constabulary made of that, and the brass after them. I grant you, Hunter is a cut above, and pretty shrewd, I'd guess. If yesterday's questions were annoying, today's beat them by a mile. One was ready to confess to any number of crimes."

"And what are you guilty of?" Addie teased.

"Good lord, I'm rusty when it comes to the Ten Commandments, but I must have broken at least half at one time or another."

Do not covet thy neighbor's wife. But Pamela did her fair share of coveting too.

"Mr. Hunter is very thorough."

"I'll say."

The footmen removed the dishes and passed the next course. Addie was getting full and decided a toasted cheese would have done very well for her too. She overindulged with her sister earlier and would pass on dessert.

Maybe she could find the inspector after dinner and fill him in on what she knew. Which was nothing, really. Her sister and Ian hadn't heard from Lucas. Hugh's friends had a crush on Pamela. Juliet had designs on Hugh.

Would he tell her anything of significance? Probably not.

"Did Mr. Hunter mention when you can leave?" Addie asked.

"Owen and I have decided to stay on to support Hugh. The funeral will be held on Friday if all goes as scheduled. I think the general consensus is that we'll all be here for it. Even the Jordan twins."

They must have guilty consciences, or realize how stupidly selfish they'd sounded, wanting to go off to have fun while their host was grieving.

Addie wasn't seeking fun but longed for her own bed and some privacy. "Beckett and I may go home and then come back for it. Compton Chase is not very far away."

"You'll be missed, Lady Adelaide."

She doubted it. It wasn't as if she'd exerted herself to be charming, even before Pamela's death.

Obediently, but with some reluctance, Addie followed Evelyn to the drawing room after dinner for coffee with the other women, leaving the men to their own devices. They paired off immediately, Evelyn waiting for the tray with Iris on one sofa, and the sisters sitting together on another. Addie was left no choice but to try to make Juliet feel at ease. Now that Hugh was nowhere near, she'd deflated significantly.

Addie sat down next to the governess on a rather spindly chair on the far side of the room. "How is John?"

"Fine. We finally went riding this afternoon. He couldn't concentrate on his studies." She fingered the fake gems at her shoulders as though she could turn them into diamonds by her touch.

"I should think not. Do you think he'll still be sent away to school?"

Juliet glanced at Evelyn, who was busy whispering to Iris. "You should ask his grandmother. No one cares what I have to say."

"I take it you don't approve."

"It's what Pam wanted. And what Pam wanted, she got. It will take a while for the household to realize they don't have to march in lockstep with her anymore." She tossed her head back in some defiance. "I know that sounds unkind. But Hugh spoiled her dreadfully—horses and rare plants and the usual jewels and furs. She had everything, and it never was enough."

Now Addie was getting somewhere. "What do you mean?"

"I've said too much already. But Pam wasn't who everyone thought she was, certainly not the perfect wife. She fooled everyone."

"Perhaps you should talk to Inspector Hunter."

"Why? I don't know who killed her."

"But you have your suspicions, don't you?"

Juliet flushed, but shook her head. "It's none of my business. But I will say it's not the tragedy everyone makes it out to be."

No, Juliet wasn't sad at all.

Chapter Twenty

Wednesday

A handful of telegrams arrived last night, too late for Dev to deal with their contents unless he wanted to roust people out of bed. He debated doing just that, burned by Waring's disappearance, but thought the better of it.

The inquest was scheduled for tomorrow, the funeral Friday. Everyone had agreed to stay at the hall until the end of the week, save for Lady Adelaide. Dev had given permission for her to leave along with Beckett, and he sensed her absence as soon as he woke up.

How very odd. He couldn't explain it, but there was a Lady Adelaide-shaped hole in the household.

He stretched. The bed was comfortable at least, despite the utilitarian nature of his room. The shared bathroom was empty, so Dev performed the necessary ablutions and was in the middle of pulling up his pants when a furious knocking made him pull them up faster.

It was Bob, red-faced and panting from climbing up the stairs. Judging from the napkin still tied around his neck, he'd presumably been enjoying an early breakfast in the kitchen. "Guv! Come quick! It's Miss Barlow!"

Dev skipped his necktie and shrugged into his jacket. "What about her?"

"She's dead, sir. Fell down a set of back stairs. One of the maids just found her and is shrieking her head off."

Dev hadn't heard anything, but the water had been running. Still, he wondered if he was losing his senses. He had the wits to put on his socks and shoes, however.

But if Juliet Barlow was in fact dead, there really was no rush or requirement of footwear.

There were numerous staircases in a house this old and disjointed, but the body was on the first-floor landing that led directly up to the schoolroom. Bob hadn't made a mistake; the woman had tumbled two flights of stairs. Judging from the angle of her head, she'd broken her neck doing so.

The position of the body was a far cry from the photograph the Cirencester police supplied him of Pamela Fernald, who lay neatly on the brick conservatory floor as if she was resting, her skirts spread out. Artificial, like a stage set death. Dev wondered when he saw it if someone rearranged her body to appear to ladylike advantage. The murderer? Mrs. Lewis claimed she wasn't responsible for the peaceful presentation.

No one had done the same for Juliet. Her robe was open, her nightgown hiked up over her thighs. There was a strong scent of gin and the usual aromas accompanying death.

"Where is John Fernald? He shouldn't see this." No one should, really.

"His grandmother is with him. Went right up. Not this way, obviously. She was in the kitchen with the housekeeper when the maid found the body."

Dev glanced below. Along with a leather slipper that matched the one still on Juliet's left foot, Trim and Mrs. Lewis were at the base of the stairs, presumably acting as guards so the other servants wouldn't come out into the hallway to gawk. Their faces were as gray as their hair.

"Lady Fernald's up early." Some women in posh houses didn't even know where their kitchens were. An exaggeration, perhaps, but then Dev remembered Evelyn Fernald and Mrs. Lewis had a cooperative relationship.

"They were talking about food for the funeral from what I overheard. I guess there will be another one."

"It appears so. Do you smell alcohol?"

"Gin, guv. Unmistakable. She must have been drunk and fell."

Dev was less sure. He bent over the body, took an unpleasant deep breath, and lightly touched the edge of her robe, then a few other places. Mindful of the butler and housekeeper, in a voice barely above a whisper, he said, "Unless she did it herself, the gin was spilled on her clothes. See? Streaked and spotted. The patches are slightly damp. We're being made to think this is an accident."

Bob's mouth dropped open. "Blimey."

"Indeed. Go round another way and see if there's any obstruction on the stairs up to the schoolroom—or string, a wire screwed into the wall, loose carpet, something. Take your time."

Bob did as he was bid. Dev called down to Trim. "Please call the Cirencester station and tell them we have another body on our hands." Dev could hear the grumbling of his local colleagues now. It was devilish early for death. But then there was never a perfect time.

"Surely Miss Barlow just took a fall," Trim said, shocked.

"We can't rule anything out yet," Dev replied. "Mrs. Lewis, when my sergeant comes back, he'll take your place. I appreciate you've kept people away, but I imagine you need to get back into the kitchen to prepare breakfast."

"I do, though how anyone could be hungry in this house after all the to-do, I don't know."

"Was Miss Barlow friendly with the staff?"

Mrs. Lewis shook her head. "Not really. I don't like to speak ill of the dead, but she put on airs. She was Lady Fernald's—Pamela's—cousin, you know. Thought she was too good for the rest of us. Mr. Trim said—" She stopped.

"What did Mr. Trim say?"

"You'd better hear it from him."

"And I will. But you're right here."

The housekeeper gave him a look that told him he'd won. "That she was all over the master at dinner last night. Pawing him and whispering nonsense. Overstepping. Everyone noticed—by that, I mean the footmen. If they did with all they had to pay attention to, I'm sure the guests did too. Poor Sir Hugh. He's so vulnerable right now."

So vulnerable he might accept the attentions of his late wife's pallid double? Did someone decide to kill Juliet Barlow to "save" him? His concerned friends? His mother? His aunt? One of the twins, jealous? A loyal servant?

Or was it a simple fall, as Mr. Trim said? Perhaps a drunken Juliet spilled liquor on herself and then took an unwise stroll down the stairs.

The lab would soon determine if she had, in fact, imbibed too much—or any—alcohol. The incontrovertible fact, however, was that she was dead.

"Does anyone besides the staff use these stairs?"

"Not usually. They go right up to the nursery on the top floor—the schoolroom now, I should say. Master John has his own bedroom down the hall now, and there's another set of stairs to that. When Miss Barlow came, Nanny Joyce retired, and not a minute too soon. She was ancient even when she took care of Sir Hugh. The stairs were too much for her at the end, and we hardly ever saw her down here."

"Where is she now?"

"Oh, she's passed, Inspector Hunter. Two years ago. Sir Hugh gave her a cottage on the estate, and I found her in bed one morning when I went to bring her my applesauce. Awfully fond of it, she was. She had very few teeth left, you see, and it was easy for her to eat. "

If the toothless nursemaid knew anything about Michael Ainsley and his disappearance all those years ago—doubtful, according to Mrs. Lewis—she took the knowledge to her grave.

"How is the list coming along, Mrs. Lewis?"

"We've put our heads together, and Mr. Trim wrote things up. He was going to give it to you this morning."

"I appreciate all your help. I know how busy you both are."

The housekeeper's cheeks pinked. "We know our duty."

Dev heard Bob's deliberate footsteps above, and eventually the man was on a step above the body. "Not a thing, guv. Carpet's tacked down, no toys or objects anywhere, no sign that anyone put a barrier across the stairs. Those slipper soles look worn. She must have just slid."

"Or was pushed." He heard Mrs. Lewis's gasp below and cursed himself. He turned to the woman. "Please keep that to yourself. Foul play can't be ruled out, I'm afraid."

"I won't breathe a word. The girls are already frightened to death with bodies everywhere, and it's impossible to get proper help, even with the good wages Sir Hugh provides. I'm not going to add to the hysteria."

"Good woman. Ah, here's Mr. Trim."

"They're on their way, sir."

"Thank you. Bob, if you'll stay with the body and keep any-one away, I'd like a look at Miss Barlow's rooms."

"I stuck my head in once I was up there. Lady Fernald must have taken the boy away from there."

"Good. Mrs. Lewis, you might want to make a big pot of your delicious coffee. It will take some of the sting away when the police get here. Wake them up properly." Dev checked his watch. It wasn't quite seven o'clock, and the weight of the day lay heavy on his shoulders.

He too found another way to get upstairs, grateful he passed no one. By rights, he should have notified Sir Hugh, but he presumed his mother or the butler had already done that. The element of surprise was always useful in police work; Dev liked to gauge people's reactions to bad news. Though he imagined that by the time he got downstairs again, the whole house would be reverberating with Juliet Barlow's death.

He entered the schoolroom. It was as neat as a pin, books lined up like soldiers on the shelves, sharpened pencils in a glass jar on the long study table. The door leading to Miss Barlow's rooms was open. He passed through a small sitting room, also neat, its quality-but-aging furniture probably castoffs from other rooms in the house. There was no sign of a bottle or a glass on any of the tables.

The little kitchen, hardly bigger than a broom closet, was spotless. Nothing was in the sink or dish drainer. A quick check in the cupboards did not reveal a stash of gin or any kind of booze. But when Dev got to the bedroom, the smell of gin was strong. The bed was rumpled and damp from it, and an empty bottle rested on the side table. There was no glass.

There was no glass. Was Miss Barlow the kind of woman who drank gin from the bottle? Dev didn't think so.

She put on airs, according to Mrs. Lewis, which definitely

would not include swigging alcohol straight from a bottle. But of course, Juliet had been in her own room, out from under the critical eyes of the rest of the inhabitants of Fernald Hall. What she did up here was her business.

Now it was Dev's.

Chapter Twenty-One

Beckett was majorly aggrieved, but Addie rang for her a little after five o'clock. She was unable to sleep a wink, was dressed, and packed up everything in her cases herself. One less thing for her sleepy maid to hold against her, although she definitely had not met Beckett's standards folding everything into the requisite tissue paper. But they were only going twenty miles or so—how wrinkled could her clothes get on the short journey?

Addie was determined to drive home in her sporty Alvis, even if it was mostly dark inside the hedgerows. She left apologetic notes to Evelyn and Hugh, claiming there was a small emergency at Compton Chase to deal with. Addie couldn't lie to one's face very well, but writing was much less of a problem. She left a generous vail for Trim to divide amongst the servants, and she and Beckett slunk out of the house before the cock had a chance to crow. She'd be back Friday for the funeral, something she was not at all looking forward to.

She let herself into her house, eliciting her butler Forbes's disapproval. He, of course, was dressed to his usual immaculate precision even at this absurdly early hour, making Addie feel a bit slovenly in her trousers and sweater, her hair every which way from the convertible top being down on what promised to be a beautiful summer day. He quickly helped Beckett upstairs with the luggage, and her terrier Fitz bounded down from her bedroom, where he probably mussed the covers rooting about, dreaming of dog treats.

He was beside himself at her return, giving her the impression he'd been desolate without her. She'd only been gone since Saturday, but it seemed like a month to her too. He yapped and spun and jumped and licked, making Addie feel wanted, if only by a silly dog.

"Oh, boo hoo. Pull yourself together, my girl. There are other fish in the sea besides your inspector."

Another welcome, of quite a different nature. Addie gritted her teeth at Rupert's teasing. There was no one in the hallway, but Addie was cognizant a few people caught her "talking to herself" in the past and wanted no repetition of the odd looks she got when Rupert made one of his surprise appearances. She had no interest in being incarcerated in a sanitarium before it was absolutely necessary.

And at the rate she was going...

"Come upstairs," she hissed. Too bad she hadn't left him behind at Fernald Hall, but she knew better by now. Rupert was impossible to shake. It was all part of his dratted mission.

"Sorry, no. Beckett is unpacking in your dressing room and hauling out the iron already. She's miffed, you know, grumbling in Gaelic. I expect she'll ask for a raise. Or a day off to catch up on her sleep."

Blast. "In the garden, then." Fitz probably needed to go out anyhow. She hoped it was too early for her gardener, Jack Robertson, and the boys from the village that made up his little crew to be working.

But alas, when she stepped outside, the distant clattering of the lawn mower told her she was mistaken.

"How about the tithe barn?" Rupert asked, a mischievous smile on his pale face.

"Damn it!" Addie had not set foot in there since last August, where her onetime neighbor had been found murdered in it. Naked, too, but that really was neither here nor there.

"Don't worry. It's not haunted, and we'll have privacy."

"How do you know it's not haunted?"

Rupert gave her a dismissive roll of his dark eyes. "Please. I'm a ghost. I have an instinct about such things. Come along."

It was inconceivable to Addie that Kathleen Grant went directly to Heaven after all her irregular relationships, but who was she to judge? Reluctantly, she followed Rupert into the cool, hushed stone building, Fitz at her heels. A few pigeons objected to their arrival by fluttering above in the rafters, causing Addie to startle and Fitz to attempt to fly.

"Don't be alarmed. They're only rats with wings. Now then. What are you going to do about Juliet Barlow?"

"What do you mean?" She looked around for a place to sit while Fitz snuffled at all the strange, delicious smells— compost, hay, and a shelf with a box filled with blocks of suet in mesh cages for the birds. Jack kept a record of the different varieties that visited the garden, and tried, with very little success, to teach Beckett to be a bird-watcher. Addie dropped down to a bale of hay, happy to be wearing trousers against the creepy crawlies that made their nests inside.

"She's dead."

Addie was glad she was sitting down. "What? That can't be! I spoke to her not even ten hours ago. She was fine!" They drank tea side by side under the rather gimlet eye of Evelyn Fernald in a very uncomfortable post-dinner gathering.

"I assure you, it is. A maid found her early this morning. She fell down the stairs, or it was fixed to look like she did."

"Oh, my God. Poor John." The two most important women in his life, gone within days of each other.

"Indeed."

"You said 'fixed.' Was she murdered?"

"It looks like it to me, but I'm not a policeman," Rupert said with modesty.

Addie stamped a foot in frustration, causing dust motes to rise and sparkle. "You're supposed to know things!"

"I can't know everything, more's the pity. I wanted to stop you from leaving so early this morning, but something came up."

Something was always coming up. Addie was very annoyed with the vagueness often associated with her late husband.

"Do you think I should go back?" Addie asked. Beckett would probably flatten her with the iron if she asked the maid to repack.

"I expect Inspector Hunter will want to speak to you, as you were the last person to see Juliet alive. Apart from her killer, that is. But he'll probably call on you here sometime this afternoon."

Addie shivered. The last person to see her alive... Well, that was incorrect. The drawing room group included Evelyn Fernald and Iris Temple. The Jordan girls. After a rushed cup of tea, the women broke up before the men joined them last night. Evelyn pleaded fatigue, which was very understandable. The twins were obviously bored in the company of such old ladies, Juliet and Addie fitting that description in their eyes as well. She and Juliet had walked up the main staircase, the chattering Jordans behind them, separating on Addie's corridor.

Did Juliet look in on John? It wasn't all that late when they went upstairs; he might have been up. Addie remembered breaking bedtime rules at his age every chance she got. Inspector Hunter would question him, as gently as possible, she hoped.

"Why do you think Mr. Hunter will come here?" she asked Rupert.

"Quite frankly, he needs a break from the House of Doom. Who knows who will kick the bucket tomorrow?"

"Rupert! You sound positively gleeful! Death is no laughing matter."

"Don't I know it. You are preaching to the choir, my dear."

Addie blushed. Sometimes she actually forgot Rupert was dead.

"Who do you think did it?"

Rupert fingered his chin, and Addie was unkindly reminded of that statue of an ape contemplating a skull.

"I know who didn't do it—Hugh. John. Those fluffy-headed chits. As for the rest—" He shrugged. "Iris and Evelyn didn't like her. Neither did the staff. And what if she had an assignation with one of the men and it went wrong?"

"We should eliminate Simon Davies."

"Why? He's not too old to climb stairs. The man moves boulders and fells trees for a living. Pushing a girl down the stairs is child's play."

Addie could not imagine that dignified gentleman murdering anyone, but she'd been fooled before.

"This is just awful." Poor Inspector Hunter.

"Why do you think that? Aren't murder cases his catnip? The more, the merrier. If all villains reformed, he'd be out of a job."

"Stop reading my mind. You know I don't like it," Addie said, standing up. She brushed off her trousers. To her horror, she realized she was starving. Was that a normal response when one heard about the death of someone one was acquainted with?

She'd consult with Mr. Hunter, who was hungry most of the time.

She wondered when he'd turn up. If Rupert was correct, that is. She should really bathe and change into something else. But not look as if she was trying too hard to attract him.

Oh, for heaven's sake. As if he would notice. He was a serious man who couldn't be bothered with her pathetic attempts of seduction, now with three murders to solve.

"You might be surprised," Rupert said, right before he disappeared.

Chapter Twenty-Two

Rupert was right. (Three words she would never say aloud and was loath to even think.) A little after three thirty, Addie looked out the diamond-paned windows of the Great Hall at Compton Chase as a car rolled up the drive.

It was a Bentley, being driven by Hugh's chauffeur.

Mr. Hunter—if he was inside—was arriving in style.

Cook prepared an even lovelier-than-usual tea at Addie's instruction. Mrs. Lewis's kitchen fare at Fernald Hall was all very well, but Cook's was superior, and she let one know it at every opportunity.

Forbes announced the police inspector with every appearance of delight, and Addie pretended his visit was a surprise.

"I'm sorry I didn't call first," Mr. Hunter said, settling himself opposite in a crewel wing chair before the empty fireplace, the tea table between them. Addie had indulged in a cup already to allay her nerves, but that hadn't worked—her stomach was bursting with butterflies. "I can't stay long. I borrowed Sir Hugh's chauffeur and car and don't want to inconvenience anyone."

"That's all right. Hugh has another car for emergencies. What brings you here?" Addie asked.

Although she knew.

"I have bad news. Juliet Barlow fell to her death sometime in the early hours this morning."

"No!" Addie gasped, quite creditably. Maybe she should give Hollywood a try if England lost its luster. Beckett would be ecstatic.

"I'm afraid so. And I suspect it wasn't an accident, despite someone's attempt to make it look like one, or worse, a suicide. I know you were one of the last people to speak to her last night, and I wonder if she said anything that might be useful to us."

Addie poured the inspector a cup of tea, not having to ask how he took it. She waited until he helped himself to a smoked salmon and cream cheese sandwich and then tried to reconstruct last night's conversation.

"She complained no one paid attention to her. She didn't think John should go away to school, especially now, but Pamela had insisted upon it. And what Pamela wanted, Pamela got, or some such phrase. I know she was resentful to lose her job and the home she had for five years, and I don't think she really wanted to go off to India. Although I'm sure it's a lovely country," Addie said hastily in case the inspector took offense on behalf of his mother.

She took a sip of tea. "She also implied that Pamela was not the perfect person everyone thought she was. I actually think Juliet had an idea as to who might have killed her, but she clammed right up when I asked her."

Mr. Hunter gave her the stern look she was very used to. "That was a dangerous question, Lady Adelaide. Who else heard you ask it?"

"Why, nobody. We weren't alone in the room—Lady Fernald, Mrs. Temple, and the Jordan girls were there, but no one paid us any mind. We sat a good distance away and spoke very quietly."

"But one of them could have overheard."

"I doubt it. They were talking amongst themselves. Then the tea trolley came in, and there was the usual pouring and chitchat with everyone participating. It wasn't the jolliest of evenings. I didn't even drink half my cup before Evelyn announced she was tired and headachy. We all got up and left—no, that's not right. Evelyn and Iris stayed behind and stacked up the cups and saucers."

"What else can you tell me? Bob said you went to Broughton Park yesterday and that no one knows where Waring is. I went to his home myself with no luck."

"I am sorry. But he's not your man."

The inspector's lips curved. "So you say."

Addie did not want to waste time arguing. "Oh! Captain Clifford was my dinner partner last night. He said he and his friends all admired Pamela, perhaps more than they should have, Michael Ainsley included. Do you suppose she had an affair with one of them?"

"Lady Adelaide, you know I couldn't tell you even if I knew." He'd already devoured two scones during her recitation and looked like he was considering a petit four from the top tier.

She nibbled on one herself. "It must be awful over there. At Fernald Hall, I mean."

"It's pretty beastly. I take it Miss Barlow was not the most popular person, but nevertheless, it's a shock to the household. Three bodies in four days. I think it's a record for me. One I don't want to hold."

"What will happen to John?"

"I gather the tutor who was hired will come a few weeks early. Once the team is finished with Miss Barlow's rooms, her things can be packed up and he can move in. She really didn't have much."

Addie looked around the exquisitely decorated Great Hall, with its gleaming two-story windows, stone floors, and thick Persian carpets. If something happened to her, it would take weeks to box her personal property. She plainly had too much and felt even sorrier for Juliet than she had before.

"You said it probably wasn't an accident…or suicide. You've ruled out the latter?"

"Throwing yourself down flights of stairs won't guarantee certain death. If she'd wanted to kill herself efficiently, she would have jumped from a top-floor window. She was up as high in the house as she could be already unless she went up on the roof."

Addie shook her head. "She'd never do that to John—to give her credit, she was concerned for him. And she didn't strike me as being that desperate or unhappy. Irritated, yes."

"Irritated enough to drink a whole bottle of gin?"

Addie laughed. "Oh, goodness, no. Juliet never drank spirits, not even wine with dinner. Her father had a drinking problem, lost his position with the family bank and all their money after fiddling with some accounts. I understand he very nearly went to jail, but his brother took pity on him and sent him out of the country. Juliet and her mother were left to fend for themselves with a little help from Pamela's family—her childhood was very unhappy. She once told me she very much approved of Prohibition in America."

Mr. Hunter's brown eyes gleamed with interest. "No one said as much to me at Fernald Hall."

"Perhaps they never noticed. As Juliet said, no one paid attention to her, and it wasn't as if she belonged to the temperance movement and marched up and down the drive with picket signs. Pamela wasn't much of a drinker either."

"Then you think it's unlikely that Juliet Barlow spilled gin all over herself in a drunken stupor and fell down the stairs."

"Very unlikely."

Mr. Hunter stood, eyeing the remaining contents of the tea stand regretfully. "Thank you—I'm glad I came. I'll see you at the funeral Friday?"

"Yes. Eleven o'clock, right?"

"Correct. You'll telephone if you have further information?"

Addie couldn't help herself. "I thought you could do without my help on this case." She tried to smile up at him cheekily but probably resembled a lunatic.

"That was before the bodies started piling up. Deputy Commissioner Olive was pretty clear when I spoke to him today. Sir Hugh is a national hero. If I don't solve the death of his wife soon—never mind the rest of it—he'll send someone else."

Her attempted smile disappeared. "That doesn't seem fair!" Addie was incensed for the inspector. He was human, not a miracle worker. The situation was getting more complicated by the day; surely this Olive person should realize that.

"I do have a few tricks up my sleeve—there were a couple of informative cables delivered last night that I haven't even had a chance to deal with. You don't know Mr. Cassidy well, do you?"

"I told you, I never met him before Saturday. He's, um, very friendly." A little too friendly, Addie thought, but as a rich, relatively young widow, she was accustomed to fending off advances. "Solicitous. Charming. The sort of man a lady has to watch out for. Why, was he after Juliet?"

"Not that I know of—she'd be beneath his ambition, I think." He paused, looking as if he was struggling with something. "It will be common knowledge once Cassidy gets back from London today, so I can tell you. I received word that Michael Ainsley was his brother."

"What?"

"Half brother, to be accurate. The War Office had him listed among the next of kin. Cassidy's mother was married to an Englishman. The marriage didn't work out, and she returned to Ireland, leaving Michael behind."

How could a mother leave her child? Addie had trouble leaving Fitz home for a few days. It had been an agonizing five months when she was in New York, and he was just a pet.

The circumstances must have been extraordinary. Perhaps Mr. Ainsley had been a brute and frightened his wife into submission. In the olden days, children legally belonged to their fathers, and many women stayed in unhappy unions to remain close to their children.

"She remarried soon after and had Patrick. The boys did not grow up together, though Michael visited once or twice when he came of age."

"You didn't get all this information from the War Department," Addie said.

"No, no. The Belfast constabulary was very thorough. Cassidy's known to them, and not for the usual reasons. He's a bit of a local hero. Had a good war and came home to take over his late father's stud and improve the business. He's got a good reputation—employs a lot of locals and is a fair employer."

Addie frowned. "This is so odd. Why is he here?"

"Well, apart from selling the Fernalds some horses, I'd wager he wanted to see the people his brother spent time with before he vanished. I'm looking forward to asking him just that."

"But he said nothing!"

"Exactly. I wonder why."

Addie picked up her teacup, then noticed it was empty. "Do you really have to go?"

"I do. Cassidy's expected back on the six o'clock train. He had an appointment in Town that couldn't wait. We'll pick him up at the station, and I'm cutting it too close as it is. Any words of wisdom for me?"

"You'll figure it out." Addie was sure of it. That's why she'd called him.

Perhaps not quite the only reason, though.

Chapter Twenty-Three

Thursday

Almost a work-week in the country. Four long days so far, with very little result to show for it. The sun was bright in the sky, almost a rebuke to the testimony Dev gave concerning the three deaths.

Not that he had much to say, or much to offer in evidence. The jury, after somewhat rambling instruction by the presiding magistrate, ruled the women's deaths accidental. Ainsley's was death by misadventure, the specifics of which were not examined.

"Water under the bridge, eh? Let sleeping dogs lie. These people have had enough grief, don't you think? Sir Hugh wants to bury his wife tomorrow," the man said to Dev as he pulled him aside afterward and patted him on the shoulder. In his private opinion, Ainsley was a possible suicide to avoid going back to the front.

Logically, that made no sense at all. If the lieutenant was afraid of death, why would he kill himself? And how he managed to get buried didn't seem to concern the magistrate one whit. The coroner Dev dealt with earlier in the week had gone to France for a long-planned holiday, and this local squire was his substitute. There were other cases set for the day, and it was obvious the man was anxious to dispense with them all and get back to his horses and hounds.

Dev was used to a more professional approach and chafed at the outcome. Cassidy wouldn't like it either, but then Cassidy wasn't here. Where in hell was he? Where was Waring?

The horse breeder was the first person to come into the conservatory after Mrs. Lewis and the maids. Coming in to check on his handiwork? Where had he been when Juliet fell down the stairs? He left the house early Wednesday morning before her body had been discovered.

But he had not returned on the six o'clock train, or any one thereafter, so Dev couldn't get answers.

He walked over to the small contingent from Fernald Hall lingering outside Broughton Magna's Women's Institute building where the inquests were held. All were servants—the Dunns, the kitchen maid who discovered Juliet's body, Mrs. Lewis, Mr. Trim. Sir Hugh, his mother, Pamela's maid Murray, Simon Davies, and Jim Musgrave were present for the Pamela portion of the testimony but left immediately after.

He half-expected to see Lady Adelaide here, even though she was not asked to testify. He'd like her opinion on the findings, not that it would change a thing. He'd been at war with himself and the facts of this case since he'd rolled up in Sir Hugh's Bentley Monday morning. He couldn't prove murder occurred, but knew it to be true, nevertheless.

At least the Fernalds were happy with the verdicts. There was no scandal attached. All three deaths were accidental tragedies. Dev supposed they'd even convince themselves eventually that Ainsley was cleaning his gun in the foundation hole on the way to the train station when it went off, causing debris to collapse on him.

"Inspector!" Mrs. Lewis smiled up at him. "Thank you for everything."

"It's I who should thank you all. You made my sergeant's and my stay here as pleasant as it could be under the circumstances."

"It will be nice to get back to normal," the housekeeper said. "If that's possible."

"Why wouldn't it be?"

"Ruthie," Mr. Trim warned.

"I'll speak my mind, Amos." She stepped away from the group. "It seems too easy, doesn't it? The mistress would never have taken something she shouldn't, even if she was—" The woman's cheeks turned bright red. "Um, distracted with the house party."

"That's not what you meant to say, Mrs. Lewis," Dev said quietly.

She angled her head. "Not in front of them. I can't."

"Very well. Let me walk you back to the house." Dev extended an arm. His briefcase with the inconclusive reports was in the other, a nuisance to carry.

"You all go on ahead," Mrs. Lewis said, and she waited for them to do so.

It was at least a two-mile tramp through back-country lanes. Dev got a ride into Broughton Magna but didn't mind the walk back if he could get new information. He hoped Mrs. Lewis was up to it; she wasn't a young woman.

He waited until the figures ahead disappeared behind a curve in the road. "Now then, what did you wish to tell me?"

"I couldn't before. I kept hoping you'd find someone. The person responsible, that is."

"Sorry I couldn't oblige," Dev said ruefully.

She bit a lip. "There was a medical exam on Lady Fernald, wasn't there?"

"There was."

"Then you know. About the baby."

Dev stopped walking. "And you did, as well. Who else knew?"

"I don't know. Murray, probably. She had to have. The woman never said a word, of course. Wouldn't stand for gossip about the mistress, and right she was. Most maids nowadays aren't so discreet. Going into service isn't what it once was."

It was very true women had more employment options since the war. Even Scotland Yard employed females now.

"How did you find out?"

"Lady Fernald didn't tell me, of course, but I remember when she was sick carrying John. There were things she ate that made it worse. Clement, the old chef, was still here then, and she asked him not to cook them. She asked the same of me a few months ago."

"She didn't explain why."

"Oh, no. Just gave orders. With a smile—it wasn't her way to be high-handed. I wondered. And I watched. She wasn't showing yet but would have soon."

They continued on the lane, Mrs. Lewis no longer clutching his arm. Dev parsed his words carefully. "Do you think it's possible that Lady Fernald decided to end her life?" Or the baby's, but he didn't add that.

"Never," she said decisively. "Sir Hugh loved her, and I think they had an understanding."

"What do you mean by that?"

She colored up again. "You know. He would have accepted the child as his own. And who's to say it wasn't? Just because he can't walk doesn't mean he can't father a child. Lady Fernald had her own rooms upstairs, but they still shared his bed lots of nights. Ask Musgrave."

"I'm afraid I'm done asking questions, Mrs. Lewis. With the inquests over, I'm expected back at the Yard on Monday. And I cannot impose on the Fernalds any longer. I plan to leave right after the funeral tomorrow. Bob's already gone." Eager to get back to his wife and baby daughter. Dev imagined his parents would be happy enough to see him, but that wasn't the same, was it?

"I just feel it wasn't an accident, Mr. Hunter. I can't explain why."

"I understand completely. What about Miss Barlow?" The toxicology report revealed no trace of poison or alcohol. Juliet died of a broken neck, but one could not guarantee that result when one pushed someone down the stairs. She could just as easily have broken an arm or been merely badly bruised. It was not an efficacious form of murder, he thought grimly.

"I don't know. It's all so very disturbing, isn't it?"

It was indeed. Dev couldn't think of a time in his career when he was less satisfied by an inquest.

Perhaps he should speak to Murray one more time. The maid was tight as an oyster when he questioned her before. Loyalty was a prized commodity, but it impeded police work.

But, when they finally got back to Fernald Hall, Murray was gone. No one found it unusual; after all, the lady she'd attended as a lady's maid was dead, and there was no point in her moping around trying to make work for herself today and crying tomorrow at the funeral. She had already boxed up Pamela's clothes for charity and removed all traces of her in her bedroom as requested by the other Lady Fernald. There were to be no shrines.

Sir Hugh did not know where Murray was headed; he'd paid her wages and a generous bonus, along with giving the woman a glowing reference. Dev wished someone might have mentioned Murray's intention to leave earlier, but he had no authority to hold her here anyway.

As frustrated as he'd ever been, he didn't expect his usual meditation or prayer would center him. The thought of hanging around Fernald Hall for the rest of the day was anathema. What would he do with himself but face his own recriminations?

There was only one place he could think of that might suit and soothe him.

It probably wasn't wise. In fact, Dev knew it wasn't.

No. He'd invaded Lady Adelaide's privacy yesterday and would have to be satisfied seeing her tomorrow at the funeral before he went back to London. Black didn't suit her—she was much too fair and lively.

Lovely, too.

Lord, he was as hopeless as the Jordan twins.

Chapter Twenty-Four

Thursday afternoon

Having nothing more exciting to do, Addie absentmindedly sipped a cup of tea in the sunshine-flooded Great Hall as she looked over the household account books. Her checkbook was at hand, her terrier, Fitz, snoozing at her feet. She trusted her steward, Mr. Beddoes, completely—a holdover from Rupert's grandmother's day, he knew the mechanics of running Compton Chase far better than she ever would. But at the moment he was in his cottage in the village suffering from an attack of gout, thus Addie was temporarily taking over.

He was so supportive after Rupert died, patiently teaching her basic accounting methods to help her make sense of the columns of figures. It was a far cry from her maths classes at Cheltenham Ladies' College all those years ago, which she hated with a fiery passion. As far as she could remember, she never wrote an accurate geometry proof, and x remained unsolved in algebraic perpetuity.

To give her late husband credit, he truly loved Compton Chase and was successful improving the estate once he inherited. The infusion of Addie's money helped, of course. It also went into the purchase of the sleek cars in the converted stables, some of which Mr. Beddoes urged her to sell. She—or her chauffeur—could only drive one car at a time, and owning seven automobiles was a bit excessive.

There had once been eight. But the Hispano Suiza met its untimely fate with Rupert and Mademoiselle Labelle.

"Don't do it. Didn't we have this conversation the other day? My cars are sacrosanct."

Rupert! Fitz continued to sleep. What a watchdog.

Rupert stared at her inky fingers. "You look…charming."

"Liar." Addie wore ancient sagging jodhpurs from her teen years when she actually tried to ride every day to please her father, and one of Rupert's old collarless shirts, not even tucked in. That the pants still fit was something of a miracle, although admittedly the top two buttons remained unfastened. If her mother saw her in this condition, she'd throw up her hands in defeat, as one was always supposed to be prepared for unexpected company.

In the dowager marchioness's universe there were rules. One's hair was brushed. Face washed. Body perfumed, but not too heavily. One wore pressed, elegant clothes, and lipstick was permitted as a grudging nod to the twentieth century.

Addie didn't qualify on any of those counts.

But then, her unexpected company was only Rupert, and he was dead.

"I've been giving this Fernald business some thought," he said. "No tea tray?"

"I'm slimming," Addie said, sucking her tummy in. "And you're too late. There's no point to thinking. The inquest was this morning."

"It's never too late to think, my dear. You don't mind if I sit, do you?" He made himself comfortable in the chair opposite without waiting for her answer. "Are you sure there's no tea tray forthcoming?"

"Positive. And I'm not ringing for one."

"Oh, you are a cruel mistress."

"You'd know all about mistresses," Addie drawled.

"A poisoned dart. Tipped with aconite."

"What are you talking about?"

"Never mind. I have a theory. What if Juliet poisoned Pamela?"

Ridiculous. "Why would she?" Addie asked.

"Jealousy. Spite. Her dream of being the next Lady Fernald."

"She was with John all Sunday afternoon, Rupert."

"So? She might have doctored Pamela's tonic bottle or something. A ticking time bomb just waiting to be ingested."

"Pamela took a tonic?"

"Several. I told you she was witchy. She was a firm believer in natural remedies for everything, and she decanted them herself. Drinks to keep one's hair shiny and face spot-free, etcetera. How do you think she kept so fashionably thin? Purging, my dear." Rupert shuddered.

Yuck. "If Pamela was dead and out of the way, why would Juliet kill herself?"

"Guilty conscience," Rupert said promptly. "I was just getting to that. Thought she could go through with it, but her courage failed her. She always was a mousy little thing. Talked a good game in the beginning but lacked confidence in the end."

"How would you—oh, my God, Rupert! Not her too! Is there ever an end to your conquests?" Juliet Barlow! And here Addie had felt sorry for the woman. Invited her to look at Rupert's damn cars!

He shrugged. "Obviously. I'm dead now. No more fun for me until I get to Heaven."

Addie simply couldn't contemplate fornication in Heaven—it wasn't…seemly. "There is a fly in your ointment. According to Inspector Hunter, falling down stairs is a very ineffective way to kill oneself. He said she should have jumped from the roof instead if she were serious."

"Perhaps she had a fear of heights."

"Rupert, you're reaching. And who spilled gin all over her? Juliet did not drink. 'Lips that touch liquor shall never touch mine' and all that."

"Well, she was fibbing there. I always enjoyed a glass or two."

Or about seven French 75s, a lethal combination of cognac, champagne, lemon juice, and simple syrup, Addie thought darkly, the cause of Rupert's demise.

"Only six. I'll have you know I was not inebriated that freezing February night. I could always hold my liquor. If Claudette hadn't—all right, all right, put your teacup down. I'll spare you the details. Accidents happen."

Addie knew that all too well. "I don't wish to discuss the past. Five days of sneaking around at Fernald Hall and this is all you have? I don't believe this will advance your cause much."

He plucked an invisible thread from his sleeve. "I agree it's too bad Juliet didn't leave a written confession in the pocket of her robe. That would tie things up."

"Too neat by half. Inspector Hunter probably already thought of it and dismissed it. However, I will mention the idea if I get a chance."

"Fine, fine. We can't all be brilliant Anglo-Indian detectives. I'm doing my best for a dilettante, and a dead one at that. But I do know something you don't. Patrick Cassidy never came back from London last night."

Oh dear. "Do you think something happened to him? Is he another victim?"

"You mean was he coshed on the head and thrown onto the tube tracks? Your inspector has made inquiries. So far, the man is nowhere to be found, dead or alive."

Addie didn't even bother with the "your inspector" bit. "He went to London on business, supposedly. Does anyone know where? Maybe he's gone back to Belfast."

Rupert shook his head. "He wouldn't leave those valuable horses behind. Hugh hasn't paid for them yet, what with everyone dropping like flies."

"Ugh. You sound so bloodthirsty."

"Occupational hazard. So, that's two of your admirers who've flown the coop."

"You can't blame me!" cried Addie. "And besides, Lucas is engaged now. I really do wonder where he is. Poor Mr. Hunter."

"Yes. Two of his suspects suspiciously scattering. You know he's not satisfied with the results of the inquest. I almost feel sorry for him."

"That won't get us anywhere. Come on, Rupert. Earn your keep! You must have some inkling of what's really going on."

"Truly, I don't. Believe me, I'm a bloody bloodhound, sniffing and snuffling all over creation. I'm as anxious to put this all behind me as you are. Third time's the charm, remember? And I'm not even counting New York or your equine disaster. Off to Heaven I'll go."

Addie thought Rupert was perhaps being too hopeful. Granted, helping to solve these murder cases was not insignificant, but he had been especially sinful the last years of his life. More might be required.

She wisely kept this thought to herself. As hurtful as he'd been to her during their marriage, she knew Rupert was making a real effort now. Was it too late? Only time would tell.

Chapter Twenty-Five

The thrum of an engine on the front drive made her glance up. Hugh Fernald's Bentley glided over the crushed stone once more. Gracious, she hoped another disaster had not occurred at Fernald Hall. She went to the two-story, multipaned window and peered out.

Rupert was right behind her. "Oh. I forgot to tell you he was on his way."

Detective Inspector Hunter stepped out of the car and adjusted his hat. She hadn't expected to see him until tomorrow and wasn't sure she wanted to now. Addie needed to firmly crush her crush for him—although he was friendly, he made it plain he had no interest in a friendship.

Well, friendship was probably the wrong word.

Look at the state of her! That rat Rupert knew all along Mr. Hunter was coming, and he let her wallow in her disarray. Not that she was especially vain—if she was, she'd never wear her eyeglasses. But her current clothes were suitable for hacking about on a horse—not that she was going to do that again anytime soon—or raking a hayfield or cleaning out a cellar.

It was too late to run upstairs, but her heart raced as if she had. She went back to her chair and household bills, ran her grimy fingers through her disordered bobbed hair (had she even combed it this morning?), and tried to appear relaxed.

Which might work if Rupert left.

"I take it you'd like me to...how did you put it the other day? Scram?"

"Yes, please."

Rupert huffed. "And I bet you'll tell Forbes to fetch tea and all the trimmings. Cucumber sandwiches. Almond crescents. Fruitcake. I'm awfully fond of Cook's fruitcake."

"Maybe."

"You are a coldhearted woman, Addie."

"If I am, you made me that way."

"Very well. I know when I'm not wanted. You behave." He waggled that annoying finger and scrammed.

As if she had a choice to misbehave.

When Forbes entered the room, she didn't even wait for him to ask if she was receiving.

"Yes, yes. Send Mr. Hunter in and have Cook make up a tea tray. It doesn't need to be anything too elaborate."

Forbes raised a silver eyebrow. "Cook wouldn't hear of such a thing. The inspector certainly enjoyed her offerings yesterday. She likes a man with a good appetite. I believe she's very fond of him."

Who wasn't?

Probably all those he'd put behind bars.

Addie rose when Mr. Hunter came through the open vaulted door and managed a smile. Fitz woke up and did his usual dance around the detective's feet, for which he was rewarded with a scratch behind his floppy ears.

"I hope I'm not intruding, Lady Adelaide. I know it's the second day in a row I've arrived uninvited and unannounced."

She might have washed her hands and put on proper clothing, no doubt changing three or four times in the process trying to look presentable. No, more than that. Alluring.

Or at least brushed her teeth.

"Don't be silly—you're always welcome. Do sit down. Forbes will bring in tea shortly."

"That's good news. I didn't have time for lunch after the inquest." He waited for her to sit back down and followed suit. Fitz made an attempt to crawl into his lap but was gently rebuffed.

Tucking the bills inside, Addie shut the ledger. "How did it go?"

A pained look crossed Mr. Hunter's face. "Accidental death for the women, death by misadventure for Ainsley."

Addie was stunned at the latter. "Really?"

"Don't ask. The coroner couldn't preside, and the magistrate who stepped in is an idiot who would have signed anything put in front of him if he could close up shop."

"Was the idiot Sir Alfred Winton? My father always thought the man's horses were smarter."

"Yes. He was more concerned about the Fernalds' reputations than getting to the truth."

"And what is the truth?"

"Damned if I know. It's officially over. I should leave it alone, but I can't. That's why I'm here."

Addie felt absurdly flattered. "How can I help?"

"I know you and Pamela Fernald were not especially close."

"That's true. Hugh was my childhood friend. You don't still think he had something to do with her death, do you?"

"I can't be sure. I'm going out on a limb here, but I trust you not to break my confidence." He drew a breath. "Pamela Fernald was pregnant."

Addie pretended to be surprised. To cement the effect, she dropped her empty teacup to the carpet. It wasn't part of her best set, but she was glad it didn't break anyhow. "Gosh!"

"No one seemed to know except for Mrs. Lewis, and possibly the maid, Murray, who's left the estate, so I can't ask her. And maybe the murderer. I had the hideous task of telling Sir Hugh myself last evening, thinking it might come out in the open courtroom, and I could swear from his reaction he hadn't known beforehand. He was...devastated."

"Oh, how awful for both of you! Was her condition made public?"

"No. Winton was good for something, I guess. I'll bet my eyeteeth someone from the Hall got to him before the inquest to hush it up."

Addie nodded. "That kind of thing does happen here." For example, when Rupert died, the presence of Miss Labelle was pretty much swept under the rug.

"I feel I'm losing my touch. There's something I'm overlooking."

Addie felt guilty for her teacup business, but how could she explain she was aware of Pamela's pregnancy?

"I certainly didn't know last weekend. Never suspected. Otherwise, I wouldn't have told you about Lucas, that is, Lord Waring," she said truthfully. "He can't be the father though. They broke it off months ago."

"The timing is still within the range of possibility, and he's still missing. You haven't heard from him?"

"I haven't, and I'm worried. It's not like him to run away from trouble, honestly it isn't. And what about Mr. Cassidy?"

Mr. Hunter gave her a sharp look. "What about him?"

Uh, she wasn't supposed to know about his disappearance either. "No one really knows him. He lied about Lieutenant

Ainsley, or at least omitted their relationship. What did you find out yesterday?"

"Absolutely nothing. He was not on the train, any of them. He could still be in London, but we've inquired at his usual haunts when he's in Town with no luck—he left behind a very organized appointment book. He had an engagement he never kept. You didn't see him before you left?"

"It was barely light when Beckett and I flew the coop, and we didn't stop down to breakfast." Addie was so anxious to get home—it was almost as if she knew disaster was going to strike again.

Poor Juliet, even if she did sleep with Rupert.

"Mrs. Lewis said he asked for a tray in his room before he was driven to the first train. The chauffeur watched him board with just minutes to spare, but that's as far as we've traced him."

"He couldn't have known about Juliet then."

"Unless he shoved her down the stairs and then went back to bed."

Addie contemplated that as Forbes rolled in an absurdly well-stocked tea tray. If Cook was trying to spoil Inspector Hunter, she was succeeding, and Addie might outgrow the jodhpurs yet.

Between bites, he outlined what he knew of all the details, starting from last Sunday, requiring nothing of Addie but her attention. Once he had eaten a rather amazing amount, albeit sharing crusts and corners with the wiggly beggar Fitz, he sat back in his chair. Addie realized she rarely saw him with the tension out of his shoulders.

"You've been very useful lending your ear. It helps to line up the ducks, as it were. Quack out loud. Bob's a capital fellow, but he tends to see things in black or white. The world is, as you know, gray. A rather dark gray, in my line of work. What jumps out at you from all this?"

"The baby business, honestly. But no one knew?"

"According to Mrs. Lewis, Pamela Fernald's maid surely did. But someone else in the household might have too. A woman would know what signs to look for, if she was looking."

Addie frowned. "Pamela was very close with Simon Davies. Could she have confided in him?"

"He'd never tell me if she had. He's a gentleman of the old school."

"You know how some of them turn out!" Addie reminded him.

"Indeed, I do, to my everlasting regret." He picked up the last raisin biscuit. "Also, according to Mrs. Lewis, Sir Hugh and his wife occasionally shared a bed. So, it's conceivable"—Here he cleared his throat at his own modest joke—"that the baby was legitimate."

"Which makes Pamela's death all the worse." How truly horrible for Hugh. "Where does Juliet fit in?"

"Could she have suspected about the pregnancy? Discovered who killed Pamela?"

"She doesn't—didn't—really mix much with the inhabitants of Fernald Hall—she was devoted to John and spent nearly all her time upstairs with him, or they rode out together. If she knew something, why wouldn't she tell you when you spoke to her?" Addie asked.

"Blackmail? Perhaps she thought she could get the upper hand."

Addie cleared her own throat, trotting out Rupert's theory. "What if Juliet poisoned Pamela, then committed suicide?"

"No note. It's highly unusual for those who kill themselves not to reach out one last time and explain why. In addition, there was no evidence of drink or drugs in Juliet Barlow's system. As I said, throwing oneself downstairs is an iffy plan if one is absolutely determined to commit suicide."

"Well, maybe her death was an accident!"

"Who brought up the gin bottle and poured it all over the poor girl?"

Addie put her hand to her temple. "You are giving me a headache. I don't know how you do this day after day, and we haven't even gotten to Lieutenant Ainsley yet."

"Three suspicious deaths are excessive, I grant you. All very different. Possibly unrelated. And a full complement of innocent-appearing people up to the roof trusses of Fernald Hall. That is, those who are still there and haven't disappeared. Waring and Cassidy both had motive and opportunity, at least for Pamela's death."

Addie objected immediately. "Not this again. I've told you and told you, Lucas is innocent."

"Why not? His mistress was pregnant, and he was about to finally be a bridegroom. He had to protect his reputation. What if Pamela Fernald wanted to make trouble for him?"

"Why would she do that? She'd only bring trouble on her own head."

"People aren't exactly logical under stress," Mr. Hunter said, which was very true.

"All right. Suppose Lucas slipped Pamela the poison somehow. He was gone when Juliet fell."

"But present on occasions when Ainsley was a guest at Fernald Hall. Two out of three, Lady Adelaide."

"You'll never convince me. I know him too well."

Mr. Hunter lifted a dark brow. "Then where is he?"

He had her there, so she shifted to Patrick Cassidy. "Let's agree to disagree. What motive does Mr. Cassidy have? He couldn't have killed his own brother."

"Revenge for his death. Perhaps he found out Pamela Fernald killed him nine years ago."

Addie snorted. "Now you're being ridiculous."

"Didn't she know how to use a gun? I was under the impression she was quite a sportswoman."

"Oh, for heaven's sake. Everyone here shoots. At birds, not people. Even my own mother." Although her eyesight was so bad, she usually missed. "Look, Mr. Cassidy is the type more likely to take a woman to bed than kill her. But I don't think he was at Fernald Hall long enough to accomplish that."

He was pretty skillful though, turning his considerable charm on Addie every time they met. Maybe she was underestimating him.

Did Pamela turn him down, and he slipped something into that silver flask he carried, telling her it was brandy?

Addie hoped he rinsed it out afterwards.

Chapter Twenty-Six

Friday

Last night, she ate a chop in solitary splendor up in her room and slept really well for the first time in days, Fitz curled up against her back in doggie reverie. If she dreamed, she remembered nothing when she woke up on this warm June morning. No kisses from a handsome dark man or anyone else.

Beckett had forgiven her for Wednesday's early rising and unprofessional packing and tucked Addie's curls under a chic black straw cloche.

"You look lovely. For a funeral," the maid said, stepping back to admire her own handiwork.

"I hate funerals." Addie had been to too many of them since last year, reminding her of the war years. She gave away most of her mourning clothes, having sworn off black once she fulfilled her year-long duty as a not-so-bereaved widow. Rupert told her he knew he didn't deserve the respect, but as her mother's daughter, she was still steeped in convention in public. In private, sometimes she chose to wear colors, but thanks to her rigorous upbringing, that felt a little too rebellious for comfort.

Where was Rupert anyway? Not that she wanted him around. Unless he could help her help Mr. Hunter.

Addie had a few minutes before one of the cars was brought around—she'd be driving herself again, looking to make a speedy getaway if she must. So, she took out her notebook from her bedside table to make some notes. Even if the inquests were over, she shared Inspector Hunter's reservations about the outcome.

Who benefits from Pamela's death?

Pamela herself, if she was pregnant and too ashamed to admit infidelity.

The baby's father, his responsibility hidden.

Her whole family, spared the scandal.

The murderer, in some way. One of the above?

She left a few lines blank in case she was struck by sudden genius.

Who benefits from Lieutenant Ainsley's death?

Addie chewed on her pencil. In this situation, not his next of kin even if he had life insurance, since the body was only just discovered. If anything, Patrick Cassidy and his family would have borne the burden of the man's presumed cowardice and desertion for almost a decade, and that was hardly a benefit.

Something happened at Fernald Hall all those years ago that caused the culprit to shoot him. Someone cold-blooded enough and familiar with firearms who could shoot a man between the eyes. One of his comrades, trained in warfare? She wrote a question mark and left several inches of space. She turned the page.

Who benefits from Juliet Barlow's death?

The governess had nothing of value to leave anyone. She hinted she knew Pamela's secret, however, or at least was aware she was unfaithful. Was that why Juliet was killed—to shut her up? Another question mark and many more blank lines.

She slapped the notebook shut. Well, Scotland Yard had

nothing to worry about from her. Inspector Hunter's job was safe for the time being, unless the murderer confessed to her at the funeral.

Addie was out of ideas.

Beckett poked her pert nose back into the bedroom. "The car's in front. Have you got everything you need?"

Addie checked her purse. Lipstick. Comb. A lace-edged handkerchief just in case, although she doubted she'd weep over Pamela unless the vicar improvised and became suddenly poetic. She knew him, though he was not as dull as Edward Rivers at her present parish, Compton St. Cuthbert's. The service was in her old childhood church, St. Mary's, in Broughton Magna. The last time she was inside, it was for her father's funeral.

She shoved the memory away and clicked her purse shut. She might need that handkerchief after all.

The day was fair and fine, but her chauffeur left the top up, a wise move, as Addie didn't want to lose her hat. The car had made the trip from Compton Chase to Broughton Magna many times, both before Addie was widowed and after.

Before, Rupert was usually at the wheel, speeding over back roads with a recklessness that churned Addie's stomach. Her mother approved of Rupert's dashing panache; he was always popular with the ladies, no matter what their age.

And now he made up for it, trying to turn over enough new leaves to make a forest. Addie wondered when he would be finally free to ascend, freeing her as well. She couldn't face another fifty years of his ghostly insouciance, popping up just when she herself was trying to move on.

Imagine if she married again—not that she was ever going to—and was still dealing with Rupert as well as a new husband over the breakfast table. She'd go mad in a month.

Addie drove through Broughton Parva, a collection of very modest cottages hugging the road that housed workers for the three major estates in the area, Ian's, Lucas's and Hugh's. There was a pub—how it remained in business with so few customers was a mystery for the ages—but no shop, church, or post office. Not quite two miles further, the spire of St. Mary's in Broughton Magna loomed over the lush green treetops, and Addie slowed the Lagonda.

A short line of cars were parked along the side of the road, and more than a few people clustered outside the lych-gate. The funeral was by invitation only, but Pamela's village neighbors, whether they were respectful or merely curious, had turned out in force. Addie knew most of them a little, and returned polite greetings, then made her way up the path to the open church doors.

Even with the June breeze, the scent inside the church hadn't changed since her childhood—dust and damp, incense and old leather prayer books. Nor had the temperature, which verged on frigid. Grateful for her gloves and the three-quarter-length sleeves of her pleated crepe dress, she entered the church and saw her cousin Ian up front in the Merrill family pew. She supposed she had as much right to sit there as he did but chose not to be so conspicuous.

Mr. Hunter had a theory—most killers couldn't stay away from their victim's funeral. To test it, Addie noted he was standing against the back wall beneath the new marble Great War memorial plaque that had far too many local boys' names engraved on it. He nodded briefly to her, then resembled the marble behind him, arms folded, stone-still except for his assessing eyes.

Addie slipped into a seat toward the rear. The church was not close to being full. The Fernald family, including young

John, and many of the servants were already in place, some houseguests in two rows behind them. If Addie hoped that Lucas—or Mr. Cassidy—would surface for the occasion, she was disappointed.

Cee called earlier. Their mother was still in London, but a black-bordered handwritten invitation for them both had been delivered. She would drive herself from the Dower House, and Addie said a prayer for the rabbits and hedgehogs and other innocent creatures her sister might encounter. Cee never wore her spectacles, which was awfully silly of her. Waiting, Addie polished her own with the handkerchief in her purse.

The organ music was soft, but sufficiently dirge-like. Sunlight streamed into the panes of the stained-glass windows, though it did not do much for warming up the church. Addie thought of applewood fires and hot cocoa, fur-lined boots and plaid wool scarves. Fox jackets. Better yet, sealskin—she'd heard it was warmer, although she was too soft-hearted to think of the animals' actual fatal contribution to her comfort. She was fairly sure despite her mighty imagination that her breath would form a cloud if she expelled it hard enough. Maybe she could just borrow a live seal to sit on her lap and cuddle.

"Scoot over." It was Cee, who would shortly be sorry for wearing a sleeveless black dress. "Sorry I'm late. I had to nip by the coffin and the pallbearers. Ugh."

"Hush."

"You may be used to being near dead people, but I am not." Cee settled herself against the hard pew and looked around with interest. "There's your inspector." She smiled and gave a cheerful wave to Mr. Hunter, totally inappropriate for the occasion. Addie bit her tongue lest she sound too much like their mother.

Cee turned to her. "Still no Lucas? I thought he might be a pallbearer, but he wasn't outside."

"No. And I'm worried."

"I'm sure he'll turn up. Unless he's the killer."

"Cecilia!" A few faces turned, and Addie felt a flush creep up her neck.

The organ grew louder, distracting people from her outburst. The rector entered with his cross and altar boys, followed by the six men carrying the coffin. Jim Musgrave was one of them, along with Simon Davies, Captain Clifford, and Owen Bradbury. The others were strangers to her.

The service was mercifully brief. Poor brave white-faced John read a passage from the Old Testament, his father from the New. Both struggled, their voices pitched almost too low for the congregation to hear. Together, they added more sprays of white roses to the mass of flowers already on top of the coffin.

Pamela had been Addie's age, and she left behind a husband and son who would never be the same, especially because of the manner of her death. They had loved her. Who would mourn Addie if, God forbid, something happened to her? Her impulsive sister? Her dignified mama? Fitz would forget her in a heartbeat, lured by a dog biscuit or morsel of meat. Addie's own insignificance cloaked her, providing no heat or comfort.

Everyone followed the procession outside to the churchyard, where more words were spoken. Addie and Cee stood to the rear, both unwilling to watch the coffin descend into its grave. A young man a few steps to Addie's right was so overcome, he was actually gulping back sobs. She passed him her own handkerchief.

"Thank you, Lady Adelaide," he murmured when he steadied himself.

"Forgive me, have we met?"

"No, my lady, but everyone roundabout knows you. And your sister too." He smiled at Cee, who was looking much too intrigued. "I'm Colin Stewart. Pamela, that is, Lady Fernald, engaged me to tutor her son. I'm to go to Fernald Hall a bit earlier than I expected."

"Oh! Then you must know about Miss Barlow."

He nodded. Stewart was indeed as attractive as Juliet described, and it was easy to see why a woman might be smitten, although he was terribly young. He was tall, dark, and handsome, looking more like a film star than a teacher. Beckett would swoon.

"I feel a fool for being so upset. One is reminded of one's own mortality at these sorts of things, isn't one?"

As Addie had been doing just that, she nodded.

"What a sinful waste of life—I can hardly believe it," he continued. "Gone much too soon. The world is a sadder place without her."

"Absolutely," said Cee, batting her eyelashes. Honestly, her sister was incorrigible.

Addie did not think he was referring to Juliet. "Yes, death at any age is tragic. John is such a lovely, bright boy. I'm very fond of him. I hope—well, I hope you're patient and kind."

Stewart looked startled. "I've never had complaints."

"These are unusual circumstances, though, aren't they? I imagine that not many of your pupils have recently lost a parent. And their longtime governess."

"That's true, but I can't let that change my approach. I've been hired to prepare him, toughen the lad up for school— believe me, he won't encounter many patient and kind masters or students. You know how it is."

Addie was grateful she didn't.

Chapter Twenty-Seven

Cee was off in a leafy corner of the conservatory, deep in conversation with Colin Stewart, fair head to dark. How very…odd… that the gathering was held in the very place Pamela's body was discovered. The rambling house had at least thirty rooms. Surely one of the several reception rooms would be more appropriate?

Maybe it was a kind of tribute to Pamela. Surrounded by her flowering plants, one saw how talented and passionate she was. The room held every conceivable specimen of orchid, all of them thriving and fragrant in their shiny new majolica pots.

Would Evelyn step in to tend them? The conservatory was her bailiwick before Hugh married Pamela. It must be hard to cede one's position to a daughter-in-law, but Addie sensed no real friction between them. Hugh was the most important person to both of them.

Although…

Pamela's infidelity was almost excusable. To be "good" one hundred percent of the time was impossible in this day and age, with so many temptations readily available. Although Addie was managing, much against her will.

She caught Ian's eye across the brick floor and waved. She

couldn't control her sister like she used to when they were young—Addie was a little general and Cee a willing foot soldier in the mischief she dreamed up at Broughton Park. No more. Cee had her own ideas and informed you at every step.

Their cousin worked his way across the room with his tea-cup, avoiding people and plants alike. He'd been the marquess for the past five years but was still reserved with his neighbors, save for Lucas. As boys, they went to school together. Probably been starved and flogged together, for all Addie knew.

"How was London?" she asked.

"Oh. It was just a quick trip. Got my business attended to and was back home by yesterday afternoon in time to receive my invitation. Terrible thing. Still can't believe it."

"It is that. I don't suppose you bumped into Mama any-where." It was so unlike her to miss the funeral of a friend's family member.

"I did not." He angled his head. "Say, who's that over there with Cecilia?"

Addie could tell he was trying to be casual, but he wasn't entirely believable.

"John's new tutor. You know his governess had an accident Wednesday."

He shook his head. "Is she all right?"

"Not really. She's dead."

Ian blanched. "Good God. Another one? How dreadful. I hadn't heard."

"Well, I don't think it's common knowledge yet, and it's not as though she had many—or really any—friends in the district. People didn't even know about Pamela at first—you didn't. So much is going on here, the servants are too busy to gossip, I guess. Pamela was Juliet's only relative, and with her gone, I have no idea what the family plans. One funeral at a time."

When Addie spoke to Evelyn earlier and offered to help in any way, the older woman was white-faced and overwhelmed. The enormity of the past few days was sinking in. Her sister-in-law Iris never left her side. Addie almost wished her mother were here—she always said and did the right thing and was a firm friend to Evelyn for decades.

"I should get out more. Who's that dark fellow with Hugh?"

Addie felt color flush to her cheeks. "That's Detective Inspector Hunter from Scotland Yard." He was bent over Hugh's wheelchair, and both their faces were as serious as could be.

"Are we suspects in something? Present company excepted. It makes for an awkward event."

"The interviews and inquest are over, and there will be no charges for anyone. The inspector is here as a courtesy." Genius struck. "I always thought the Jordan sisters were innocent, though. Have you met them?"

Ian stood a bit taller. "Those blond girls over there? I don't believe so."

"Let me introduce you," Addie linked her arm through his and led him to the wicker table where the twins sat. They brightened measurably at the sight of a young, good-looking, unmarried marquess, and Addie left Ian to fend for himself.

Perhaps Cee would notice. The twins, for all their faults, were very pretty girls. If Mama was not in favor of a well-connected doctor, she would probably have a stroke over Cee's attraction to a small-town solicitor's son, a tutor several years her junior. Addie couldn't fault Colin Stewart's looks, though. He was almost too handsome. In some ways, he reminded her of Hugh when he was young.

She caught her breath. Had Pamela thought so too? Stewart was awfully emotional at the cemetery for someone who wasn't even employed at Fernald Hall yet, and would "toughen up"

John when he was. But Addie couldn't very well saunter across the conservatory and ask him if he had an affair with the late Lady Fernald. For one thing, her sister would resent her interference, and the other—she was too hot now, as opposed to freezing in church.

She needed air. Addie walked through the open glass door onto the lawn to think—even with windows and doors thrown open, the conservatory was like an oven on such a sunny day. Again, she wondered who'd selected this particular room when there were so many in the house to choose from.

She looked for her handkerchief to blot her throat and remembered Mr. Stewart had it. Was Pamela in pursuit of the young tutor before she died? In books, it was always the opposite—the innocent governess got in trouble with the brooding master.

"Huh. What a cunning mind you have."

Addie stopped her handbag from slipping off her wrist onto the grass. "Go away," she whispered, turning her back to all the windows.

"No one can hear us," Rupert said, adjusting his necktie, which had looked perfect to start with. Addie was beginning to wish he'd change out of the clothes he was buried in, but apparently that wasn't part of his improvement program. He shaved, however, knowing how much she disliked his moustache. Without it, he looked much younger and more innocent, the latter a very false impression. "They're all busy gabbing away, pretending they didn't kill Pam and Juliet, no matter what the findings were."

"How come you didn't see that coming anyway? Or was it just an accident?"

He shrugged. "I can't be everywhere at once. And there's no 'just' about an accident that leads to a death."

"I didn't mean it that way and you know it!" She set her

purse down on an overturned flowerpot by the door and moved through the garden at a rapid clip. If Rupert couldn't keep up with her, too bad.

Of course he could, even when she was practically running. Out of breath, she sank down on the grass behind a bank of blown pink peony bushes, their sweet-scented petals scattered everywhere, as if she was a girl playing hide-and-seek.

"Your bottom will get damp," Rupert said.

"Stop thinking about my bottom! Why are you badgering me again?"

Rupert dropped down next to her. "I just thought I'd pay my respects." He produced a ripe strawberry and a slice of seedcake from his pocket and ate them.

He had come for the food. "You have no new information for me?"

"I'm trying, I'm trying. You simply don't appreciate the lengths I've gone to."

"Like spying on Mr. Hunter in the bath," Addie said accusingly.

"A minor skirmish. I feel I'm on the verge of a breakthrough, though. I'm going into the village tonight."

"Broughton Magna?"

"The very one."

"What are you going to do there?"

"I'm sure the spirit will move me in the right direction."

Addie hoped it would move him to a higher plane. And soon.

She shivered, even though she'd been too warm not ten minutes ago.

"You're going to miss me when I'm gone," Rupert said, confident.

"I missed you when you were gone the first time." Although it didn't make sense. Her guilty relief had been tinged with regret.

A marriage that was so promising in the beginning foundered with Rupert's infidelity. Addie lost count of the betrayals.

He took her hand, and she didn't pull away. "I know it was all my fault. Every bit of it. You are a priceless pearl, and I didn't value you enough."

"Let's not get carried away." Rupert always had a way with words. Most times he talked himself out of any jam he got into.

A stone wall, however, was obdurate.

"Oh, you snore when you sleep. Now, now, it's true—you don't know it because you are asleep. Fitz won't tell you—he snores too. Besides, dogs don't talk. But any flaws you have are minor in comparison to mine. I do want you to be happy, Addie. Never doubt it." He passed her his handkerchief.

"I don't need that."

He gave her a look, and she blew her nose. "It's the peonies. I must be allergic to them too." Which would be unfortunate, as they were her favorite flowers.

"Funerals are no fun. I've been to too many of them." The war years had been hellish on his friends.

"Were you at yours?" So many of his lovers were.

"No. I'm not sure where I was—it's rather hazy. But then last August I more or less woke up, and here I am. At your service."

"I should get back." She gave him the soggy handkerchief, and it miraculously returned to its starched condition. "How do you do that?"

"Beats me. I'm getting damn sick of this tie, you know. You could have buried me in my uniform. I'd have more gravitas."

"You always said living up to your heroic exploits was a bore," Addie reminded him.

"It's all a bore." He waved his hand between them. "This entire premise. Guardian angeling. But I shall do my best, never fear." And with a salute, he was gone.

Chapter Twenty-Eight

When she returned to the conservatory from her tête-à-tête with Rupert, Mr. Hunter wasn't there. According to Hugh, he was on a call with Scotland Yard.

She hoped he wasn't in trouble. Everyone was satisfied with yesterday's results except the detective and herself. Surrounded by his son, good friends, and neighbors, Hugh even laughed a time or two. Life would go on here.

The mourners began to thin out. Addie waited for Mr. Hunter as long as she could without looking obvious before deciding to drive home. Cee was still entranced by Colin Stewart, and the twins were eating Ian up with two spoons, so she abandoned her matchmaking. Kissing the Fernalds goodbye, she asked Trim to have her car brought around.

The sky was forget-me-not blue, too pretty a day for memories of death. Addie tried to lift her spirits, mostly in vain.

They were all missing something. Someone. Too many "accidents," in Addie's not-so-humble opinion. No wonder Mr. Hunter was not happy and couldn't let it go.

She rumbled over a cattle grate, startling her from her grim thoughts, and decided to appreciate the beauty around her.

When she got home, Addie changed into something more comfortable. Not as comfortable—or sloppy—as yesterday's wrinkled shirt and jodhpurs, since she had a niggling feeling that Mr. Hunter might stop by before he left the area.

At least she hoped he did. She wanted to say a proper goodbye, even if they both were not convinced of the proper disposal of the cases.

It might be the last time she ever saw him.

Butter-yellow linen sheath, matching yellow shoes. She was a ray of sunshine, except her hair was a trifle flat from being underneath her hat all day. Addie clasped a string of amber beads around her neck and went downstairs with a book.

She didn't have too long to wait. The Bentley deposited Mr. Hunter in her drive, suitcase and briefcase in hand. Fitz barked at the doorbell and raced out of the Great Room.

Even her dog knew a good thing when he saw it.

Forbes announced Mr. Hunter and he entered, holding Fitz in the crook of his arm. The dog was vibrating with happiness, and Addie envied him.

Mr. Hunter set him down. "Third day in a row. You'll be glad to see the back of me."

"Not at all! I missed you after the funeral. Thank you for coming by. May I get you anything?"

"With reluctance, no. The next train to London leaves soon. I just stopped to say goodbye."

"Thank you. Won't you sit down at least?"

"Only for a minute."

He lowered himself into the embroidered wing chair, looking weary. It had been a hard week for everyone.

"What's next for you, Inspector?"

"More theft and murder, I expect."

Addie shuddered. "I don't know how you cope."

"Someone has to. There's a lot of evil in the world." He gazed around the paneled room, with its vaulted ceiling and sparkling windows. "Not here, though. Your home is very…cozy, Lady Adelaide. Peaceful. And you are good company."

"Th-thank you."

"Thank you for your help. I know you did your best."

It was all thanks to Rupert, but Addie couldn't say that.

In fact, she couldn't say anything. She was afraid if she opened her mouth, she'd blurt out something entirely inappropriate for the occasion.

The awkward silence was broken by Forbes, who carried in a tea tray. It was hastily assembled, with just a pot, cups, and a plate of biscuits. Four kinds, since Cook was still trying to impress. She always had water on the boil.

"I know you don't have much time, sir, but Cook insisted," Forbes said. "There's always time for a cup of tea."

Addie was grateful that pouring the tea gave her something to do and something else to look at besides Inspector Hunter's dark eyes. She handed him a cup.

"I'll miss our chats," he said.

Oh, he really was making this difficult.

"I will too." She bit into a biscuit, which tasted like sawdust.

"And I'll miss Cook. You are lucky to have such devoted servants."

"Yes, I am." She wondered who cooked for Mr. Hunter in London. His mother? She knew they lived in the same building.

He swallowed half the cup at one go. "I should be leaving."

Through the window, Addie saw a taxi come up the drive. "Did you arrange for a car to take you to the station? That was unnecessary—my chauffeur can take you. Or I can, if you don't mind driving with me again." She referred to last spring, where she was behind the wheel, a murderer at her side, Mr. Hunter tied up in the backseat.

He looked out the window. "Not I. It appears you have another surprise visitor, Lady Adelaide." He whistled, and Fitz cocked his head, ears lifting. "Speak of the devil."

In less than a minute, the devil pushed past Forbes in the doorway. His face was…green, or close enough, his suit stained, his hair rumpled.

"I'm glad to find you here, Hunter. Someone tried to kill me."

"Sit down before you fall down, Mr. Cassidy." Mr. Hunter gave up his chair and guided the man to it. Patrick Cassidy was so unsteady he nearly toppled over despite the detective's firm grip.

"May I pour you some tea? I think it's still hot," Addie said.

Mr. Cassidy shuddered. "Not unless you want me to ruin your carpet. Persian, isn't it?"

"It was Rupert's grandmother's." Only slightly moth-eaten, the colors still vibrant. But Mr. Cassidy was obviously not here to discuss home furnishings. "Why do you think someone tried to kill you?"

"Because I nearly died. Had to get off the train at Swindon, I was in such agony. Stopped at the first hotel I found near the station and spent two days…well, I don't want to disgust you with the details. The doctor the hotel management called in told me I had food poisoning and gave me something wretched to take, and I lay abed wanting to die."

Mr. Hunter dragged another chair over to the fireplace. "Why did you come here?"

"I wasn't about to go back to Fernald Hall and risk a second whack at me, was I, even if all my belongings are in my room. I thought the lovely Lady Adelaide could put me in contact with you in case you were still there without arousing any suspicion from those wicked people. Somebody's out to get me, just like they did Michael."

"Ah, yes," Mr. Hunter said, leaning forward. "Why didn't you tell me he was your half brother?"

"I didn't want that lot to know who I was. Thought I might nose about and find out what really happened to him. Desertion!" Cassidy's face twisted in anger. "The shame of it killed my mother. She never recovered, wondering where he was. Why he did such a thing. She might not have raised him, but he was her firstborn son, and she loved him, maybe more than she loved me. It was easy for the influenza to carry her off, and my father with her. Someone topped Michael, and let the world think he was a coward." He paused, trying to gain control. "How did you discover we were related?"

"Telegrams came late Tuesday." Mr. Hunter looked thoughtful. "Someone else might have read them before I did."

"And that someone put something nasty in my breakfast early Wednesday! Food poisoning, my arse. Begging your pardon, Lady Adelaide. I was running late and never ate it all, thank the good Lord, or I might not be sitting here."

"Who brought your tray up?" Mr. Hunter asked.

"One of the maids. I didn't pay much attention. As I said, I was dashing about to get dressed and told the girl to put it on the table. I didn't even look at her face."

One didn't, Addie thought ruefully. For many, servants were just part of the domestic landscape, like so much moving furniture. She liked to think it wasn't that way at Compton Chase.

"I can ask Mrs. Lewis. Somehow I don't see her or the maid as the culprit, however."

"Could it have been a simple case of food poisoning?" Addie wondered aloud. "Accidents happen even in the best of households. Food does spoil, even with modern refrigeration. Did the doctor test any of the, uh, effluvia?"

Mr. Cassidy shook his head. "By the time he saw me, the worst of it passed. I didn't think of poison at first—why would I?—but the longer I lay in that hotel room, the more sense it made. I was meant to disappear in London and die there in the street like a dog."

Good heavens. The man was dramatic, but Addie supposed he had every right if what he suspected was true.

"What did you ingest?"

"Coffee. A few mouthfuls of porridge. Half a slice of toast. As I said, I was in a rush."

"Sugar, cream, butter, and jam as well?"

Mr. Cassidy thought for a moment. "No jam. There was some on the tray—marmalade and honey, too, if my recollection is accurate, but I never used any of it. The coffee tasted bitter, even after sugar and cream."

"Did the kitchen know your preferences? For example, that you use sugar in your coffee?"

"I have no idea, do I? I'm not a cook. Does it matter?"

"It would be helpful to know how the poison got into your system, if poison it was. Mr. Trim keeps a book of guests' menus—they're very organized over there. I'll have to take a look at it."

"You mean if I drank black coffee, they wouldn't bother tampering with the sugar bowl."

"Precisely. If someone at Fernald Hall wanted to kill you, they'd make sure you actually drank or ate what was contaminated." Mr. Hunter looked over to her. "Lady Adelaide, I intended to go home tonight. Would it inconvenience you to put me up here for a day or two, as well as Mr. Cassidy?"

"Of course not! You're both welcome." One a little more than the other, to be truthful.

She'd have to say goodbye all over again, wouldn't she?

"I think it best if Mr. Cassidy lays low. We don't need to advertise he's here, especially to the inhabitants of Fernald Hall. May I count on the discretion of your staff?"

"We're a good twenty miles away, practically in another world in some ways. I'll speak to them."

"As will I. And if I could borrow a car tomorrow, I'll pay another visit to gather up your things, Mr. Cassidy, since you are now officially a missing person."

Cassidy smiled for the first time. "I am? Who reported me?"

"Let's see. You were to meet with a Mr. Garvin for lunch at Rules on Wednesday, were you not?"

"You are thorough."

"You left your appointment book behind. No wonder we didn't find you in London if you've been holed up in Swindon all this time."

"I'm sure the town has its attributes, but I'm not aware of them," Mr. Cassidy said with another smile. He was looking slightly less green, which was a relief. "What's to happen with my horses? I'd guess you're not going to bring them here."

"I'm sure they'll be well taken care of at Hugh's stables. Pamela was very particular about her horses, and the grooms were hired with that in mind," Addie said. She might not be much of a horsewoman, but it was indisputable that Fernald Hall was famous in Gloucestershire and beyond for its hunters.

"When do I become unmissing?"

"When I'm satisfied that no one tried to kill you. It will be hard to prove, but then everything that's happened this week falls into that category," Mr. Hunter replied.

Addie rose. "I'll inform Forbes and Mrs. Drum that you'll both be staying, and I'll see you at dinner." Cook would be pleased; Addie lived so quietly now that the woman had little opportunity to show off her culinary skills. Even at short notice, Addie knew dinner was bound to be delicious.

She left the gentlemen to discuss the recent events and went down to the kitchen wing. Forbes was observing a footman who was polishing already perfectly polished silver in the butler's pantry and took the news with his usual sangfroid. Mrs. Drum and Cook (whose real name was Mrs. Oxley) were sharing a pot of tea and seemed exceptionally pleased that their mistress was entertaining two gentlemen for the foreseeable future, even if no one was to mention it. Cook disappeared into the larder for extra provisions, and Addie went up to her room to freshen up.

Rupert lounged on her bed, looking much too comfortable, as usual.

"Now what?" she snapped.

"Now, now, pet. Someone has to chaperone you. All the old things you employ will turn a blind eye to any hijinks. And Beckett will try to bully you into someone's arms. My presence is absolutely necessary."

Where was Beckett? Her presence was absolutely necessary too to make some semblance of order to Addie's person.

"Lurking about the kitchen garden, last time I looked. Jack is weeding and she is trying desperately to distract him. She has turned up the hem of her uniform by at least two inches, the little minx."

"Stop listening to my thoughts!"

"Entirely inadvertent, I assure you. Are you satisfied with Cassidy's explanation, or is it a bunch of malarkey?"

Addie tried to fluff up her hair with little success. "He certainly looks dreadful."

Rupert sat up and smoothed down his jacket. How could he be so immaculate when he was so very dead? "He could have dosed himself, don't you think?"

"Why would he do that?"

"To gain sympathy. To cast aspersions upon the residents of Fernald Hall and deflect his own guilt."

"You are suspicious."

"Always, when it comes to the males of the species. You are far too trusting, Addie."

Guilty as charged, at least when it came to Rupert. Talk about turning blind eyes—she wore a sack over her head for much of their marriage. "What do you think he's done?"

"We can assume he didn't kill his brother, but really, how do we know? He could have got leave, snuck up on the poor fellow, and pulled a Cain and Abel. We only have his word for it that they were on good terms."

Addie put the hairbrush down. It was hopeless, requiring the talents of her absent maid. "It should be easy enough to check if he had leave at the time. I expect Mr. Hunter has already done that."

Rupert snorted. "Do you honestly think our government is one hundred percent reliable when it comes to keeping paperwork? You've never been in the British Royal Flying Corps. It's either fifteen smudged copies which are entirely illegible or none at all. No, mark my words—there's something off about Patrick Cassidy."

Chapter Twenty-Nine

Friday evening

Rupert's words lingered in Addie's head. Thank heavens he wasn't seated at the other end of the table eavesdropping, although for all Addie knew, he was under it, hiding like a naughty child. She pulled her skirt down and made sure her ankles were crossed.

Mr. Cassidy's color had improved, although his appetite remained delicate. However, the inspector made up for that and then some. Mr. Hunter enjoyed his food and was able to pack it away without adding any extra pounds to his superb masculine physique. Addie was a trifle jealous, already feeling as if she was born in the wrong decade. Even if she starved herself, which she would never do for fear of Cook, the boyish figure that was all the rage at the moment would never be hers. The current crop of Merrill women were curvy, curly-haired, and nearsighted, and that was that. One could not fight biological destiny, no matter how many puddings one reluctantly pushed away.

Addie was anxious for Mr. Cassidy to go upstairs to bed, as she wished to discuss Rupert's reservations with the inspector.

Did the Irishman make up his story? At this point, she didn't believe anyone. She was gullible once, but those days were long gone, thanks to Rupert and the dead bodies that kept accumulating.

The three of them adjourned to the drawing room for coffee. Conversation lagged despite her effort to be a good hostess. Her mother, the dowager marchioness, would be disappointed at her lack of vivacity. They'd exhausted Irish politics, the current dry spell, and whether a woman could realistically infiltrate a criminal gang dressed as a boy. Clara Bow was going to do just that in *Lawful Cheaters*. The film wasn't out until next month (Beckett read all about it in one of her magazines), and Addie wanted to give the actress the benefit of the doubt.

How amusing it would be to masquerade in men's clothes! However, Mr. Hunter and Mr. Cassidy thought the plot was ridiculous. According to Mr. Hunter, in his professional opinion, no self-respecting gang member would be so stupid, and Mr. Cassidy (as a professional ladies' man, Addie supposed) agreed a man would have to be blind and deaf both to fall for such a thing. Men were men, and women were women. Period.

Addie held her tongue. The odds were against her.

Mr. Cassidy finally stifled a yawn.

"Goodness! We're keeping you up after your dreadful ordeal. Why don't you go on up to bed?"

Mr. Cassidy gave her a crooked smile. "I'll need an escort, I'm afraid. I've forgotten where my room is. Your house is quite ancient, isn't it? All higgledy-piggledy."

Forbes took both men to their rooms earlier to settle in before dinner, but Addie could empathize. When she was a new bride here, she often got confused in the Jacobean part, much to her embarrassment.

Before Mr. Hunter could volunteer to guide the way and she

lost him for the evening, she sprang up and rang for Forbes. The butler appeared almost instantly and escorted Mr. Cassidy out of the room.

"I'm rather tired myself," Mr. Hunter said, trying to make his own escape.

"I won't keep you too much longer. I know you have a busy day tomorrow."

"Turning up like a bad penny. They probably think they saw the last of me and won't welcome me with open arms." He sighed. "I admit I'm not looking forward to it."

"No, I imagine not. Do you think someone at Fernald Hall will slip up and reveal themselves?"

"I can hope, but—" He paused. "There is not one thing that is straightforward in any of this. After the verdict yesterday, I know I'm expected to leave everything alone. This Cassidy business adds a new wrinkle, but I'm not certain I believe him."

Addie nodded. "Exactly! I've had, um, a hunch. What if he's pretending to be poisoned?"

Mr. Hunter smiled. "Lady Adelaide, you have a diabolical mind. It's too convenient, isn't it? Him disappearing the morning Juliet Barlow is found, then claiming someone's trying to murder him. But he was quite convincing, didn't you think? The color of his face was unnatural."

Addie nodded. She saw her fair share of plays, however, and knew stage makeup could produce amazing effects. Had Mr. Cassidy ever aspired to be a thespian? Maybe Clara Bow could give him some pointers. "I don't know who to believe anymore. It's very vexing."

"As a detective, I've found it best to believe no one at first. But one can't go through life as a civilian like that. It's too... dispiriting."

"Speaking of spirits, would you like a brandy?" He passed on the wine at dinner, probably because he felt as if he was still on duty interviewing Mr. Cassidy. His conversation was skillful, lulling the man to disclose more about his half brother than he might have.

"No, thank you. But don't let that stop you."

"You know I don't have much of a head for alcohol." Last summer, she had far too much to drink, thanks to Rupert crashing her dinner with the detective. Mr. Hunter was required to put her to bed.

Chastely, damn it. Or at least she was pretty sure. He removed her shoes, but he was not the sort of man who would take advantage.

Not like Rupert. He was not meant for marriage, and she had very nearly forgiven him. Edward Rivers, the newish vicar at Compton St. Cuthbert's, went on at great lengths every Sunday about forgiveness. Some of his words inevitably penetrated, even though Addie often composed her weekly to-do list during the service.

But back to the problem at hand. She noted Mr. Hunter pretended not to remember her inebriation and was grateful for his gentlemanly forbearance.

"I'm trying to winnow the suspects down to a manageable number. It's a shame Juliet Barlow had her accident—she'd be a fine murderess. The alienation and bad blood between the cousins."

"She practically threw herself at Hugh at dinner Tuesday evening. Evelyn couldn't have liked that."

"Hmm." He tapped his chin. "Lady Fernald is an interesting woman. Imposing."

"Like my mama. They're good friends, actually. They both put family first and have wills of iron." Addie reflected that Evelyn Fernald was an outsize force in her son's life from her widowhood on. When he'd come home so injured, talk was that he'd not survive for long. Between Evelyn and Pamela, they'd made Hugh prove the experts wrong.

But Evelyn Fernald wouldn't shoot Michael Ainsley or poison her daughter-in-law. Push Juliet down the stairs. Try to kill Patrick Cassidy with putrid porridge. It was simply unthinkable.

"A bit like you then."

"Me?"

"You're loyal to your family. You saved your sister's life," he reminded her. "To the untrained eye, you may appear to be soft and fluffy, but any sensible person wouldn't want to cross you. You are every bit as stubborn as your Fitz with a bone."

Was this a compliment? Addie rather thought it was, and barely knew what to say. Fluffy? Really? When in doubt, just smile, her mama would say. So she did.

Mr. Hunter looked pointedly at his watch. "It's late. I want to make an early start in the morning. May I borrow one of your cars?"

Addie's cheeks grew hot. Rupert's cars were famous in the area. The Fernalds would know who provided the policeman's transportation, and tongues would wag. But it wasn't as if they were unchaperoned. There was Mr. Cassidy. A houseful of servants.

And Rupert.

"Of course."

He quirked a dark brow. "You do have something that's not too flashy, don't you? I wouldn't want to give the wrong impression. Or get accustomed to the high life."

"There are seven to choose from. It's really quite ridiculous to keep them all." And all were fairly flashy. Her late husband had a need for speed.

"My father is fond of his Morris but doesn't really use it much.

He rarely leaves Chelsea, and between you and me, I don't believe he sees well enough to drive anymore. He'd be better off with one of the horses he rode when he was with the Military Mounted Police. Those animals know their way around."

"Does he still ride?" Addie asked.

"He does. He and an old army friend ramble about in Hyde Park every so often on rented nags. He claims it's much too tame after India, but the outings never fail to raise his spirits, even if he aches like the devil afterwards."

"My father had great hopes for me as a horsewoman, but I'm afraid I don't live up to them."

"Not everyone can be a Pamela Fernald. I'm sure you have other accomplishments," he said politely.

Did she? Addie couldn't think of one right at the moment. Oh, she was charitable, but really, how much money could one woman spend on herself? She had everything she needed.

Almost.

Chapter Thirty

Saturday

In the end, there was a choice between seven utterly unsuitable cars, and the truck that young Jack Robertson used to fetch gardening supplies. That vehicle, because it was part of the Compton estate, was so immaculate that one could have dined happily on its flatbed without incident. There was only the vaguest whiff of spent blooms and compost, and the leather seats gleamed with saddle soap, thanks to the elderly grooms who maintained the garage and clearly missed their horses.

Jack had no objection to Dev borrowing the truck for the morning. It was his day off, and he and Beckett were to picnic later but would walk to their preferred spot on the land. Dev had no idea how many acres Lady Adelaide possessed—hundreds, probably. He was very much out of his element here, although everyone made him feel accepted.

But he felt remorse—he was using Lady Adelaide's home as a base of operations, hiding a potential suspect there, and possibly giving her the wrong impression about their relationship again.

The devil of it was, when he was with her, he enjoyed their conversations. Enjoyed looking at her.

Far too much.

He kissed her a few months ago. But that kiss was not to be repeated. She was a distraction he didn't need, and couldn't afford, in all senses of the word.

So Dev did what he did best—compartmentalized, focused solely on the family and friends at Fernald Hall and reviewed the case in all its opaqueness as he drove those twenty miles through the green countryside.

For a city fellow, he had an unexpected appreciation for Gloucestershire. When he was here on the Grant case last August, he very much enjoyed tramping down the lanes to think.

He wished a good brisk walk would help him now. A policeman for more than a dozen years (with a hiccup in the middle for his war service and recuperation when his foot was nearly blown off), he had never encountered anything quite as baffling as this Fernald business.

A beautiful, young, unfaithful wife, poisoned. The husband would be the obvious suspect in other circumstances, but Hugh Fernald, because of his immobility and clear affection for his wife, was unlikely. But could someone have acted under his direction?

A poor relation, with little to no influence. Why would someone arrange her death to appear to be a drunken accident? No one would benefit from her death, unless it was to silence her.

A soldier. Friend. Shot and buried for nearly a decade. What had the man done to deserve such a fate?

Dev knew these three disparate deaths were related, but damned if he could see how. And Cassidy's alleged mishap was just the icing on a most indigestible cake.

He drove through the open gates of Fernald Hall, its distinctive Tudor chimneys visible over the trees at the end of the long driveway. If anyone spotted him in the truck, they'd think he was a tradesman and expect him to go round to the back. But he rolled up to the nail-studded front door, and it wasn't long before Trim opened it, a frown upon his face until he saw the vehicle's occupant.

"Inspector Hunter! Are you expected? No one told me."

"I should have called first." Dev deliberately had not. He hoped to arrive before the household was awake, although any element of surprise was going to be lost once the servants got wind of his presence.

"We thought you returned to London."

"I would have, save for a directive from Deputy Commissioner Olive," Dev fibbed. "Patrick Cassidy has been reported missing."

Trim looked flummoxed. "Missing, sir? We thought he stayed in Town to, uh, avoid the unpleasantness here."

"No. He never met the fellow he was to have lunch with Wednesday. An important business acquaintance who reported it, he was that worried. It's been more than seventy-two hours since Cassidy was last seen. I'd like to speak to everyone who had an interaction with him before he left. And if you would be so good to see that his belongings are packed up, I'll take them with me."

"Is that usual, Mr. Hunter? What if he comes back here?"

"Scotland Yard is reliably safe, Mr. Trim. It even has a safe. I'll make sure his possessions are returned to him intact."

The butler nodded. "Of course. I'll see to it. I presume you'd like to interview the kitchen staff. One of the maids brought up his breakfast tray—I'm not sure which one. Mrs. Lewis will know. And then there's Evans, the chauffeur."

"You didn't see Cassidy leave?"

Trim winced. "I did. I opened the door for him, as I was nearby when he came down. But that was all. I don't even think he wished me a good morning. He was late leaving for the first train. It wasn't our fault—his breakfast was brought up at the time he requested, but he was still getting dressed. Evans waited for him in front of the house for quite a while."

"What was your impression of him that morning?"

"Well, as I said, he was in a rush. He seemed annoyed." Trim paused. "His hair wasn't combed to its usual standard, but then he put on his hat."

"He showed no signs of illness?"

"I wouldn't say so. Mr. Cassidy looked perfectly healthy to me, but of course I'm no expert. Do you suppose he's fallen ill somewhere?" the butler asked.

"Anything is possible. Cassidy definitely left before Miss Barlow's body was discovered on the back stairs?"

"Oh, yes. A good half hour before. And well after Lady Adelaide departed."

Dev pulled out his new notebook. "I'm curious if he had any dietary requirements or preferences. Would you recall offhand, or do you need to consult your book?"

"I'd have to look in the book. The past week has been very stressful, you know."

Didn't Dev just. "Thank you, Mr. Trim. Will you also notify Sir Hugh that I'm here when he's awake? I don't want to disturb him, but I'd like a word with him too when it's convenient."

Strictly speaking, he should ask the baronet's permission to speak to the staff first. But damn it, three murders had been committed, no matter what was decided at the inquest. "I know my way to the kitchen."

It was good that Dev's sense of direction was impeccable, for the layout of Fernald Hall was Byzantine. He passed several surprised housemaids, who were carrying breakfast trays upstairs.

So much for his attempt at stealth.

Mrs. Lewis was squinting at a list in her hand, bedecked in a spotless cap and apron. She looked pleased to see him, a welcome he was not generally used to.

"Mary, you finish Mr. Davies's tray. It's just the tinned fruit left. What can we do for you, Inspector? I didn't think to see you again."

"I had a change of plans. Mr. Cassidy is considered a missing person, and I have a few questions for you and the kitchen staff."

"Really! We wondered where he'd got to, didn't we, Mary? He and Lord Waring both, though at least Lord Waring took his things with him. I do hope they're all right somewhere."

"Are the other guests still here?" Dev asked.

"Mr. Davies is staying until a decision is made about the improvements. Everyone else plans to leave after lunch tomorrow. To try and make the best of the week and support Sir Hugh." The Jordan sisters, Clifford, and Bradbury. The captain was cutting it fine joining up with his regiment, wasn't he?

"Can you remember who brought Mr. Cassidy's tray to him Wednesday morning?"

"I did, sir," Mary said, vigorously cutting into a can of grapefruit segments with an opener. "But when I brought it down, he'd barely touched it."

"What was on it?"

"Everything he asked for," Mrs. Lewis said. "Coffee, Irish oatmeal, wheat toast."

"Who made the tray up?"

"I did myself. I remember, since I cooked a special pot of porridge for him every morning. He said it was like a good bran mash to his horses for him. Got him ready for his day. Very fussy, he was."

"Who else knew of the oatmeal?"

"Why, it was in this year's book." She pointed to the Welsh dresser, where a diary lay next to a wooden bowl of walnuts. "Are you thinking he's been poisoned too? I wouldn't do such a thing, Inspector! Surely you know that!"

Mrs. Lewis was offended, and Dev regretted the thrust of his questions. But really, he couldn't omit Mrs. Lewis from his list just because he liked her.

"No, no. I just wondered how he seemed before he left, and if anything he ate might have caused him distress. He never arrived at his luncheon appointment."

"Well, you can take the oatmeal away and have it tested!" The housekeeper went into the pantry, emerging with a tin that had "Mr. Cassidy" written on a strip of masking tape. "He brought it with him in his suitcase! As if our old-fashioned English oatmeal wasn't good enough for him."

"Thank you." Anyone who visited the kitchen had access to it, then. Cassidy himself was in the kitchen with Lady Adelaide. Had he tampered with it while he was wooing her with hot milk?

The young maid picked up the tray, looking anxious to escape Mrs. Lewis's wrath. "Mary, before you go upstairs, how did Mr. Cassidy seem to you Wednesday morning?"

"I dunno, sir. All I did was set his breakfast on the table in his room. He never said nothin' but 'enter.' He was doing up his tie in the mirror and never looked at me or even said thank you."

"Well, I thank you, Mary." Dev smiled at her, and she turned scarlet as she fled the kitchen.

"Now, what's this all about, Mr. Hunter? The man's probably gone to meet a lady friend somewhere. Thinks he's God's gift, doesn't he?"

"Did he flirt with you, Mrs. Lewis?"

The housekeeper gave him a look that reminded him of his mother. "Don't be silly. But he was even after Lady Adelaide's little maid, her eyes as big as saucers. I don't need a man like that around my girls."

Did she dislike the fellow enough to make him sick? Dev really hoped not.

Chapter Thirty-One

Mr. Cassidy was sleeping in. Understandable. He had a scare, and Addie asked her servants not to disturb him. Whenever he awoke, he should be given whatever he wanted.

Just like the old days, when guests slept their hard-earned hangovers away at one of Rupert's wild house parties. The staff at Compton Chase was unused to company since her husband died, and even before that. Addie found it difficult—to say the least—to entertain his mistresses and rackety friends the year or two before he landed in Limbo. As a hostess, she felt like the soggiest of wet blankets, but it was very hard to remain cheerful when one's husband was cheating with virtually anyone of the female persuasion.

Addie wondered what kind of progress Mr. Hunter made some twenty miles away as she sat at the breakfast table. She didn't envy him one bit, returning to the scene of multiple crimes. No one, including the guilty party or parties, would like that. Would he be safe?

Her heart stuttered. A few months ago, she thought he was dead. Until he winked at her. The overwhelming feeling of joy—

And of her own guilt too. It was her fault he came so close to being murdered himself. Addie shook the memory away, locked it up in a padded room just like the perpetrator was in now.

"My, you've a hard case of the blue-devils, haven't you?"

Rupert was inspecting the covered dishes on the sideboard. Thank heavens Forbes left the room to get her a fresh pot of tea.

She whispered anyway. "What are you doing here?"

"I caught a ride to Fernald Hall with your inspector and am back to make my report."

Addie didn't even bother correcting him. Really, what was the point? She supposed Mr. Hunter was as much hers as anybody's.

Rupert fished out a mushroom from one of the chafing dishes and popped it in his mouth. "In the truck," he said, chewing. "Reminded me of my flying days, bumping along the French countryside to the airfield, adrenalin flowing. Young Jack's truck does not, as you might expect, provide the smoothest of rides. I must say your policeman friend is overly cautious in terms of speed, so it wasn't too hair-raising or bone-shattering or much fun, really. But I'm glad I went."

Did Rupert ride in the back, or next to Mr. Hunter? On top of the cab, like a genie on his rug? The image was preposterous, but then, this entire situation was preposterous.

Including Forbes entering just then with the tea. Rupert waggled his tongue at him and thumbed his nose. He never really cared for Forbes, as Forbes never really cared for him. The butler was always proper and deferential, but there was a slight hint of disapproval at his master's life choices, shown by a discreetly raised eyebrow or a nearly silent sniff on requisite occasions. He knew Addie since she was ten years old and was a very loyal retainer.

"Thank you, Forbes." Addie reached for the sugar. "I think I'll take a cup with me out into the garden. It's a lovely day, isn't it?"

"It is, indeed, my lady. Though some might like a little rain to fall. I understand the farmers are concerned."

Which reminded her of Lucas. She wondered if Rupert had word of him and hurried out the morning room's French door that Forbes held open for her.

"Alone at last!"

"Not yet! We're still too near the house," she muttered. It was unfair that Rupert could read her mind when she didn't have the faintest clue about what made him so puffed up with pride this morning.

She whisked him through the lavender-lined walkway, sloshing tea onto the saucer. At the end of the path was a weathered bench under an arbor of pink climbing roses. Jack was doing a yeomanly job keeping the garden watered, as their part of the world was in near-drought conditions. The ornamental lake on the estate was low, though the ducks hadn't noticed.

Addie sat down, pointedly placing the teacup beside her so Rupert would have to stand. "All right. What is it? You look like the cat who's drunk up every last drop of cream and is too full to ask for more."

"This is a bombshell, my dear. I've cracked the case. I have every right to be proud. " Rupert straightened his straight tie and shot his cuffs. It was as if he expected celestial trumpets. Alas, only crickets and birdsong were audible.

Addie rolled her eyes. "What makes you think so?"

"I can read, can't I?"

"I don't think that's ever been in question." Rupert was a Cambridge graduate, whose degree was more than adequate even if he paid very little attention to his tutors. He told her it wasn't until the war, when he was surrounded by danger and death, that he'd come alive.

"Aren't you the least bit curious to ask what I've read?" he huffed.

"I expect you'll tell me, whether I beg you to or not." Addie took a sip of her tea, enjoying Rupert's disappointment.

"You are a flat tire."

Addie had to agree with him there. She had not enjoyed herself much in weeks.

Months.

Years.

He threw up his hands in disgust. "I don't know why I even bother. Here I am, offering the murderer's head on a platter, so you can inform your inspector and get all the gold stars. I'll never be able to take any credit."

"Pooh. Every good deed you do here is in aid of you finally getting into Heaven. Don't be so disingenuous." For the hundredth time, Addie wondered how many more good deeds Rupert was required to do before they were both released from their unwanted partnership. She had a large bone to pick with the Fellow Upstairs when she saw him.

If she went in the right direction. Which she had every good intention of doing.

Rupert plopped down on the grass. "All right. I'll tell you anyway, so you can get over to Fernald Hall in time to stop the madness. Evelyn Fernald is being blackmailed."

"By the murderer?"

"Don't be silly—she is the murderer. Or murderess? I'm not sure what's grammatically correct."

"Rupert! Stop joking!"

"Oh, now I've got your attention." He gave her a superior smile, and she squelched her urge to slap it off his face. Violence was never the answer. Or hardly ever the answer. But when it came to Rupert, it was all too appealing, no matter how reformed and sympathetic he'd become.

"I don't believe it. Not one word, no matter how grammatical you are."

It couldn't be true. Evelyn and Addie's mother were friends. It was like accusing the dowager marchioness herself.

"Believe what you want. But yesterday evening the kitchen boy from the Pig and Shilling in Broughton Magna delivered a very interesting letter to Lady Fernald from Pamela's ex-maid, Murray. She took refuge there before seeking new employment. If she has to ever work again. She accused Hugh's mama of putting something in the fruit cordial Pamela drank every afternoon, and wants a substantial sum to keep quiet about it. A really substantial sum. The poor woman has delusions of grandeur, I'm afraid."

Addie was almost too shocked to speak. "You read the letter?"

"But of course I read the letter. I explained my reading prowess earlier, didn't I? Keep up, my dear. I could have brought the thing with me, but that would alert the old gal that the jig is almost up. It's in her unlocked jewel case where any idiot can come upon it. Hunter should find it with no problem."

Addie refrained from calling Rupert an idiot himself with some difficulty. "You went through Evelyn's things?" The thought made Addie very uneasy. It wasn't...cricket.

"Oh, for heaven's sake! The woman has killed people! It's not as though I was rummaging through her brassieres and panties for prurient purposes. I do have some standards. She's old enough to be my mother. You've got to tell the man to arrest her."

Addie shook her head. Rupert was obviously off his own. "But that letter doesn't sound like proof," she said reasonably. "It's just an ex-employee's attempt at extortion. Which, may I remind you, is against the law too."

"Well, damn it! Murder is a hell of a lot worse than blackmail. Have him arrest Murray too, I don't care. Where there's smoke, there's fire. Murray is pretty convinced that Evelyn poisoned Pamela. Your inspector is a persuasive fellow—I'm sure he'll get somebody to confess to something in one shake of a lamb's tail."

"He'll want to speak to Murray first before he does anything," Addie mused. Mr. Hunter did not go about half-cocked. Especially to accuse Lady Evelyn Fernald of murder! He was an ambitious man, and that would be the height of folly without something substantial to link her to Pamela's death.

"He'd better hurry up then. They're meeting tonight at the pub, or at least Murray demanded Evelyn's presence. Says she'll be sorry if she ignores the 'invitation.'"

"Hm. Maybe Inspector Hunter can catch them red-handed. Eavesdrop somehow." Not that Addie believed he'd hear anything worthwhile. Rupert's "radio signals" must be getting crossed.

"I personally wouldn't want to wait that long," Rupert said, examining his fingernails.

"Why? What's Evelyn going to do beforehand?"

"One doesn't like to think of it. Murray, in my humble opinion, is in way over her head. It's very foolish to threaten someone as formidable as Evelyn Fernald. She's a dangerous woman."

Addie picked up the teacup and rose. She might as well humor him. "I'll go talk to Murray myself. Tell her to be careful."

"Tell her to leave the area and put aside her greed. I wouldn't put it past Evelyn to set fire to the pub."

Was Rupert exaggerating? He had the ability to capture fleeting thoughts of those around him, which was too provoking when they were Addie's thoughts.

"And then," he continued, "you can go over to Fernald Hall and inform your policeman of the latest developments. Tell him Murray confided in you because of your kind face and trusting nature." He lay back on the grass, closed his eyes, and was gone.

What was she to do? Ignore Rupert at her peril? He hadn't been wrong before, just…incomplete. Still, what he told her seemed entirely out of the question.

Addie walked back to the house, stopping by the garage first to ask her chauffeur to ready the Rolls for her. After changing her clothes to make herself more presentable, she touched up her lipstick and ran a comb through her curly bob. She put on a pretty hat that Inspector Hunter had not seen.

Did gentlemen even care about hats? Probably not, until they had to pay the bills.

Perhaps she spent too much time primping. According to Rupert, this was an emergency situation, although Addie simply couldn't take him seriously. He was desperate to get all this over with and was grasping at straws.

Addie found Forbes and informed him of her various destinations and set off for her old stomping grounds. The late morning really was remarkably fine, although gray clouds swirled inside Addie's head. She spent a good portion of the drive working up a convincing explanation as to why she wanted to see Murray.

She hardly exchanged a word with the woman when she was a guest at Fernald Hall—why would she? Addie might gossip with Beckett, but most maids did not enjoy such warm relations with their so-called betters.

Addie had a front-row seat at the crumbling of British social stratification, and she was generally all in favor. The war had changed so much, despite people like her mother and Evelyn clinging to the familiar old ways. And it wasn't as if they were deliberately unkind, merely traditional.

For example, in their view, men were meant to take care of women. Addie was aware her mother still had marital expectations for her, continually casting about for some eligible man to mend Addie's opinion of husbands. But one husband was very much enough, especially since she couldn't seem to shed him.

Deciding it was best to "accidently" bump into Murray somehow and commiserate with her over Pamela's death meant that Addie had the barest of plans. How she would get around to bringing Evelyn into it was a mystery.

Evelyn! It was too absurd.

But Rupert was convinced. She hadn't been able to trust him when he was alive, but now...

Addie prided herself on making the best of difficult situations. Her mother had raised her to get along with both dustmen and debutantes, and she hoped she could earn Murray's confidence before—if Rupert was right—another awful thing happened.

If, if, if. Such a tiny word freighted with so much power.

She arrived at the pub, where lunch was in progress. Several people she recognized sat in the beer garden, their pints and pies in front of them. After being suitably polite as a favored daughter of the late marquess, Addie excused herself and went inside, her eyes adjusting to the cozy dark room. All the tables were occupied, a big change from the war years.

The landlord, Bill Parks, greeted her effusively. A dozen years ago, she spent many an evening here with Lucas and other young friends, nursing a cider while the boys proved their manliness by arm-wrestling and drinking a little too much away from their parents' eyes. Bill never let them get out of hand, though, and had taken many a lad—and a few girls—home in his pony trap after last call.

Between sets of darts and heated disagreements about the village cricket team, they had discussed the problems of the world as only the naive and innocent can do. The world still had more than its share of problems, but Addie was smart enough now to know she couldn't solve them, with an infusion of cider or without.

And too many local boys had never returned to play cricket again.

She gave Bill a hug and caught up with his laconic version of local affairs, conscious that the clock was ticking. But she didn't want to be rude, so let him ramble on uninterrupted. When she finally asked if she could see Murray, he shook his head.

"Up and left this morning, she did. Came here Thursday with her carpetbag in quite a state. Don't blame her for not wanting to stay at Fernald Hall one minute longer. So much sadness there. The poor woman said she couldn't even bear to go to the funeral. But she must have forgotten something back at the house—she sent a note with one of my boys after supper, and Sir Hugh's mother came to see her about it first thing today."

So Rupert was half-right. "Lady Fernald was here?"

"Don't sound so surprised. She's not as top-lofty as all that. Why, I fixed her a lemon shandy myself a time or two. Lovely woman." He sighed. "Awful business. Those poor people. Haven't they had enough trouble? I gather they still have to bury the governess, though that won't be as much of a fuss as it was for young Lady Fernald."

"Did she say where she was going? Murray, that is?"

"Sorry, Lady Adelaide. I expect Miss Murray has to earn her bread like most of us and walked to the station. What with one thing and another, I didn't notice—she was all paid up for the two nights and didn't give me a goodbye kiss. She's probably bound for London and an employment agency. Told me Sir Hugh gave her a fine recommendation; I imagine Lady Fernald will speak highly of her as well. They were upstairs half an hour or more."

"Da—uh, drat. My friend Lady Grimes needs a lady's maid, and I thought Murray would be perfect. On the odd chance she comes back, could you tell her to get in touch with me?"

"Of course, my lady. I trust your mother and sister are well?"

"Yes, thank you for asking. How is Mrs. Parks?"

"Just the same. Keeping me on my toes. She'll be sorry to have missed you, but she's gone to the outdoor market in Stroud. Left me on my own to deal with the tourist crowd."

"I'm so glad business is good! Please give her my best."

Once she was outside, her smile wavered. Addie slid back into the driver's seat and put on her gloves. There was nothing for it. Lady Grimes to the rescue once more.

Chapter Thirty-Two

There was a time when Fernald Hall's evergreen-lined drive did not feel so menacing—just a week ago, in fact. Addie now dreaded every inch of the journey through it. She hoped Murray made a safe escape and refrained from eating or drinking anything from Evelyn's hand.

Of course she would have, if she suspected Evelyn of poisoning Pamela. What had transpired in their half-hour chat? Certainly no screaming or shouting, or Bill Parks would have mentioned it. He didn't discover Murray's dead body in her room, either. Was she somewhere on a train, getting sick like Patrick Cassidy?

Addie never believed one could entertain two completely opposing thoughts at the same time, but it seemed one could. How could she think Evelyn was a murderer? She'd known her all her life.

Trim opened the door immediately. "Good afternoon, Lady Adelaide!"

"Is Mr. Hunter still here?"

"He is. I believe he's in the study with Sir Hugh and his mother. If you'll follow me—"

Oh, dear. Addie did not feel equal to running into Evelyn at the moment. She was sure her confusion would be visible at twenty paces.

"If you don't mind, could you just tell him I'm here? I only need a quick word with him in private and don't want to bother the family."

"I hardly think they would be bothered, but you know best, I'm sure."

Addie didn't know anything of the kind. Perhaps didn't know anything, period. Maybe Rupert was all wrong. After all, Evelyn hadn't burned down the pub when she was there earlier, had she?

And his track record in life had been less than stellar. Addie hadn't been able to depend upon him for years, if ever. Just because he was eager to help now didn't mean he wasn't the same selfish man she'd known and loved.

Trim led her to a small parlor off the entrance hall. Addie kept herself from pacing by looking out the window. Pamela's gardens were green and lush, as Addie's own were growing to be. During the war, the plantings at Compton Chase had been confined to vegetables and a scraggly lavender path. Its late gardener, Mr. McGrath, had been too old to do anything fancier afterward. When Rupert inherited the house and brought her there as a bride, she did not want to make waves. But her new employee, Jack Robertson, despite losing a leg in France, was like a mighty Neptune. His ambition was admirable and, if Addie was honest, a trifle overwhelming.

After waiting long enough for Addie's nerves to get the better of her, Mr. Hunter entered, his concern evident. "Lady Adelaide, what's amiss?"

She swallowed. "I—I wouldn't have come to interrupt unless there was a clue."

"Sit down and breathe. I won't bite."

A naughty thought flitted through her disordered mind, and she promptly batted it away. She dropped into a chair, pulling her skirt down and examining a sharp pleat. "It has come to my attention that, uh, Pamela's maid, Murray, may have been trying to blackmail Lady Fernald. She wrote her a threatening letter. That is, Murray wrote to Evelyn. Not Pamela. She's dead."

God help her.

He sat down opposite and fished his notebook out of a jacket pocket. "What? Why?"

"Well, she thought Evelyn might have been responsible for Pamela's death. That she tampered with the drink she gave her every afternoon for her nausea. That is, Murray administered it, and it was Pamela's nausea." There were altogether too many "shes" in the sentence, and Addie knew she wasn't making sense.

Maybe Murray was right in a way—Evelyn might have been trying to help with the concoction and miscalculated somehow. Addie felt obliged to give her the benefit of the doubt.

Mr. Hunter raised a dark eyebrow. "How did you come by this information?"

She swallowed again, harder this time. "You know my friend Lady Grimes? Of course you don't—you've never met. She doesn't go out much, hardly at all. Her husband died, you see, and she's quite alone in the world with very few friends. I'm lucky to be amongst those fortunate few." Mr. Hunter's pencil was poised over his notebook. Addie could see she was trying his patience.

"Anyway, she's been looking for a lady's maid and I thought Murray might suit. They, uh, spoke on the phone early this morning and apparently Murray blurted out her suspicions. Josephine—that's Lady Grimes—called me right away wondering if Murray was reliable or just plain mad. I admit I hardly know Murray, but Pamela seemed pleased with her service, so I thought it was safe to recommend her in the first place."

"Where is Murray now?"

"I'm not sure." That was perfectly true.

"And this Lady Grimes? How can I get in touch with her?"

Addie crossed her gloved fingers and hid them under the pleat. "She said she was going away. Leaving today, in fact. I forgot to ask her where she was headed—somewhere in South America, perhaps? The Virgin Islands? A long sea voyage, at any rate. But she'd wanted to engage a new maid before she left."

"Perhaps she hasn't left yet. Do you have her number?"

"Oh, gosh. It's in my address book at home. I didn't think to bring it."

He must think she was the stupidest woman alive.

"So, let me get this straight. You'd like me to arrest Lady Fernald because a blackmailing maid told a potential employer what she believed happened last Sunday, discrediting herself on a telephone job interview."

"I never said arrest. But perhaps investigate further. I realize it's hearsay two times over. Or perhaps three. But I figured you might be...interested."

"Why wouldn't Murray tell me this herself? I interviewed her."

"I'm not privy to her mental state." In truth, Addie was hardly privy to her own at the moment.

"And how am I to prove any of this?"

"There's the letter. It's in Evelyn's jewel case."

Both his eyebrows raised. "How on earth would you know that? Have you been upstairs snooping?"

"No! I'm just assuming. That's where I would keep important blackmail letters."

"Do you get blackmailed regularly?" he asked dryly.

"Not yet. But there's a first time for everything," Addie said. Damn Rupert! He was the source of this lunacy and she couldn't very well confess to Mr. Hunter that he was being assisted by the ghost of her late husband, who had been upstairs snooping.

It would be a tremendous relief if she could confide in somebody about Rupert and not get clapped away in one of the discreet nursing homes which catered to nervous, drunk, and drug-addled aristocrats. They must be doing a booming business, judging from society's current excesses.

Mr. Hunter rose. "I don't have a search warrant. In fact, I probably shouldn't be here at all, even with Cassidy's accusations. For all we know, he's lying. This case—these cases have been closed. The family is satisfied with the jury's verdict."

"But you aren't."

He sighed. "You know I'm not. But that's a long way off from accusing Lady Fernald of the murder of her daughter-in-law based on the word of two women whose whereabouts are unknown, one of whom admits to being a blackmailer to a perfect stranger on the telephone."

Addie should have explained things differently, but it was too late. What if he wanted to interview Lady Grimes when she returned? Addie would have to send the woman permanently to someplace where twentieth-century communication was impossible. Antarctica? Tierra del Fuego? Addie's geography knowledge was sketchy at best. She'd have to consult John's maps in the schoolroom.

She had a feeling Lady Grimes was about to meet her fate somewhere in the Caribbean. Did she wash overboard after too many rum punches? Perhaps she swam with dolphins and attracted the attention of a shark. And weren't there still pirates in the area who were cruel and bloodthirsty? Addie would hate to lose dear Josephine, but she and Beckett could work out some other arrangement.

There was a knock on the door, and Trim entered, holding a leather suitcase in each hand. "I've seen to Mr. Cassidy's things, Inspector. Shall I put them in the truck?"

"I'll do that, Trim. Thanks for your assistance."

"Are you finished here already?" Addie asked in surprise. "You won't, um, ask any more questions of you-know-who?" Trim was still hovering.

"I was just informing the Fernalds of Mr. Cassidy's missing person status, Lady Adelaide. They'll let me know if there's any word from him. And I believe any more questions are quite out of order. I'll return your truck and be on my way to London, if you can arrange a lift to the train for me."

Well, she had tried, and would tell Rupert that his crackpot idea was rejected. Addie was swept by disappointment that Mr. Hunter was leaving so soon but hoped he wouldn't notice. "Very well. I'll follow you home."

"Shall I have the vehicles brought round?" Trim asked.

"No, that's all right. I'd like to stop by the stables before I leave, and I'm sure we can find them in the service yard."

Once they were outside, Mr. Hunter set the bags down. "These are heavier than I expected, even without the custom oatmeal tin. Trim is an old marvel, isn't he?"

"Pardon me?"

"Never mind. A bit of an inside joke. I promised Cassidy I'd look in on the horses. I do have one bit of good news for him— Sir Hugh has agreed to go ahead with the purchase, providing Cassidy can be 'found.' So that's something."

"I'll come too."

He smiled down at her. "I was under the impression you're not all that fond of horses."

"Oh, no. I didn't inherit the family horse-madness, but I like them well enough." At a distance. Addie realized her mother was missing an opportunity to sell the advantage of being the next marchioness of Broughton to Cee, who was horse-mad. Broughton Park's stables were chock-full of prime horseflesh, and while Cee borrowed them almost daily when she was in the country, it would be far better to think of them as hers. Addie would mention this strategy when her mother returned from London.

And Ian was really a catch. He might be a little straitlaced, but that was precisely what Cee needed. Her dance with disaster last spring should have settled her down some. But usually Cee did not do what was expected, and everyone around her paid the price for it.

Mr. Hunter picked the luggage back up, and they walked around the house to the cobbled yard between the kitchen door and the outbuildings. Both vehicles shone in the sun. Someone had wiped then down, which was thoughtful, but they were bound to get dusty again. The local roads needed to be oiled in the worst way, but better dry than muddy.

He put the cases in the cab and extended an elbow. "Shall we inspect your four-legged friends?"

"Friends might be too strong a word."

He stopped mid-stride. "You aren't...afraid, are you?"

"Of course not." Not if the horses were safely in their boxes, merrily munching hay rather than her fingers. It wasn't as if Mr. Hunter was going to toss her up onto a saddle; she certainly wasn't dressed for riding in her powder-blue pleated Chanel dress. How hard could it be to stroke a velvety nose for a second and murmur something soothing and not sneeze her head off?

Chapter Thirty-Three

Addie recognized Timothy Hay immediately and hung back while Mr. Hunter quizzed the groom about the horses whickering at their intrusion. He was careful not to show a particular interest in the new arrivals but was regaled with their details, nevertheless. Nose tickling, she pretended to examine the various rosettes lining the window of the stable master's office. He was not present, only the young man Mr. Hunter spoke to, and one even younger who waxed a saddle with grave determination.

It was kind of the detective to try to set Mr. Cassidy's mind at rest. The man was sure to be pleased that the sale was going to go through after all, and he couldn't doubt that the horses would have a good home. From the gleam of their coats and the immaculate condition of the stable's interior, it seemed to Addie that they lived a far better life than a great many people nowadays.

There was a cracked leather sofa in the office, and she slipped inside to wait. She checked her wristwatch, estimating which train Mr. Hunter would be able to catch once they returned to Compton-Under-Wood. She wished he'd consider staying one more night, not relishing being alone with Mr. Cassidy. But perhaps the Irishman would go back to Town with him and leave her in peace.

To do what? She could hardly accuse Evelyn of being a murderess again. And Rupert would still be underfoot until all of this was settled. Addie was developing one of her headaches. She simply was not cut out for detection, or, really, death of any kind.

"Oh, I wouldn't say that." Rupert appeared on the couch and patted her arm reassuringly.

Addie stopped herself from yelling and slid down so she wouldn't be visible through the window. She didn't need to be seen talking to herself again. And by now, Rupert's sudden appearance shouldn't surprise her into making any noise at all.

"What are you doing here?" she mouthed.

"Speak up, love. I can't hear you."

He was so annoying. She glared at him, and he responded by glaring back.

"Fine. If you refuse my help, I will not be responsible for the consequences. I believe you're still holding a grudge about my less-than-perfect performance as a husband."

"That's an understatement," Addie muttered. "And I'm not holding a grudge. I've forgiven you." More or less.

Perhaps less.

"I suppose I would hate me too if our positions were reversed, but I cannot undo the past. Believe me, if I could, I would—I'd be a regular choir boy, pure as the driven snow. Immaculate as the Conception. An archangel."

"You're not even an angel yet."

"A mere technicality. I'm doing the best I can."

"By sneaking and spying!" she hissed.

"What do you expect me to do but sneak and spy? My options are somewhat limited. It's not as if I'm going to lower myself and put on a cut-out sheet and chains and frighten people into a confession."

"Do ghosts do that?"

"Those with inferior intelligence," Rupert replied, mulish.

Addie knew it was pointless to argue. He was as fed up with their current situation as she was. "Are you absolutely sure that Evelyn is guilty?"

"One cannot be sure of anything in this life—well, your life, can one? I'm told things are properly sorted in Heaven, all black and white, cut and dried, good and evil, sweet and even sweeter, not that I seem to be any closer to finding out for myself. But all the arrows point to her. I'd be very careful around her if I were you."

Addie shivered. "I have no intention of seeing her."

"You know what they say about best-laid plans. She's about to turn up here very shortly."

"What? How do you know?"

"How do I know anything? Consider yourself warned. You should take your policeman and scram." With that, Rupert blew her a goodbye kiss and disappeared.

"Oh!" Addie leaped up from the sofa. He might have said a little sooner, and she would have dragged Inspector Hunter out of the stable as quickly as possible. The very last person she wanted to bump into was Evelyn Fernald. The hell with Mr. Cassidy's horses.

She waved through the window trying to get the detective's attention to no avail. Stepping out of the office, she brushed a bit of straw from her skirt and marched over to the men, who were deep in horse-y conversation.

"I have to go." Addie felt like a coward, but Rupert had spooked her in more ways than one.

"I'll be right with you," Mr. Hunter said.

"No. I need to leave now." In her sudden panic, blood was surging to Addie's skin, spine tingling, hair raising. Something was going to happen if they stayed, she was sure of it. She hadn't felt this frightened since she was held captive by a crazed killer.

Only three months ago. She really needed to make significant changes to her life, or she soon would be crazed herself.

But even if Evelyn came to the stable, surely Addie could pretend that nothing was wrong. Make polite small talk. She had plenty of practice pretending; it's what ladies did approximately seventy-five percent of the time. One was always interested in whatever one's dull dinner partner had to say. One prayed in chilly, musty churches when one was unsure that the Fellow Upstairs was paying attention. One plastered on a smile when one wanted to scream.

One turned a blind eye to one's husband's infidelities and kept up appearances if it killed one.

It was all make-believe.

Mr. Hunter looked at her with concern. "What is it, Lady Adelaide? Are you unwell?"

"Yes! That's it. My, ah, allergies."

"Perhaps we should go back into the house. Mrs. Lewis strikes me as a woman who knows what to do when one is ill. Or shall I drive you home straightaway? I'm sure arrangements can be made to get Jack's truck back."

Addie would feel better with Mr. Hunter behind the wheel. She loved to drive, but right now her hands were not too steady and quite damp inside her gloves. "Yes, please."

But it was too late to flee. Hugh's mother strode through the open doorway in her elegant black riding habit, stopping short when she caught sight of them. The groom whipped off his cap and tried to stand taller.

"H-hello, Evelyn," Addie squeaked.

"Robby, get Jupiter ready for me, there's a good lad." She turned to Addie as the boy dashed off. "Trim told me you'd come but had mysterious business with the inspector. How are you, dear?"

"Uh. Not quite the thing at the moment. Mr. Hunter and I were just leaving."

Evelyn took a few steps forward and placed a cool hand on Addie's forehead. It was all Addie could do not to flinch. "No fever. What seems to be the trouble? Headache? Tummy upset? I have everything you might need in the stillroom."

"No!" Addie mustn't shout. "No, thank you. I'm simply tired and a little stuffy-nosed. I don't need to tell you what a difficult week it's been. How is Hugh managing?"

"He's strong. Everything happens for a reason, don't you agree? Or at least that's what our vicar says. I don't imagine Mr. Hunter agrees with that, however."

"That's not been my experience in my line of work, Lady Fernald. Often a criminal's reason makes very little sense to the average person."

"Aren't the usual motivations love, money, and revenge?" Addie asked. At least that was true for the mystery books she'd read.

"Generally. But then, it's always a mistake to generalize. Each case is unique."

"Well, I'm sure you're happy this one is over and anxious to get back to London," Evelyn said. "It's all been a tempest in a tea-cup here—three very unfortunate accidents. Unlucky, but we at Fernald Hall will survive. We always do."

Addie seized her chance. "I have a question for you before we leave, though. Would you perchance know where Murray has gone? I have a friend looking to employ a lady's maid."

"Goodness, how should I know? Hugh dealt with her."

"Oh. That's odd. When I stopped by the Pig and Shilling, Mr. Parks said you spoke with her only this morning." Mr. Hunter shot her a warning look, but she pretended not to see it.

"And so I did. But she didn't reveal where she was bound, I'm afraid. A peculiar woman, really. I don't think she would suit your friend. Pamela, being so good-natured, was a trifle lax with the servants, and Murray took advantage."

"I got the impression when I interviewed her she was devoted to your daughter-in-law," Mr. Hunter said.

"Well, yes. As I said, Pamela spoiled the servants. Allowed far too much fraternization. Murray really didn't know her place and wasn't all that bright to boot. A bad combination."

Mr. Hunter mustered up a charming smile. "You must be relieved that she left your employ, then. I'm curious—why did you visit with her this morning if you disliked her so? Why waste your time?"

Evelyn's face went blank for a few seconds, then she recovered. "Really, Inspector I can't see how that's any of your business. I was under the impression your work here was finished."

"So it is. But should any new evidence come to light, I'm obliged to act upon it."

"New evidence? What on earth do you mean?" Her tone was mocking.

"I understand there is a letter."

Addie was stunned that he was using her Rupert-acquired information when he said he wasn't going to. Did he have prickles up and down his spine too?

"You are quite mistaken," Evelyn said.

"You didn't ask me who sent the letter or what its contents are," Mr. Hunter said.

"Because there is no letter! I have no idea what you are inferring, but I must insist you drop the subject. I've received nothing whatsoever in the post that could be seen as 'evidence' for anything from anyone. Unless, of course, you're curious about my tradesmen's bills. I did order a new hat last month, which I really didn't need. Evidence of my profligacy, I'm sure. Shame on me. But hardly a crime. Now, if that's all, Inspector, I'm going for my ride."

"Sorry, I must have misunderstood my source. So, no one is trying to blackmail you? That's a relief. Blackmailers are never satisfied."

"Your source? This is ridiculous! Who in the household has fed you such rubbish?"

"I'm afraid that's confidential. But if I were to go upstairs and inspect the contents of your jewelry box, you wouldn't object?"

Mr. Hunter was taking a dreadful risk, and it was all Addie's fault. For all she knew, Evelyn had burned the letter before she came out to ride.

What if Evelyn complained to Deputy Commissioner Olive? Mr. Hunter could lose his job!

Oblivious to the tension crackling in the air, Robby brought the horse to his mistress. "Leave us. Take Liam with you."

No please. No thank you. The boys didn't ask any questions, just filed out of the stables on an unexpected break. Evelyn waited until they were gone before she spoke.

"What are your ambitious plans for me, Mr. Hunter? You'll never be able to prove a thing, and then what will your future be at Scotland Yard after I'm done with you?"

Chapter Thirty-Four

Addie gasped. Evelyn appeared no different than she always had—so familiar. Fit, shiny dark hair interlaced with threads of silver, perfectly made-up.

But perhaps under the powder and rouge was the face of a murderer.

"I'm not afraid of you."

"Don't be dishonest. It's unbecoming for a detective to dissemble, don't you agree? Think of all the corruption you try to distance yourself from—that hasn't made you so popular with your colleagues, has it? No one will care if you're ruined. I've asked around the week you've been here, you know. You're a regular Boy Scout, according to your superiors. Surprisingly intelligent for one of your class. Addie wasn't wrong to ask for you, although I'm sorry she did. I was hoping I could keep my secrets."

Mr. Hunter wasted no time. "Did you poison your daughter-in-law?"

Evelyn stroked the horse's nose, and at first Addie didn't think she would answer. Why should she? Murray was gone. Evelyn had gotten away with it so far, and one could hardly call Rupert to the stand to testify. But then—

"Yes. And I'd do it again, given the opportunity. Actually, she poisoned herself."

My God. Rupert was right after all. Addie felt light-headed, but now was no time to faint, even if she could do it in a marchioness-approved manner.

"What do you mean?" Mr. Hunter asked.

"She made up a potion to help her with her stomach upset, ginger, a slice of lemon, some peppermint leaves. I added a little something to it. Murray saw me in the stillroom and must have realized the extra ingredient caused Pamela's death. The little fool drank it right down in a nip of blackberry cordial as she did every day. Typical Pamela—she didn't get morning sickness, but afternoon sickness. I didn't force her—I wasn't even there."

"But Murray was?"

"They'd gone down early to check that the conservatory was ready and the orchids were properly arranged. Murray panicked when Pamela fell after she gave her the dose. Thought she'd be blamed for mixing up the medicine and ran off. But she isn't totally stupid—as you noted, she's trying to bribe me now. Quite foolishly, I gave her some money this morning but told her that would be the end of it. Generous severance pay and a letter of recommendation evidently aren't enough these days."

Not enough to keep quiet about a killer! Addie should think not.

"She's all right then?" Addie asked.

"Why? Did you imagine I'd poison her too? Adelaide, I'm surprised at your lack of judgment, but then you've always been ingenuous. Look at what that husband of yours did to you. With my daughter-in-law on occasion, I might add. He was just another local conquest for her."

Addie almost rose to the bait but caught Detective Hunter's eye.

And anyway, one couldn't argue with Evelyn's conclusions. Even Rupert would admit she was right.

"You knew Pamela was pregnant."

"Of course. I practically caught her red-handed with that boy a few months ago. Colin Stewart. Interviewing him for a job, my eye," the woman said in disgust. "Upstairs in the Bear of Rodborough in Stroud, where anyone in our circle could have seen them leave together. I'd known for years she was having affairs, though usually she was discreet. But Stewart, her son's future tutor? Completely unsuitable. If she thought to bring him under my roof so she could dally at will, she was mistaken, wasn't she? One doesn't shag the help."

"Wasn't it possible the child she was carrying was your son's?" Mr. Hunter asked quietly.

Evelyn looked down at her hands. For the first time, Addie noticed they showed her age, faint brown spots dotting her fair skin. "I don't know," she said. "I couldn't take that chance. Hugh put up with enough. To raise someone else's child—which I'm sure he would do out of a misplaced sense of duty—crossed the line for me. What if the child was a boy, and something, God forbid, happened to John? Fernalds have been here since Henry the Seventh's day with nary a cuckoo in the nest as far as I'm aware. It's no time to start now. When Simon told me—"

"He knew?"

That meant Murray, Mrs. Lewis, Evelyn, and Mr. Davies were all aware. Addie was beginning to wonder if the old gardeners were in on it too—Pamela's pregnancy was the least secret secret she'd ever heard of.

"Poor Simon. He's always harbored an unfortunate weakness for the Barlow women. Pamela buttered him up and sicced him on me. He thought he could appeal to my better side. But I haven't one, have I? I couldn't afford to be understanding. Make excuses. Not when it came to Hugh's happiness. I've sacrificed too much. I wasn't going to leave him in a mess."

Oh, really? Just what exactly constituted a mess, if a murdered wife and a motherless grandchild were not one? Addie practically had to bite her tongue to shut herself up. To think that this monstrous woman was a lifelong friend of her mother's—it was all too sickening.

Mr. Hunter made a few notations in his book, then put it back into his pocket, his face impassive. "Why don't we go into the stable office where you can sit down, Lady Fernald?"

"I don't want to sit; I'm fine. Do you want the full story? Not that you'd ever find out on your own, no matter how bright they say you are. I already told you I was not going to have my Hugh taken advantage of again. Not by Pamela. Certainly not by Juliet."

"In what way?"

"She was a grasping little nobody, so jealous of Pamela, ungrateful for the opportunity we provided her. I'm afraid I didn't anticipate her gall. With my daughter-in-law out of the way, I saw that it was only a matter of time before Juliet tried to move in to entangle my son. I couldn't have that. Not after everything this family has been through. Hugh has worked damned hard to be strong, both physically and emotionally, but he's vulnerable as well. I watched the little witch try to sink her claws into him at dinner the other night and knew I had to move quickly." Evelyn shrugged. "What he put up with from Pamela because of her pretty face—I couldn't let him fall for a pale copy of the original. One Barlow mistake was enough."

Addie remembered Pamela in their debut year—glittering balls, an even more dazzling Pamela, her dark pompadour sprinkled with diamond clips, when everyone else was in modest and virginal pearls. Hugh was stricken with her beauty, as was every other young man of Addie's acquaintance. The competition was stiff, but he won her.

"And you made Juliet's death look like an accident."

"I only meant to frighten her and didn't expect her to run down the stairs like a madwoman after our little talk." The woman paused. "I overplayed my hand. It really was an accident. You can't make me feel sorry. The Barlows are unworthy. Bankers," she said with distaste. "At least there was money for Pamela, although that can't buy breeding."

"Why the gin?"

Evelyn shrugged. "I didn't want people to think she was pushed."

She didn't meet the inspector's eyes.

Did that mean she had pushed Juliet? Perhaps she hadn't intended the fatal outcome, but Juliet was dead just the same.

"As long as we're telling the full story, what about Patrick Cassidy?" Mr. Hunter asked.

"What about him?"

"He was Lieutenant Ainsley's half brother. Did you fear he'd discover the truth?"

Evelyn gave him a sour smile. "And what is the truth, Inspector?"

"I'm not sure yet."

Addie looked at him. He was calm, almost placid, a contrast to the fierceness Evelyn projected.

His composure was nearly as frightening.

"If I wanted him dead, he would be. Pamela was not the only herbalist at Fernald Hall. I taught her everything she knew."

Mr. Hunter had said nothing about Cassidy's poisoning.

Another confession.

"It's nice to know you have some compunction," Mr. Hunter replied mildly.

The woman had murdered at least once, and caused the death of another, no matter what she said. What was a little poisoning to her? An upset stomach, an inconvenience. Enough to warn Mr. Cassidy away.

But Lieutenant Ainsley's death was still unsolved, and Addie couldn't quite work out what had happened.

"And yes, I read your telegrams before they were handed on to you Tuesday night. I wish I'd known who Cassidy was to begin with—I would have forbidden him to come. He practically invited himself, you know. And if only those idiot Dunns didn't start digging. Men. Trust them to be in thrall to Pamela even if she were dead. I hoped with her gone, we'd have a reprieve from the new construction and Ainsley would stay where he was put—it was all so unnecessary anyway. The estate was fine without her so-called improvements. But nothing was ever enough for her."

Evelyn's dark eyes glittered with malice. "Do you know who shot that soldier? Pamela did! He made advances, and she put him in his place quite smartly. We covered it up for her."

Addie couldn't believe it. It just wasn't possible, was it? She felt she needed to sit down.

"Who did?" Mr. Hunter asked.

"One of the servants. Me. It's useless to ask who helped— he's long gone. And don't blame him. I'm sure he's felt terrible about it all these years, but he was only acting on my orders."

"Sir Hugh didn't know?"

"Of course not! He didn't know much of anything at that time. Pamela kept him drugged and docile. He was very badly off. Wasn't expected to survive."

Addie still had a great deal of difficulty picturing Pamela shooting a man between the eyes, no matter what the circumstances. Yes, she was a crack shot, as was Addie herself when she wore her spectacles; they lived in the country, after all. She'd been on enough shoots with Pamela to know her prowess.

But shooting birds was one thing. Lieutenant Ainsley was not a bird.

"Did he try to, uh, molest her?" Addie asked.

"What difference does it make? He was too forward, chasing after her like a puppy. Maybe she didn't mean to kill him, but she did. She came to me, and I took care of it."

"You buried Ainsley?" Inspector Hunter sounded doubtful.

"Yes." Evelyn lifted her chin, daring him to contradict her. "And now, if it's all the same to you, I'm going to go on my ride. When I come back, you can try to arrest me. Or shoot me. I don't much care. No one will believe you anyway."

With that, she mounted her horse with an agility for her age that the much-younger Addie could only envy. No mounting block, no groom's assistance. Mr. Hunter leaped for the reins, only to miss by inches. The horse knocked him into the sharp corner of the box and down to the floor for his trouble. He lay stunned for a moment, blood dripping from the cut on his forehead.

Whipping the horse, Evelyn Fernald rode hell for leather out of the stable.

Chapter Thirty-Five

Addie was useless, not even crying out. Evidently, she still could be surprised by evil.

And surprised further still. Mr. Hunter brushed himself off and was saddling up Timothy Hay.

"You ride?"

"My father was in the Military Mounted Police. What do you think? Go to the house and call Cirencester. And say nothing to anyone inside." He tightened the girth. "Do you have any idea where she'd go?"

"Not really." She pulled a handkerchief down out of her sleeve and tried to clean off the detective's face.

"I'll do that." He snatched the linen out of her fingers and pressed it to his temple.

"I know she rides in the local hunt. It goes over Fernald land. To the west. She might go that way—we did Saturday when we all rode out together. You can gallop for miles." Addie paused. "Won't she—won't she come back?"

"Who knows what that woman will do? I'm not going to wait around to welcome her home."

Addie took Mr. Hunter's hands in hers and looked up into

his startled brown eyes. "Whatever you do, don't sneeze. Timothy Hay—that's his name—doesn't like it." She ran off before he could question her, heart thudding. Entering the house through an open Dutch door, she found herself in an unfamiliar hallway.

There was a telephone upstairs in a bedroom wing, where Rupert eavesdropped on Lucas's call to his solicitor. She'd have more privacy there, with less to explain to Trim. Praying she wouldn't encounter anyone, she climbed the first set of stairs she came to and miraculously came across a phone sitting on a cherrywood credenza. A handy chair was nearby, and Addie sank into it to catch her breath.

It took the Cirencester desk sergeant much too long to unscramble her message, and she had to repeat herself four times before he took her seriously. He promised to send people as soon as he could and advised Addie to let the police do their work this time.

Addie had no intention of interfering; she wanted to get out of the hellhole Fernald Hall had become as quickly as possible. But she worried about Mr. Hunter. Silly, she was sure—he knew what he was about. Like Evelyn, he had not needed a groom to help him with anything. Timothy Hay seemed cooperative, too, sensing Mr. Hunter's heretofore unknown skill.

She left the house the same way she entered and dashed off to the Rolls. Starting it up, she sped down the pine-shaded avenue. Addie had watched the local hunt from various vantage points since she was a little girl growing up at Broughton Park and knew the turnout where she'd have the best view of the countryside. Most of her old neighbors regularly came out to see the spectacle of dozens of horses flying through the fields, to hear the horns and bays of the dogs, but she wouldn't have to jostle amongst them today.

Addie never much liked the idea of the fox being torn to shreds. In fact, it horrified her, and she had many an argument with her father about it. He once told her if she was a boy, she'd understand, which had cut her to her core. Cruel was cruel, and it shouldn't matter if you were male or female. She got nowhere with him, and now she never would. His death still hurt, even if he was stubborn and set in his ways.

And it was true, she acknowledged, that she owned a beautiful silver fox jacket, and several stoles. Other animal pelt coats besides. She was being inconsistent. But at least she didn't have to witness the death of the terrified, helpless creatures when she shopped at Bradleys in Chepstow Place. They were the biggest fur specialists in Europe—even members of the Royal Family patronized the store.

This was the sort of philosophical conundrum she might discuss with Mr. Hunter.

If she ever spoke to him again.

On this hunt, there were no dogs, just a determined detective. She hoped the beautiful Irish horse would behave, and not balk at hedges or stumble into a badger's sett.

Addie turned down a narrow bumpy road which crested ahead. Pulling off to the side, she got out of the car and shielded her face from the sun. Some of the patchwork squares below showed signs of cultivation, but there was a broad green swath closer, perfect for riders. The local master of the hunt who had replaced her father made sure the track was adequately groomed and mowed. She'd been out this way herself last weekend before she was thrown from the damned horse.

A modest stone farmhouse with several buildings hugged the sandy lane running along the greensward, and Addie spotted a woman hanging laundry in the side yard. A man was pushing a plough behind a huge piebald horse in the distance. She wished she had binoculars but squinting through her spectacles would have to do.

Clouds' shadows scudded across the landscape in the breeze. It was a perfectly bucolic June day, belying the darkness she'd just witnessed.

What if Evelyn didn't come this way? Then Inspector Hunter would be on a wild goose chase. But surely he could track her in some fashion. Watch for hoofprints and dust clouds. It had been so very dry that she must have left her mark.

Addie leaned up against the Rolls, trying to calm down. Worry about the future never accomplished anything but ruin one's present. It was all up to the Fellow Upstairs, as Rupert would say.

How did one recover from the ugly truth? Poor John. Would Hugh tell him what his mother and grandmother had done? She hoped not. But how could such secrets be concealed? Addie supposed if anyone could pretend that all was well, it was the inhabitants of Fernald Hall. They had years of experience prevaricating.

How had Pamela been able to withstand the tension and guilt and threats of her mother-in-law? Every day must have been like navigating a minefield.

In comparison, the only thing Addie ever concealed in her life was Rupert in death—and his numerous peccadilloes when he was alive. She chose not to air her dirty laundry then, hiding her broken heart. Well, she was pretty much healed now, and strangely enough, Rupert was responsible for that. He'd been properly contrite over the past ten months, admitting his responsibility, and making every effort to keep her alive.

And, once, out of jail. The thought of the Dowager Marchioness of Broughton bailing her out of the pokey, and holding that over her head, paled against Pamela's situation, however.

Addie listened, hoping to hear the thunder of hooves in the valley. Contrary to popular opinion, the country was a noisy place, with birds, bugs, and farm machinery making their own music. Maybe it was too much to expect to hear a couple of horses—it wasn't as if the hunt was about to come roaring by. Her gaze swept back and forth, and she began to think she had sent Mr. Hunter the wrong way.

Then Evelyn emerged from a gap in the copse, bent low over her mount. She was going at a frightful speed, but suddenly reined in the horse. Turning to look behind her, she reached into her velvet hacking jacket, then held her arm out straight. Metal glinted in the sun.

Oh, God. She had a weapon and was going to use it as soon as Mr. Hunter rode out of the trees. Addie screamed, and screamed again, but not nearly loud enough to catch anyone's attention.

She had to get down the bank as quickly as possible, run Evelyn over if she had to. But before she had the chance to climb back into the car, Mr. Hunter raced into the sunshine.

There was a flash and a popping sound. He fell off the Irish horse almost as though he were a trick rider in a circus, rolling and tumbling in one smooth motion. Evelyn fired again, then kicked Jupiter and they tore off.

Addie swallowed back another scream, her body shaking. She started up the car, backed it into the road, and pointed the bonnet toward the edge of the embankment. Before she released the brake, to her great relief she saw Mr. Hunter stand up. If he was wounded, she saw no sign of it—in fact, he was now loping off after the horse, which had sensibly looked for safety in the stand of trees.

Odd, Timothy Hay could withstand gunshots, but not sneezes.

Mr. Hunter couldn't mean to continue to ride after Evelyn.

She tried to kill him! Who went riding with a pistol in one's jacket unless one intended someone harm? This wasn't the Wild West of Beckett's cowboy cinema stars. Gloucestershire was the consummate country idyll.

But perhaps...perhaps Evelyn meant to harm herself. Everything she did for Hugh was about to blow up in her face.

She was still in view, at one with the black horse. Addie would go after her if she didn't wreck the car first. She hoped her reflexes were as good as the detective's, for likely Evelyn would shoot at her too.

Addie was determining the most direct route through the stones and scrub when Evelyn reined Jupiter in again. She looked behind her. Mr. Hunter was still coaxing the horse out of the trees, too far away to shoot, thank God.

But then, she reached into her jacket again.

Not a gun this time. Evelyn held something to her lips, tipped her head back and drank, then tumbled off the horse to the ground.

Addie barreled down the hill in a storm of dirt and flying rocks, sliding as the gears locked when she tried to shift. What she needed was one of those new tanks they used in the war, but speed was not a factor now.

Below, Jupiter was rearing and whinnying in fear. Rupert stood over his mistress, then looked straight in Addie's direction and shrugged. She could not see his features, but she knew.

Evelyn Fernald was dead.

Chapter Thirty-Six

Engine smoking, the car lurched to a stop, and Addie staggered out. She wondered if her teeth were still intact after the riotous ride she'd had down the slope. She was still some distance away from Evelyn and realized how foolhardy she'd been. The car could have easily tipped on the uneven terrain, and then how much help would she be?

Rupert strode up, looking like thunder. "What in God's name are you thinking, driving my Rolls down that bloody hill? You could have killed yourself and very probably killed the car!"

At least she had come first in his scolding. "It's only a machine, Rupert."

"The best of the bunch. I'm beginning to regret leaving them to you in my will. You simply don't appreciate the finer aspects of automobiles. Hold still, you have a burr stuck on your hat. So, that's that. Was I right or was I right?"

"She's really dead?" Addie whispered.

"Yes. Can't hear you or me. I have a feeling I know where she is, too, and she won't be bothering anyone else for eternity. Good riddance. I hope I might say the same after this very delightful interlude, not that I expect to head in her direction."

"You mean you think you will ascend?" Did she dare hope?

"Who knows? I should get some credit for my successful sleuthing. Oh, look. There's your inspector racing toward us as if he's heading for the finish line at Ascot. Cuts a fine figure on a horse, doesn't he?"

"I hadn't noticed," Addie lied.

"Go on with you. Well, I'd best scram, as you so succinctly put it. Fingers crossed we don't meet again for a good long time, if ever. I'd say something more flowery and foolish and fitting for the occasion, but that policeman is in something of a hurry." He kissed the palm of her gloved hand and met her eyes. *"À bientôt!"*

He would speak French, wouldn't he? And as she recalled from her school days, it meant see you soon or see you later, which Addie hoped was very much not the case. He vanished, and she shut her eyes against the sun and the dead woman only yards away. When she opened them, Inspector Hunter was standing over the body, the Irish horse grazing companionably with a calmer Jupiter nearby. Screwing up her waning courage, she stepped forward.

The detective met her halfway. "Are you all right?"

Addie nodded. "Are you? She shot you!"

"Shot at me. A very welcome preposition in this case. But getting shot at is a habit I'd like to break." He took her elbow and moved her back toward the Rolls. "You don't need to see her."

Addie hadn't wanted to, her eyes everywhere but the twisted form on the ground, allowing herself only a quick look at Evelyn's polished riding boots. Addie rested against the car, hoping it wouldn't explode and that her knees would remember what they were designed for. Mr. Hunter spotted a fringed plaid blanket in the rear seat and returned to Evelyn, gently tucking it around her body.

Addie closed her eyes again against the dancing black spots.

He was back, speaking softly. "Take a breath. It will be all right." He touched her cheek with a fingertip, and Addie was surprised to find she was crying.

She'd given her handkerchief to Mr. Hunter in the stable, and now he gave her his own. "Will it?"

He stood next to her, a proper distance between them. "It has to be, doesn't it? There might be a scandal but no trial." He held out a small brown bottle. "I found this in the grass. We'll have to get it analyzed. Did you see what happened?"

"I think she took it out of the pocket of her jacket. At first I—I thought she was going to shoot you again. At you." Did Evelyn carry around a vial of deadly poison on her person like some people did a lucky penny? Always prepared. Addie shivered. "Will you tell Hugh what she said?"

A shadow crossed his face. "I'll have to, won't I? But..."

"But what?"

"Something's not right about it. I believe Evelyn killed Pamela, almost believe she didn't mean to kill Juliet Barlow. Cassidy's situation is not really a factor, not that I want to make light of it. But Ainsley's death—it's too pat. I can't see Pamela Fernald intentionally killing someone."

"I can't either. Maybe it was an accident." Pamela might have slept with Rupert and Lucas and Colin Stewart, but adultery was a far cry from murder.

"I could accept that." He almost smiled. "Funny, isn't it? I never knew the woman. I should be more judgmental, shouldn't I? She was a bit of a vamp, carrying on with who knows how many neighbors besides Waring and, uh, your late husband. If she was having an affair with Colin Stewart, that makes her a cradle-robber, too—I bet the lad's not seen his twenty-second birthday yet."

"So, what will you do?"

"All I have are the accusations of a self-confessed murderer against a woman she secretly hated. I don't think I need to involve my colleagues in this aspect—in fact, I'm sorry I asked you to call them."

"I only told the desk sergeant about Evelyn—that she said she'd poisoned Pamela and had ridden off with you in pursuit," Addie said. The rest had seemed too convoluted—and far-fetched—for a telephone call.

"Good. Can I trust you to keep that information between us? And yes, I'm asking you to collaborate in perverting the course of justice. Jesus." He raked his hair back from his forehead. "I wish I hadn't come today. Ignorance is bliss, isn't it? Even if Thursday's verdict stuck in my craw, I find no satisfaction in being right."

"Then must you say something to Hugh?"

"I owe him the truth, whatever it may be." Mr. Hunter paused. "I thought it was difficult when I told him about his wife's pregnancy. I'll not forget the look on his face anytime soon."

"But if you doubt the veracity of what Evelyn said—"

"I do, and I'll tell him that. She may have been right in principle, but the extenuating circumstances would tell the full story. Now we'll never really know."

They were silent for a minute or two, then Mr. Hunter touched her elbow. "I have to leave you, Lady Adelaide. I need to ring for a doctor and guide the men from Cirencester. Do you think you can manage?"

"Of—of course."

"You'll have to mind Jupiter too. I'll send one of the grooms down to get him. We can tie him to the car if you're wary of him."

The sad thing—she was, a little. What if Rupert popped up again to say a more substantial goodbye? Animals were sensitive creatures, although her dog, Fitz, didn't seem to respond to

Rupert at all. But then, Fitz was pretty unresponsive in general unless food was involved. Ghosts didn't faze him one bit.

"No. I'll walk him and try not to sneeze."

"You're sure?"

"I'm sure. Please don't worry about me—you have more important things to do. Go on back to the house."

Mr. Hunter whistled, and both horses ambled to him. He handed Jupiter's reins to Addie, then mounted the powerful Irish horse and was off. He definitely had a good seat, and Addie pictured him in one of Mr. Pink's hunting coats, riding to the hounds. Or better yet, playing polo as they did in India, where no hapless foxes would be harmed.

"Well, here we are. You poor darling."

The horse whickered and shook its head.

"I'm glad you can't talk and tell the world about Rupert," Addie said. "Who would believe you anyway? There are no such things as ghosts, right?" She looked around the area, praying her late husband was long gone, hopefully to his final reward. She didn't relish getting kicked in the head by a thousand pounds of frantic horse.

She continued to walk the horse over to the narrow strip of lane where the ground was more level. The farmhouse lay up ahead, but she turned in the other direction.

There was a lump in her throat, and her vision blurred. Addie cried for the woman she thought Evelyn Fernald was all her life, not the one she saw today in the stables. Addie's mother would take the death hard; the women had been close, not only because they were neighbors. She wished she knew where her mother was staying in London so she could tell her first before she read the news in the papers.

Jupiter was docile enough, pausing on the track now and again to swish his tail and snort. Addie couldn't see a hint of the plaid in the grass, which suited her very well. She walked aimlessly with her new friend, murmuring encouraging words, happy that her feet were on the ground instead of in stirrups. Her nose twitched with the merest tickle. The moving clouds gave her just enough shade, but she would not turn down a glass of cold lemonade when she returned to Fernald Hall.

Addie stepped onto the grass when she saw the police vehicle making its way slowly down the farmhouse lane. Mr. Hunter had returned with two men from the Cirencester constabulary and Robby. The car stopped long enough for the boy to jump out and take Jupiter away from her, and then it rumbled over the field to where the corpse lay.

Soon there would be a doctor. An ambulance. Her own car was probably a lost cause, so she decided to walk back to the house. She caught Mr. Hunter's eye and mimed her plans, and he waved her off.

If she had seen how the day was going to unfold beforehand, she would have chosen different footwear. A different dress, since the light blue was sadly spattered with dirt. A hat with a wider brim to keep out the sun. But she was alive, and that would count for something.

Chapter Thirty-Seven

*Late Saturday evening, the Pig and
Shilling, Broughton Magna*

Dev was lucky a room was available. Nothing fancy, and very
small—he could barely turn around—but it didn't really matter.
His personal belongings were still at Lady Adelaide's, and he
would make do tomorrow with a borrowed razor from the landlord before he returned the truck and retrieved them.

It was too bad he had sent the suitcases back to Patrick
Cassidy—Dev and he were about the same size and he could
have done with a clean shirt after pitching himself off that horse.

Earlier, Cassidy had told Dev on the telephone that he was
heading for London on the first train from Compton-Under-
Wood tomorrow morning, expecting a much smoother trip this
time. Maybe he was fanciful imagining he was poisoned. He still
wasn't especially happy about the inquest, but what could one
do after all these years?

At least he was getting paid for the horses.

Dev did not disclose the accusation against Pamela. He never
met the woman, so why did he have such doubts?

Let sleeping dogs lie.

Mr. Parks gave Dev the use of his private office, all the paper and pens and ink he could need on a well-ordered scarred golden oak desk. The noise and smoke from the pub barely filtered back here. From what little Dev heard, the customers were having a typical rollicking Saturday night, unaware of the mourning at nearby Fernald Hall.

There would be two reports, one sanitized for public consumption and one for his own edification. Dev would recount certain things all over again on official forms, but he wanted to write the true events up while they were still so terribly fresh in his mind.

Lady Adelaide would be left out as much as possible, although he'd be forever grateful to her for driving down that rutted bank in a madcap attempt to make sure he was uninjured and would stay that way. The undercarriage of the Rolls-Royce would probably never be the same.

By mutual agreement, she would say nothing of Lady Fernald's extraordinary revelations before she killed herself. Lady Adelaide cared too much for Hugh and John to carry tales, and it was no one's business, not even the Crown's anymore. One couldn't receive the death penalty from beyond the grave.

So it was left to Dev to have the worst hour of his career informing Sir Hugh of what had transpired in the stable and afterward. He couched what facts he knew as gently as he could, wondering with each word if the baronet would somehow survive the conversation with his sanity intact. Dev wasn't sure of his own at this point.

If all the truth ever came out, the tabloids would have a field day. And for what? Nothing could be changed or improved. Both women were dead, and there was not a shred of proof to link them to their crimes. Fernald and his son had lost enough.

There was a knock on the frosted glass of the door. He shoved the papers aside and hoped Mr. Parks would be quick at finding whatever he was looking for.

"Come."

"A word, Inspector."

Dev looked up to find Captain Clifford and Owen Bradbury in the doorway.

Now what?

Bradbury shut the door behind him. "Hugh told us you were spending the night in the village."

"Yes. I didn't want to intrude any further upon Sir Hugh's hospitality."

Dev needed to get away from there—it wasn't every day he abandoned an investigation. Got shot at and nearly broke a shoulder too. From the stabbing sensation every time he moved, he thought it might be dislocated and gave it an absent rub, wishing for some aspirin or perhaps a strong brandy to dull the pain.

He would make do with the soothing effects of nicotine. It was past time for his daily gasper. Dev reached into his pocket gingerly and pulled out a crushed pack of Pall Malls and held them out. "Sit down, gentlemen. Join me?"

Clifford unstacked the two bentwood chairs in a corner and placed them in front of the desk, while Bradbury pulled out a gold cigarette case. "Here. Have one of mine. They look to be in better shape than yours."

"Thank you."

The men sat and a matching gold lighter made its way around the desk. There was no attempt at small talk. Both his unexpected guests looked pale but resolute. Dev braced himself for another confession, and it wasn't long in coming.

"There's really no way to say this," Clifford began.

Dev thought all along they knew more than they had told him. Friendship. Loyalty. Perhaps even love. All were admirable traits, but wreaked havoc with a police investigation.

This case had more layers than a harem girl's veils. These men had protected Pamela Fernald's reputation for almost ten years.

"Try," Dev said. "I won't judge."

"But you might," Bradbury said. "Maybe enough to try to arrest us both."

Dev raised an eyebrow but said nothing.

The captain shot a look at Bradbury, who nodded. "Go on, Denny. Get it over with."

Clifford took a long drag on his cigarette, as if he might never get the chance to smoke again. When he exhaled, he cleared his throat. "Pam didn't kill Michael. Hugh did. But he...doesn't remember."

Dev stopped himself from dropping his own cigarette. "How do you know this?"

"We were there, weren't we?" Bradbury said. "Saw it all."

Dev stubbed out his cigarette in a clean copper ashtray and took out his notebook. "You are saying you were both present in the autumn of 1916 when Lieutenant Ainsley disappeared... and was killed."

"Don't bother writing down what I'm telling you. We'll deny it," Clifford said. "I have my career to think of, and one day Owen will be Baron Hurst."

Bradbury grimaced. "Don't count chickens, Denny. My cousin is a hale and hearty fifty. He might outlive me yet. Or have half a dozen sons if he marries again to go along with his six daughters."

Dev didn't care one iota about Bradbury's genealogy. "Then why tell me? Why now?"

"It's time. Hugh told us what you said—that while you had no proof, his mother had blamed Pam for Michael's death before her…accident. It isn't true, and we told him that. Argued with him, really. Swore up and down we would have known if that was the case since we were there."

"The man's a wreck. Hugh needs to know that his wife was completely innocent, at least of this. It was all so long ago. What difference does it make now?" Clifford asked.

"We'd like you to back us up by saying you've given it some thought, and in your professional opinion you don't credit what his mother said. Hell, I bet you even wondered about the probability that she did it," Bradbury added.

Dev had. But it was altogether too convenient to blame someone who could not defend themselves, just as Evelyn had tried to pin the deed on Pamela. She had been oozing with spite at the end, which was just one reason he hadn't believed her.

"He's had enough tragedy. He loved Pam—he shouldn't think she's a cold-blooded killer."

No. His mother deserved that description.

But right to the end, she was protecting her child, wasn't she?

"You know there is no statute of limitations on murder." He plumped up one of his own Pall Malls and lit it. "And I still don't understand. You say he doesn't remember. How is that possible?"

Clifford sat back in his chair. "Didn't you see him the other day? How happy he was that his friend's honor was restored? He doesn't remember. And if he does, it's like a dream, all mixed up with the war. Musgrave says he has nightmares sometimes, but Hugh truly doesn't know what he did. I'd stake my own life on it."

Dev examined the men before him. He was used to fabrications and half-truths but saw none of the tells from either of them that revealed a lie. "Sir Hugh doesn't know that he was the one who killed Ainsley," he stated, mostly to himself. It sounded ludicrous.

"That's right. And we don't want him to," Clifford continued. "He didn't mean to. If he'd been himself—well, he'll never be himself again, will he? John needs his father, especially now."

"Then why are you telling me this?" Let sleeping dogs lie.

"It's for Pam." Dev could barely hear Bradbury's voice over the pulsing in his ears. "She always felt responsible. Said she might as well have pulled the trigger herself." He drew a deep breath. "It wasn't really her fault. She and her mother-in-law gave Hugh things to try to ease his discomfort beyond what the quacks prescribed when he got home. To help him sleep and breathe and so on. They did it out of love, the both of them. But they weren't doctors, and it took a while to get it right. Hugh didn't know what he was doing half the time that fall. Didn't know where he was. Carried his service revolver at all times so he could defend himself from the bloody Huns."

Clifford gave Dev a rueful smile. "Musgrave kept taking the bullets out of it. It was almost comical the lengths he went to hide the gun or the bullets. But this was one time he failed."

Bradbury's words flowed faster now, as though he was eager to get rid of this long-held secret. "We were just dancing to records that night, you know? Taking turns pushing Pam around the drawing room like we did every night since we arrived. She was a good sport, and it was perfectly harmless. Of course, Michael liked her—we all did. She was…Pam. He kissed her after he spun her around. Just as a friend, mind. She laughed and pushed him away. All in good fun. But Hugh came in to say goodnight and saw. Musgrave tried to grab the gun away, but it was too late."

"It could have been any of us." Clifford shuddered. "Pam fell to pieces."

"Lady Fernald sorted it all out. Kept it quiet somehow from the servants. Musgrave got Hugh dosed and settled, and then we buried the body in the dead of night where Evelyn told us to. The next morning we pretended Michael just decided to leave. That makes us accomplices, and if you want to arrest us, you have every right, but it will be the devil to prove, won't it? We kept silent for Hugh all these years. And for Pam," Bradbury said. "And we'll stay silent."

Except for tonight.

"So you wouldn't sign a statement corroborating what you've told me? And Musgrave won't either, am I right?" Musgrave, who owed his life and employment to Captain Sir Hugh Fernald.

The men looked at each other but said nothing.

What good would it do to arrest Fernald for a crime he couldn't remember committing? In effect, Dev would orphan Hugh's son and cause complications far worse than what the boy was presently experiencing. No mother. No father. No grandmother. Even his governess was dead.

And there was nothing concrete to produce as evidence except the word of two men who wouldn't repeat themselves.

"What do you want me to do?" Dev asked.

"We told you. Tell Hugh you doubt his mother's story. That she was simply deranged at the end. She shot at you, didn't she? Tried to murder you. Killed herself! There, a madwoman! Tell him you're happy with the jury's finding at the inquest. Nobody will ever know for sure just how Michael managed to get himself killed. It could have been a passing tramp."

Everything Bradbury said went against Dev's conscience and training. Right was right and wrong was wrong. There was nothing more important than truth and justice. What would Cassidy make of his complicity? To withhold the facts and protect a killer—

Dev had never done such a thing. What he had done for Fernald this afternoon was use discretion, not deliberately obstruct. Oh, he knew with certainty there was corruption within the force, as Evelyn Fernald had so accurately pointed out. His colleagues were offered bribes to see one thing and not see another all the time. He was tested himself when that banker set a fat wallet in front of him last year. The rich and privileged often felt the rules did not apply to them.

Bradbury and Clifford asked him to bend those rules, but not to benefit themselves. They covered for their friend for nearly a decade and must long to truly bury the past.

But nobody was above the law, not even the Prime Minister.

"We only want to help Hugh. He shouldn't go through the rest of his life believing a vicious lie. He's got enough to deal with, don't you think? His mother killed his wife. He was always the best of us," Clifford said with feeling. "We're alive because of Hugh's sacrifice. It's time a sacrifice was done for him."

Dev's sacrifice.

Of his own morality.

Here he faced the very thing he'd studied in the abstract all these years in his spiritual questing. But what choice did he have really? There were three witnesses who wouldn't cooperate. The other three witnesses were dead.

He wished these men had not come forward to relieve their burden and pass it on to him, but it was too late to call back the truth.

Dev would write to Fernald. He didn't trust himself to look the man in the eye and lie.

That was the best he could do.

Chapter Thirty-Eight

Sunday

Addie set her toast down before she choked on it and gazed out the breakfast room windows. It was another perfect June morning, but she couldn't appreciate it.

She watched a woman die yesterday and was completely unable to prevent it.

What with Rupert's investigation, she might be considered responsible for it.

No, Addie didn't hand Evelyn the bottle of poison, but if they hadn't confronted her in the stable—

She would have gotten away with it all.

Evidence against Evelyn was entirely illusory—Detective Inspector Hunter had only her own brazen words, with Addie as witness. She could have been lying right to the end.

Despite his questions when she returned to Compton Chase yesterday, Addie was less than truthful with Patrick Cassidy, giving him the barest bones of the story. What good would it do to accuse Pamela of killing Michael Ainsley now? She'd already been punished.

So, poor Evelyn had simply fallen from her horse and died.

Mr. Cassidy was grateful to escape another horror at Fernald Hall. Visibly moved by Hugh's plight, he hoped the family would recover from yet another tragedy, no matter what transpired in the past.

For a moment, Addie thought the man might kiss her over the coffee cups after they dined together—he was back to his flirtatious self, his face no longer the color of an unripe lime. Instead, he leaned forward to give her a business card from a silver case, with the offer of private lessons should she ever purchase one of his horses and consider riding again. At the word "private," his auburn eyebrows actually waggled. Addie tore the card up as soon as she reached her bedroom. Beckett was apt to be perpetually disappointed.

To Addie's relief, he left at daybreak. She could easily have seen him off, for she was wide awake most of the night, but she preferred to hide in her bed behind a locked door. She managed to keep him at bay so far and didn't want to tempt fate by any awkward goodbyes. Addie suspected Mr. Cassidy was a man who could turn a friendly handshake into a fiery embrace without a smidgeon of guilt.

Maybe she should go back upstairs for a few hours and try to start the day all over again. One thing she knew—though she was dressed for church, she simply couldn't face it. About to ring for Forbes to cancel the car, he entered before she had the chance.

"The Marquess of Broughton has come to call, Lady Adelaide. He is in the Great Hall. Shall I tell him to come through to the breakfast room? He says he's already eaten, but that it's very important that he speak with you at your earliest convenience."

Addie looked at her plate of congealing eggs. "No, Forbes,

tell him I'll be in to see him shortly. Please take him some coffee and rolls in case he changes his mind."

If it had been anyone else—except for Mr. Hunter—she would ask Forbes to say she was not receiving. She crumpled the monogrammed napkin and examined her face in a knife. Dark circles which had been impervious to Beckett's powdering were clearly visible beneath the tortoise shell frames of her spectacles.

It was unlike Ian to make such an early morning call. Perhaps he wanted more information about the awful events at Fernald Hall, although he'd never struck Addie as being at all macabre.

She wore one of her old mourning dresses. Black was suitable for so many reasons—she had lost friends—and very probably Rupert again, one could hope. Her late husband, surprisingly, did not come home to gloat last night, and she waited up for him until fitful sleep finally overtook her.

Did that mean his duty here was done? Addie hoped with all her heart that it was so.

She made her way to the Great Hall. Sunshine flooded into its two-story windows. Her cousin was looking through them at the ornamental lake and its family of ducks, but he turned quickly at her footsteps.

"Good morning, Addie. I hope my visit has not disturbed you. I know I should have called."

Addie rose up and kissed his cheek. "Nonsense. You're always welcome, and anyway, I've been up forever. You must have made an early start, though."

"It's a glorious day for a drive. Tonneau cover off, of course." His curly fair hair was ruffled, adding to his attractiveness. Really, she and Cee needed a heart-to-heart. Someone was bound to snap Ian up any minute.

"Let's sit. I assume you've heard about Evelyn Fernald." But not everything, she hoped.

Ian followed her to the wing chairs in front of the massive fireplace. "I intend to stop at Fernald Hall on my way back home. I can't imagine how Hugh is managing."

Neither could Addie. Keeping her promise, Addie said nothing to alarm Hugh before she was driven home with Mr. Cassidy's cases. She hadn't envied Inspector Hunter his grisly task.

Forbes entered with a fresh pot of coffee, a basket of hot rolls with butter and jam, and a dish of early strawberries. She was proved right as Ian helped himself to a second breakfast as they discussed the bad luck of the Fernald family.

"In a circuitous way, that's why I'm here," Ian said, setting his coffee cup down. "I've got a confession to make, but first, read this." He reached into his pocket and drew out an envelope.

The handwriting was as familiar to Addie as her own. Startled, she glanced up at Ian, who looked uncomfortable.

"I meant to get this to you right after the funeral, but I was sidetracked." By the twins, she guessed. "I'm sorry for the delay."

"What—"

"Just read it first, and then ask me anything you wish."

She took her glasses off and rubbed the bridge of her nose. The envelope was unsealed, and she pulled the letter out.

Dear Addie,

By the time you get this, I will be in Paris on my honeymoon. Yes, I convinced Pip to elope and flee the country. Probably not my finest hour, robbing the girl of a proper wedding and running away from the police. But with Pam's death, I realized just how short life is. I simply do not want to waste any more time. Tempus fugit and all that. Pip, bless her, knows everything and is taking me as I am. I am humbled and truly a lucky man.

Your cousin Ian has been a brick through all of this, arranging for the special license and our safe transport to France. I trusted him with my future and am not disappointed. He's the best friend a fellow could have.

Pip says hello and to expect an invitation in the fall to a formal reception to celebrate our marriage. By then I pray we'll have even more to celebrate.

Please give my regrets to Detective Inspector Hunter. I trust he's solved the case by now, or at least removed me from his list of suspects. I hope Lady Waring (!!!) and I may call on you upon our return.

Yours as ever,
Lucas

"You knew where he was this whole time?" Addie asked. "You lied to me!" And very well.

"I did. I'm sorry, Addie, but Lucas is one of my oldest friends. I couldn't have that detective chap haul him away in handcuffs over a misunderstanding."

"More than a misunderstanding. He should have told the truth about his relationship with Pamela. Detective Hunter would have listened." She hoped so anyhow.

"Come now. From what Lucas told me, he was suspect number one." Ian cleared his throat. "He, uh, told me about Pam's condition. He was insistent he was not responsible. That he'd ended the affair. But it could have been another local man." He looked down at his hands.

Today was chock-full of surprises. "Ian, are you saying you had an affair with Pamela too?"

"A gentleman doesn't discuss such things with a lady, even if the lady is his cousin. But Pam was a dear friend and will be sorely missed."

Addie tried to recall his reaction when she told him Pamela was dead. He had known all along—had already been colluding with Lucas—and played dumb.

It seemed her cousin had unknown and devious depths, and she couldn't decide whether to be angry with him or not.

Ian was not as straitlaced as she thought.

He rose and went back to the window. "I don't want you to think less of her. Or me. Or Lucas, for that matter. Pam loved Hugh, but was…restless. There were perhaps a half dozen of us—if that—over the years whose company she sought on rare occasions. I was honored to be amongst them." He drew a breath and turned from the light. "I would very much appreciate it if you didn't mention any of this to Cecilia. I'm not sure she would understand."

One more secret to the pile that Addie was already balancing. Who said nothing ever happened in the country?

"Of course not."

"If, ah, I were to ever marry, you have my word I would be a faithful husband."

"I'm glad to hear it."

Infidelity definitely put the kibosh on a happy marriage.

Chapter Thirty-Nine

The church bells rang half an hour ago as Addie waved Ian off. She would invite the Reverend Rivers for tea to make it up to him for shirking her Christian duty. He was doing the best he could at Compton St. Cuthbert's; it's just that his best was not so very good.

It was a relief to hang her black dress back in the closet. But she did expect Mr. Hunter to come along eventually, so, like yesterday, she chose her second outfit of the day with care.

This might be the final last time she ever saw him, and she wished to be memorable.

Addie was fully cognizant that she was an idiot. No matter how kind Mr. Hunter had been to her, he was not romantically inclined. Yes, he could wipe tears and loan handkerchiefs and not rub her nose in the fact that her husband had been an unfaithful bastard. He wanted to protect her from getting mixed up with criminals. He never made her feel ignorant, even though his interests were far more intellectual than hers. He liked her.

But not enough.

Did he think she was too "good" for him? It was entirely the other way around. He was a hero, and she was adrift, having accomplished very little in her almost thirty-two years.

Like Rupert, it was time for her to turn over a new leaf, only while she was still alive. She was going to find a purpose this summer even if it killed her.

But right now, her only purpose was to cause the inspector just the tiniest regret for his scruples. She kicked off her black pumps and rummaged through her wardrobe. The peach voile and lace shift skimmed her curves nicely and would do. Soft cream leather T-straps wouldn't hurt the blisters she'd acquired walking back to Fernald Hall. Addie had gotten sun on her cheeks as well, so rouge was not necessary, just more powder under her eyes. A dab of coral lipstick, a fluff of her hair, a string of pearls, and she was done.

And now to wait and look like she wasn't really waiting.

She took a straw hat out of its box. It had a lush pink-and-peach silk rose on its band and had come at a wicked cost. "Come, Fitz, let's take a stroll through the garden and commune with nature."

The dog opened one eye from his position on the chintz window seat cushion and made no attempt to move. How many hours of the day did he sleep anyway? She clapped her hands and he struggled to sit up, one ear up and one ear down.

"Do you want to go out?"

Ah, those were words he recognized. He hopped down to the floor and wagged his stubby tail.

Addie gave instructions to Forbes and left the house. As she walked, she trailed her hand through the lavender hedges that bisected the lawn, stirring up their heady scent. She took a breath and tried to relax. Lavender was famous for its soothing effects, but it was failing her today.

The last time she was in the garden—gracious, was it only

yesterday?—Rupert had been with her. She half-expected him to be hanging from the arbor like a monkey, but so far she was still alone, with the exception of Fitz, who bounded ahead after a butterfly.

Addie seated herself beneath the canopy of roses and crossed her ankles, fidgeted, then got up. She didn't wish to look like she was posing. Why hadn't she thought to bring a book? Or a pair of secateurs and basket so she could be caught in the ladylike act of cutting flowers? She simply wasn't good at staging an appearance. She didn't even have a ball to toss at Fitz.

Who sat around alone outside dressed to impress anyway? Her clothes were suitable for a lavish garden party, and she didn't even have a cup of tea with her.

She whistled to Fitz, but he ignored her, as she didn't have any streaky bacon either. Addie was being silly. Trying too hard. And unless she was stark naked, Inspector Hunter probably wouldn't notice anything.

She unpinned her hat and fanned herself with it. Maybe she should go back indoors before the heat got to her.

But then the sunlight glinted on glass as the terrace's French doors opened, and Forbes stepped out with Mr. Hunter. Addie gave a little wave and waited on the path, worrying the brim of her hat with her fingers.

Mr. Hunter looked rumpled and tired, but then he didn't have the benefit of Beckett and a powder puff.

"Good morning! May we get you some breakfast?"

"Thank you, but no. Mrs. Parks gave me a massive fry-up before I left. She said she was sorry to have missed you yesterday."

"She's a dear. Um, how are things?"

"If you mean whether you'll be reading about Evelyn Fernald in the newspapers, the answer is no. I think I managed to convince everyone involved to…let sleeping dogs lie. The results of the inquest will stand."

"Poor Hugh. How did he take it?"

"As you might expect," he said shortly, rubbing a shoulder. Was he injured from his fall? Before she had a chance to ask, he spoke. "I only came out to say a quick goodbye. I hope you don't mind, but when I dropped off the truck, I fixed it up with your chauffeur to take me to the station." He glanced at his watch. "I should go. Thank you for all your help, Lady Adelaide."

My, he was so distant and formal. Addie swallowed back her disappointment and held out her hand. "I hope we meet under less stressful circumstances someday."

"That's unlikely, I'm afraid. Well, good luck. It's been as much a pleasure as possible seeing you again." He pumped her hand in business-like fashion, but she held on longer than she should.

"Dev!" Her voice cracked.

He hadn't let her go yet either and the warmth of his hand was almost unbearably comforting. "Yes?"

All around them, birds twittered without a care, but Addie had trouble finding the right words. She tried to smile as she looked up, counting those dark eyelashes. "Good luck to you too. I hope life brings you nothing but joy."

"And you as well." He paused. "Addie."

She watched him walk toward the house, his posture as rigid as the soldier he used to be. He didn't look back.

But then the glass door opened again, and Addie blinked through the annoying tears that were building up. Forbes was back on the terrace, this time with her sister, Cee, who flew down the steps straight into Mr. Hunter's arms.

"Thank God, I've found you! You must help me! Us!" Cee clung to Mr. Hunter like a limpet, and Addie hurried over as fast as her sore feet could take her.

Her sister was still wearing her pink cotton pajamas, her hair in pin curls under a net cap. She'd driven twenty miles in such a state? Something was seriously amiss. Cee was addicted to fashion, even if she dabbled in revolutionary ideas.

"Cee, what on earth! What's wrong?"

"It's Mama! She's been arrested for murdering her l-lover! I don't know whether to laugh or cry."

"What?" both Addie and Mr. Hunter said at the exact same time.

"She called me this morning from a police station. We have to get to London right away. Call one of the Mr. Pullings or their partner, Mr. Stockwell. She didn't care which one."

"The solicitors?"

Cee nodded.

"But it's Sunday," Addie said stupidly.

"I have her address book in the car. She has all their home numbers, because of course she does—she's the Dowager Marchioness of Broughton." Cee looked up at Mr. Hunter, in whose arms she remained, causing Addie a sharp stab of jealousy. "She asked specifically for you, Mr. Hunter. Said if anyone could straighten this out, it would be you."

"She did?" He looked as if someone had hit him in the head with a cricket bat.

"She says she has complete faith in you, even if you almost had Addie killed. Twice. Obviously, she's gone off the deep end and must be desperate. A lover! And he's dead to boot. Can you believe it, Addie? This is Mama we're talking about!"

Addie was indeed having trouble believing. But her mother had requested Mr. Hunter's assistance, and who could argue with Mama and win?

ABOUT THE AUTHOR

Maggie Robinson is a former teacher, library clerk, and mother of four who woke up in the middle of the night absolutely compelled to create the perfect man and use as many adjectives and adverbs as possible doing so. A transplanted New Yorker, she lives with her not-quite-perfect husband in Maine, where the cold winters are ideal for staying indoors and writing.